FIREFLY EMBERS

FIREFLY COVE
BOOK 2

ASHLEY TEMPLIN

To all of us who have darkness hanging heavy over our heads and the unrelenting pressure to fight it tooth and nail—even if the battle seems unending—I see you, you matter, and you are loved beyond measure.

A NOTE FROM THE AUTHOR

Firefly Embers deals with themes that may be heavy for some readers. While I have done my best to portray these topics with the sensitivity and tenderness that they deserve, the truth is— emotion is raw, unfiltered, and sometimes oppressive. Please know that your mental health is of the utmost importance to me and I encourage you to read through the content warnings on the next page before reading.

If you're like me and like to be surprised, proceed to the front of the emotional roller coaster. Keep your arms and legs inside the vehicle at all times, and welcome back to Firefly Cove.

CONTENT WARNINGS

FIREFLY EMBERS INCLUDES THE
FOLLOWING SENSITIVE CONTENT:

Traumatic Spinal Injury
Grief and Discussions of Loss
Brief Discussion of Suicidal Ideations
Descriptive Depictions of Rodeo Accidents
Family/Sibling Trauma
Intense Therapy and Healing
Explicit Sexual Content
Rope Play

PLEASE PROCEED RESPONSIBLY AND
REMEMBER THAT SHOULD YOU FIND
YOURSELF IN A DARK PLACE, REACH
OUT A HAND. SHOULD YOU NEED THEM,
THE NUMBERS FOR MENTAL HEALTH
INTERVENTIONS ARE LISTED BELOW.

NATIONAL SUICIDE PREVENTION
HOTLINE
1-800-986-5990 OR DIAL 988

PLAYLIST

JUST PRETEND- BAD OMENS
HEAVIER-RAIN CITY DRIVE
BURIAL PLOT - DAYSEEKER
FIRE AWAY - CHRIS STAPLETON
FRIENDS DON'T - MADDIE & TAE
I DESERVE A DRINK - MADISON HUGES
BACK IN THE SADDLE- CHRIS STAPLETON
THE FALL- CODY JOHNSON
COWBOYS CRY TOO- KELSEA BALLERINI
MIGHT BE DANGEROUS- TYLER BRADEN
SHE WAS MINE- ROMAN ALEXANDER

Check out the entire playlist on Spotify

PROLOGUE

"They say I changed a lot; I said a lot changed me." —Derez De'Shon

WHITE-HOT SEARING PAIN scorches its way through the flesh of my back. Even though the pain is imaginary, it feels as real as any physical touch. As many times as I will my mind to block out the pain and reminder of my accident, my body refuses to forget. I close my eyes, begging my body to follow my mind into oblivion and give me the reprieve I crave. Of course, with my rotten luck, I am trapped in this cycle of agony.

I can feel the bite of the bullet as it pierces my skin, tearing through the flesh of my back as if it were nothing thicker than paper.

My mind still forces me to relive the terror that swept over me as I fell, my legs heavy and unable to move.

The doctor's words, "never ride again," were a haunting

refrain in my mind, reminding me of the life I could no longer live. A life I had built, brick by painstaking brick.

Anger, fiercer than any before, poured in through my scars, raced within my blood, and boiled ferociously through my veins, filling my body with an untamed fire.

Every night, it's the same song and dance, a constant cadence of agony tangoing with anger. The crescendo, a gut-wrenching pain that threatens to overtake my senses, draws me further and further into the darkness of my grief.

Under the cover of darkness, I beg my body to forget the feeling, the sound, the anguish. I'm silently pleading with my mind, hoping to quiet the ceaseless churning of dark thoughts. I drown the pain in alcohol, constantly trying to lighten the weight of oppression that these memories hold over me.

The nightmare plays out in the dark recesses of my mind. I am lost, drifting out to sea with no life vest to keep me afloat. Kicking my legs, their stillness an icy tendril of remembrance.

I desperately try to scream, but no sound emerges from my throat. The waves crash over me, drawing me farther and farther from the surface as darkness threatens to consume me, to pull me under.

Looking skyward, I can see the sun. Its rays are a beacon of hope and warmth, beckoning me to keep trying, keep kicking. I stretch my arms up, reaching for the surface, but my fingers fall short of breaching the inky depths. I'm drowning.

I refuse to surrender to the darkness, but every second I'm stuck under, I find my resolve weakening. I don't know how much fight I have left before this relentless grief swallows me whole.

WADE

I WATCHED as everyone around me toasted their drinks to the radiant bride and groom, a profound sense of sadness flooding my weathered soul.

Sure, I was happy for my brother and his new wife, Stella, as they accepted their well-earned congratulations with beaming smiles permanently etched on their faces. They deserved this. They had been through hell and back for their happy ending.

I was happiest, though, with the glass of top-shelf bourbon resting against my palm, its cool bite a reminder that I could feel something, anything. The warmth of the amber liquid pooled low in my belly, radiating out to every inch of my skin, burning away the one fuck I had left to give.

Hell, I was even happy sitting back and watching my best friend, Ray, flirt with every single warm-blooded man in attendance. Well, maybe I wasn't *happy* about that one. I was indifferent; that was the most accurate way to put it.

The indifference was new; normally, the thought of Ray with another man would have sent me into a blind rage.

Lately, all I could feel was the emptiness left by my losses —a hollow reminder of what life had taken from me. There was a pivotal piece of my soul missing. Like a phantom limb, I felt the ache of a piece of me I wouldn't ever get back. That reminder was the catalyst for my ever-present bad mood.

The searing pain of a bullet narrowly missing my spine had become a recurring nightmare. That was about the only thing I felt in excruciating detail; everything else was shrouded in a haze of indifference.

The reminder that I would likely never get on a horse again brought with it a crushing realization I had been forced to accept.

Though the word "never" still tasted like acid on my tongue. I wanted to see it as a challenge, but the alternate reality of becoming a quadriplegic should something go wrong wasn't a reality I wanted to entertain.

Here, at what should have been one of the most joyous moments of our family's life, I felt the scrutiny of societal standards, being that I was the last single Daniels man.

I guess being thirty and a perpetual bachelor loses its appeal when your twin brother settles down and becomes a stepdad all in one fell swoop.

Although everyone was breathing down my neck, wondering when I was finally going to get hitched, I couldn't find it in myself to take a step in that direction.

Realistically, I couldn't force myself to make a move in *any* direction.

After all, who wants to date a washed-up cowboy with an alcohol dependency, a fucked-up back, no job, no house of his own, and debilitating trauma he refused to acknowledge?

Yeah, I sure sound like a fucking catch.

I swirled the amber liquid around my glass before taking a

hearty swig. The bourbon burned its way down my throat, pushing down the bubbling anxiety threatening to overtake me.

I'd never been a particularly heavy drinker, not even in my early twenties. I'd have a beer or two out with my brother and our friends at the local dive bar, but getting obliterated and not remembering what or who I'd done held very little appeal.

Especially when my days consisted of being up at the ass crack of dawn doing manual labor.

But after "the incident," as I like to call it, I refused to take anything stronger than some ibuprofen. I didn't like the way the pills made me feel—floaty and uncontrolled. Alcohol temporarily numbed the pain, physically and mentally, without the side effect of a dependency on narcotics.

Although I am certain that I was simply replacing one dependence with another, I added that to the increasingly long list of things that I had lost the ability to give a fuck about.

A loud laugh broke me from my self-deprecating spiral; the joyous sound was hearty and unrefined. There was no denying whose laugh that was. I'd been hearing it since I was thirteen years old.

Rayna Cortez.

Ray was the one thing that could brighten even the darkest of my days. She had been my best friend since we were kids. Ever since she had gotten lost in the woods between our houses and had adamantly declared us best friends, we were attached at the hip.

Her presence was as warm and bright as the sun itself, which is how I'd come up with her nickname. Every time she walked into a room, all eyes were on her. For some reason, whenever she was around, I felt like I could breathe again.

Champagne in hand, she giggled at the bartender's words,

her dainty fingers playfully toying with the glass as I watched her flirt shamelessly. His eyes trailed over the soft curves of her breasts as he blatantly looked her over, making zero effort to hide his interest.

There was absolutely no denying that Rayna Cortez was a knockout. Men were always left speechless around her, their jaws dropping in awe as she unknowingly commanded their attention.

Standing at five foot four, she compensated for her lack of height with a healthy dose of sass. She had curves, but not in a way that made her disproportionate. She filled out a pair of Wranglers better than any woman I'd ever seen, and I'd seen a lot of women in Wranglers around the rodeo circuit.

The dress she wore tonight was like a second skin, as if it were painted directly onto her luscious body. It hugged every single one of her curves, dipping in at her slender waist and flaring out over those beautiful, God-given hips. She had pulled her dark brown hair into an elegant updo, highlighting the slender slope of her neck.

Fuck, she was stunning.

As if she could feel the heat of my stare on her skin, she turned her hazel eyes in my direction, her mouth pulling up on one side in her signature devilish grin she reserved just for me.

Her knowing smile was undoubtedly a challenge. She was watching to see if her conversation with another man would push me over the edge and make me want to show her how much I wanted her.

The two of us had been playing with fire for years. Ray and I were both exceedingly attracted to each other, but we knew that being together was a direct risk to our friendship.

So, instead of taking the risk, neither of us dared to discuss the true extent of our affection.

If we did, there would be no turning back.

I watched with rapt attention as she tapped her manicured hand on the top of the bar and mouthed a "thank you" to the bartender before heading in my direction.

Anticipating Ray's inevitable meddling, I finished off the rest of my bourbon, hoping the liquid courage would do its job.

I watched as her strides ate up the distance between us, the undeniable tug of lust thrumming through my veins.

"Dance with me?" she asked, holding out one of her hands in offering.

There wasn't much I'd say no to when it came to Rayna Cortez. She had me wrapped around her little finger and a vice grip on my balls.

"Do I ever say no to you?" I questioned, my voice husky from lack of use.

I had barely uttered a word since I had walked down the aisle at the church with my brother, watching him marry the woman who was the reason I currently hated my life.

As I put my hand in hers and moved my chair back to stand, Ray gave me that same trademark smirk.

Even though I had a significant height advantage, she remained unfazed as I towered over her. She could easily take my six-foot-three frame and make me feel two feet tall with the flick of her wrist.

Had I mentioned that I was an absolute goner for this woman?

She led me out onto the makeshift dance floor, where couples were swaying to a crooning country song. Never one to hesitate, she grabbed my other hand and placed it right where her hip dipped in and pulled me close. I rolled my eyes at her not-so-subtle insistence.

She smelled intoxicating, a heady mix of vanilla and cinnamon that had me wishing I could pull her closer and trail my nose down her neck.

"What's up with you tonight?" she questioned bluntly, her tone snippy and straightforward, not one to beat around the bush.

I looked over the top of her head at where my brother and his new wife were sitting at the newlyweds' table, not an inch of space between them.

Sleep threatened to overtake Charlie, my now niece, but Max kept her perched on his lap, her head resting on his shoulder, one arm wrapped around each of his girls, always the protector.

A sudden, hot wave of anger flared within me. Why did they get the happily ever after, and I get the bullet in the back?

"Wade…" Ray reached up and cupped my cheek, noticing where my eyes had wandered, and forced my gaze back to hers. The worry and concern reflected in her eyes were undeniable.

Great, the last thing I needed was the most beautiful fucking woman in the world pitying me.

"Wade, what's wrong?"

"Nothing, I'm fine," I snapped.

A scoff escaped her lips as she brought her hand to my chest, pulling me near, focusing my attention on the sensation of our bodies almost touching instead of the anger burning its way through me.

"And here I thought I was the girl in this relationship," she huffed, a frustrated sigh puffing through her plush lips.

"Ain't no relationship here, Sunshine," I grit out between

clenched teeth. The words felt wrong as they tumbled past my lips.

I didn't have a single logical explanation for why I was acting like a dick toward Ray. *She'd* done nothing wrong. She had been nothing short of smotheringly supportive since the incident, and I was, some days, grateful to have her help. Even if I did a shitty job of showing it.

"You're being a dick, Wade Daniels."

"I'm being truthful."

I could see the hurt that washed over her eyes, but I couldn't find it in me to care. She didn't need my baggage. There were so many men at this wedding whose focus never left her that she could have had her pick of them.

Hell, she could have her pick of the men of Firefly Cove. Ray was a catch. She was smart, sweet, strong, and she sure didn't need to be hung up pining after my washed-up ass.

The hand that had been resting on my chest was once again on my face, this time gripping my chin between her thumb and index finger, demanding my undivided attention. Her grip was unwavering, and her eyes bore into mine, with a stern look of determination on her face.

"Listen here, you sulky motherfucker. I know what happened to you sucked."

I jerked my chin from her grasp, a scoff escaping my lips. It more than sucked, but I would let her continue her clearly long overdue reprimand if it got her off my back for a night or two.

"Wade." Her tone was gentler as she skated her fingers across my jaw, tiny pinpricks of electricity in their wake. "I'm sorry that life's dealt you a shit hand lately. It's not fair; that's for damn sure. But you're walking around this place like Stella is the one directly responsible for you getting—"

I cut her off by gripping her wrist harshly and removing her touch from my skin.

Taking a step back and running my fingers through my hair, I scoffed. "Isn't she, though? I wouldn't have been there if she hadn't gone off on some fucked-up vigilante mission because she couldn't let your dad handle things like he'd asked us to." The words burned as they left my lips, but Ray and I never shied away from speaking our truths to each other.

Well, most of them.

Feeling the anger bubbling up to the surface, and not wanting to make a scene, I stalked off, leaving Ray on the dance floor, a look of defeat marring her face, as I sulked to the bar. I slammed my hand down on the bar top, startling the bartender mixing drinks.

That's what he gets for flirting with my woman.

My woman. Fuck.

Ray wasn't my woman. She wasn't anyone's woman. She sure as hell wouldn't want to be my woman now. I'd just pissed her off, bashed her best friend, and left her on the dance floor alone at a wedding. I'd no doubt hear about it tomorrow after she let me stew in my fuck up for a while.

"Bourbon, top-shelf, neat," I gritted out to the pansy ass motherfucker behind the bar. He wouldn't even stand a chance if Ray got her claws into him. She needed a man who could challenge her. She needed a man who would stand beside her as she took the world by storm, ready to battle anything in her way.

She needed someone stronger than me, that's for sure.

The bartender slid a rocks glass in my direction, and I tossed a five-dollar bill into his tip jar.

Max and Stella had opted for an open bar, and I was going

to take full advantage of the constant flow of liquor while I wasn't paying for it.

I looked out across the dance floor, drawn by an irresistible magnetic pull. Ray stood on the opposite edge, a warrior on her battlefield. She lifted her chin defiantly and schooled her features back to the bubbly and vivacious girl everyone knew and loved, slipping her mask of indifference back into place, effectively shutting me out.

The only problem was, I knew Rayna Cortez better than anyone at this wedding, and she wasn't going down without a fight. She saw the rage simmering under my skin, and it had become her mission to bring me back to the light.

What she didn't realize, though, was that I had gladly accepted the darkness that had become me, and there was no reason to pull me back from its shadowy claws.

What did I have waiting for me on the other side?

RAY

I SCHOOLED my features as I sauntered my way back over to the head table, an extra sway in my step, knowing I was being watched.

Wade wasn't going to keep me from enjoying my two other best friends' wedding.

I wanted my happy-go-lucky, bubbly, full-of-life cowboy back—but I feared he had died the moment the doctor read off his test results. The killing blow came with his demand, echoing with finality, that Wade stop riding.

For Wade, riding was a form of therapy. Without it, he lost all sense of who he was at his core. The man had been born to be on the back of a horse, and I couldn't imagine the pain he was in without the ability to escape and feel the wind in his hair when he needed the space to breathe.

But his insistence on pushing me away wasn't going to fly. I knew Wade better than anyone else. We had been best friends since I was eleven, and he was thirteen. We had moments together that were special, things we didn't share with anyone else.

Wade had seen me grieve the loss of my mom, get my first period, have my first broken heart, get rejected from every college I applied to, start my business, and so many more seemingly insignificant moments through the years.

Wade and I were kindred spirits. What he felt, I felt… deeply.

I watched as he walked back over to his table, a fresh glass of bourbon in his hand, and lifted his glass to his lips, taking a hearty sip. The dim lighting of the makeshift dance floor, accented by the facing sun, accentuated the furrow between his brows.

He'd been drowning himself in alcohol since he'd come home from the hospital. We all knew there was going to be a breaking point, but none of us knew how to approach him about it without causing an emotional blowup.

Max had tried talking to him before the wedding, hoping to keep the brooding to a minimum for his big day, but Wade was having nothing to do with him.

"Ray." My best friend Stella's voice, cheerful and insistent, broke my stare at the handsome and broody cowboy drowning himself in alcohol at a table across the dance floor.

"Yeah, sorry. What were you saying?" I asked, not having any clue what the conversation going on around me was about.

"I was saying that we were thinking about heading out," she said as she stroked an errant curl away from her daughter, Charlie's forehead, and placed a tender kiss on her temple.

Charlie was curled up in the lap of Stella's new husband, Max, who was Wade's fraternal twin brother and the remaining piece of our best-friend foursome.

Stella had stumbled into our lives the year prior after running from the drug dealers who had killed her ex-boyfriend, Charlie's father. She and Max had danced around each other's feelings for months before finally accepting that they were obsessed with each other.

Wow, what a thought!

The three of them had survived so much together in the past year. Someone had abducted Charlie, Stella had gone after her, and Max had saved them both.

That night had changed everything for everyone in our friend group. It was also the night Wade lost the one thing that was possibly most important to him.

Due to an unfortunate series of circumstances, Wade was shot in the back while he was leaving the building with Stella in tow.

Although the attacker was shot by my father, the sheriff, things had already been set in motion, and Wade lay crumpled on the floor, bleeding out and unable to move his legs.

As a lasting result of the incident, he was advised that riding a horse again could potentially put pressure on his spine, which would eventually lead to a permanent loss of function in his legs.

It had been a huge emotional blow to all of us, but the notion that Wade wouldn't be able to ride again was a bitter pill to swallow, and he'd come home a different man than before that night.

Wade's life was suddenly defined by the distinction between who he was before and after the incident.

He was lost, and the blame for his unfortunate circumstances being placed on Stella was unfounded. Stella hadn't forced him into the building with Max to save Charlie; she had been perfectly content doing everything herself—much to her own detriment. Wade had gone in willingly because we were a *family,* and family sticks together.

I looked over at the happiness radiating from the newly-weds and the little family they'd been through hell for. I knew in my heart that Wade would survive this. If they could work through the trauma of the year prior, Wade could find his way back.

Max and Stella had done the hard work of going to therapy, dealing with the trauma of the event, and leaning on each other.

Wade had opted to forgo therapy and to lean into a bottle of bourbon instead. I'd never seen him so emotionless as right now.

His gaze caught mine from across the room, and the hollowness in his eyes gutted me. I felt the aching chasm that was once the man I knew. I needed to figure out a way to get my best friend back before it was too late.

"Do you think he's going to be okay?" I heard Max ask hesitantly through the haze that Wade's haunted stare had caused. I knew he was concerned; we all were, but I also knew Max had his own demons he was dealing with.

I sighed, not knowing how to answer his question. Did I think he was going to be okay? Eventually, yes. Did I think he was going to lose himself along the way? Maybe.

I went with the more diplomatic answer, not willing to bear the breaking of another Daniels boy's heart. "I think he will be, eventually. He's hurting, Max—badly. Right now, he can't see the forest for the trees. He's lost and self-medicating. Give him time."

I patted his knee, offering comfort even if it felt somewhat hollow. I wanted to believe that Wade was going to be just fine. He just needed time to heal, but this was as reserved as I'd ever seen my best friend, and I wasn't so sure the man I knew before was still in there.

"Thanks, Ray," Stella chimed in, taking my hand in hers. "For everything."

I shrugged off the compliment with a flick of my wrist and a forced smile.

There wasn't much I wouldn't do for the Daniels family, and that extended to Stella and Charlie now.

"It was nothing," I insisted.

"Nothing, my ass," she added. "You planned, organized, and executed the wedding of our dreams. All while dealing with Broody McBroodface over there."

I didn't bother looking in Wade's direction, but I could feel his eyes on me. I could always feel when his eyes were on me.

"Honestly, Stell. It was nothing. You're family, and you should know by now that family sticks together, no matter what."

I watched as her eyes caught her new husband's gaze, and an effervescent sense of peace washed over the pair of them. What I wouldn't give to have someone look at me the way Max Daniels looked at Stella. The unspoken love that coursed through them radiated from every look and simple touch.

I sighed wistfully and flicked my wrists in their direction, again effectively shooing them away.

"Go home. I've got this," I promised, standing up to start the teardown process of the nearly empty venue.

I smoothed out the skirt of my dress and turned around, catching Wade's heated stare. Refusing to give him any more of my time this evening, I broke our standoff and began cleaning.

RAY

RAY

IT TOOK me a couple of hours to tear down the venue and get everything ready for the rental company to pick up in the morning.

Since the wedding had been on D&D Ranch property, it wasn't far for me to get back to my house. I walked through the door mentally and physically exhausted, the weight of the evening pressing down on me.

I still lived at home with my dad, Emmanuel. He was the current sheriff of Firefly Cove, having received his badge and title back once he'd been cleared of any wrongdoing in Wade's attack.

Though he technically lived here, his second home was undoubtedly the police department, as he worked long hours and overnights.

With the last of us kids being old enough to fend for ourselves, Dad seemed to be at the station more and more.

It wasn't that Firefly Cove was a bustling metropolis of police activity; I think he just needed to stay busy after spending so many years chasing toddlers and kids alone.

Our property and D&D Ranch, the Daniels' property, backed up to each other, the middle point being the semi-hidden cove that the town had got its name from. Technically, the Daniels family owned the cove.

Penny—Max and Wade's mother—had insisted it be open for the public to use whenever someone from the town wanted to go there.

Normally, the locals didn't venture out that far, and the cove stayed vacant, which sure proved beneficial in our teenage years when we needed a place to go make out with our significant others behind our parents' backs.

Thinking back on the cove always brought back a swirling torrent of memories. The Daniels boys and I had spent good times, and bad, at the edge of the small creek that flowed through its center.

It stood as a place of solace amid the ever-moving landscape of our lives. Whether we needed a place to talk, express our emotions, grieve, or just *be*, the cove was there to welcome us with open arms. The surrounding foliage made us feel like we were enveloped in a comfortable silence, and it was the perfect place to unwind.

I made the split-second decision to make the hike out there, needing to clear my head of the image of Wade's hollow stare and the subsequent anger I was feeling toward his indifference.

I changed out of my bridesmaid dress, tossing it on the bed and throwing on a pair of black leggings and a threadbare Firefly Cove Police Department tee I had stolen from my dad years ago.

I snagged a hoodie off a hanger in the closet and tucked it under my arm. The cove was often chilly down at the water's edge, and I planned on sitting out there until I couldn't feel my feet—or my feelings.

I walked back through the house, stopping by the living room where I could see my dad's snoring figure posted up in his big chair.

He had gone from a twenty-four-hour stint at the station straight to the wedding, and I knew he had to be exhausted. Instead of waking him up to let him know I was leaving, I grabbed the quilt that was draped over the back of the couch and covered him up softly, turning out the lamp beside him, and bathing the living room in darkness.

His peaceful frame and lack of a deep furrow in his brow caused my heart to constrict almost imperceptibly. Since my mom died, I hadn't seen him relax much—if at all. Lately, he was either busting his ass down at the station or carting the twins and Benny to and from sporting events.

Thankfully, there were only four of us kids left at home, and I helped out where I could.

I was the oldest of ten, and my mom passed when I was thirteen. Complications during her pregnancy with my twin sisters had led to an emergency surgery post-delivery. The doctors weren't able to save her, and she bled out on the operating table.

There were days I wished I had my mom to give me guidance, but Wade's mom, Penny, had stepped in when she could after her passing.

She could never take the place of my own mother, but she was a wonderful stand-in when I needed some motherly advice. When we subsequently lost Penny, it left a gaping hole where a mother's love should have been—for all of us.

On soft feet, I padded my way toward the door. I turned the knob slowly, hoping to avoid the creak of hinges that desperately needed to be oiled.

Managing to get outside without making much noise, I shut the door with a soft click and turned around, coming face-to-face with my fifteen-year-old twin sisters.

They had the audacity to turn around and attempt to walk in the other direction, feigning as if I hadn't already seen them.

"Lucia y Sofia Cortez. Détente ahí mismo." *Lucía and Sofia Cortez. Stop right there.*

"Shit," Lucy mumbled under her breath, realizing they had been caught attempting to sneak back in.

"Shit is right. And you're going to be in deep shit if you don't get your asses inside and in bed. You've got school in the morning." I placed my hands on my hips, doing my best to act as an authoritarian and control the situation.

Being the oldest often came with the responsibility of stepping in as judge and jury when the single parent wasn't available. Not having Mom around for the entirety of the girls' lives meant they respected me, their oldest sister, as the motherly figure in the household.

They turned, dejected, and hung their heads, padding their way to the house. When Sofia's hand grabbed the doorknob, I spoke.

"Chicas."

"Si, hermana?"

Their Spanish was choppy, as Dad hadn't bothered with speaking it much after Mom passed. They could get by, but they weren't fluent like the rest of us who grew up in a bilingual household, and they didn't possess the fluidity of a native speaker.

"La próxima vez, usa la puerta trasera. Te amo." *Next time, use the back door. I love you.*

It took them a second to decipher my rolling words, even though I'd done my best to slow them down. After they mentally translated, wicked grins spread across their faces, and they nodded, entering the house.

Once the door shut and I heard the lock flip, I made my way toward the clearing of trees that led to the cove, shaking my head.

I hadn't been much different in my teenage years, but being on the receiving end of it, I now knew why Dad's hair had gone grey at the temples.

Walking through the woods between the Daniels ranch and my father's house always gave me a sense of peace and comfort.

It was eerily quiet, accented only by the sounds of the night, but the silence never felt oppressive. The chirping of crickets and the rustling of leaves were the soundtrack to some of my best memories, and the sound washed over me like a soft hug.

Easing up to the water's edge, I closed my eyes, feeling the cool bite of the wind on my skin.

Although it was chilly, I didn't reach for my hoodie. I let the icy breeze seep into my flesh, covering my arms and legs in a fresh layer of goose bumps. A small breeze blew through the cove as if whispering promises of solace and peace.

"You're gonna catch a cold," a gruff voice snapped from behind me, bursting my bubble of serenity. I didn't need to turn around to know that it belonged to the broody cowboy who inhabited the body of my best friend.

"Like you care," I groused, ignoring the pleasant warmth

of his body as he stepped up beside me. We lowered ourselves to the damp earth at the edge of the small creek.

"Sunshine…" he started, but I effectively cut him off by holding up my hand.

"Don't *Sunshine* me, Wade Alexander Daniels."

"Oh, I get the full name tonight," he said with a sardonic chuckle, and the sound floated across my bare skin like a tingle of electricity.

The glare I shot in his direction could have rivaled the icy chill that was washing over us.

I wasn't in the mood for his bullshit, which lately, there had been a lot of. I was tired of walking around in circles, attempting to ignore the elephant in the room. This shit was getting on my last nerve.

"¿Me estás tomando el pelo, Wade? ¿Tienes el descaro de venir aquí, a nuestro santuario, y burlarte del hecho de que nos trataste a mí y a todos los que te rodeaban como mierda en la boda de tu propio hermano gemelo? No, vete a la mierda."

Are you kidding me, Wade? You have the nerve to come here, to our sanctuary, and mock the fact that you treated me and everyone around you like shit at your own twin brother's wedding? No, fuck you.

His confused silence let me know that he didn't understand most of what had just come out of my mouth, but the way he wouldn't meet my eyes told me he understood the bite of my tone. The dejected way he hung his head also told me that he had been effectively scolded.

I wished that thought brought me satisfaction, but it only brought pain. I didn't want to scold Wade. I wanted him to open up to me like he had so many times before.

I closed my eyes, breathing in deeply to calm my racing heart. I didn't want to fight with Wade. He was my best friend, for fuck's sake. He knew me better than anyone else in the world.

I knew this angry side of him wasn't normal, but it didn't hurt any less when he lashed out. It hurt more knowing he didn't feel like he could reach out to anyone, especially me, in his time of need.

Opening my eyes, I was met with the image of a broken man begging for relief from the overwhelming pain and sadness he'd been feeling. The despondent look on my best friend's face gutted me to my core.

The vibrancy that normally surrounded Wade Daniels had faded, and in its wake was a shell of the man he used to be. His long, sandy-blond hair was pulled back into a bun at the back of his head. His chocolate-brown eyes that normally twinkled with mischief were lifeless, dark purple bags underneath, hinting at the sleepless nights I knew he'd been fighting through.

I tenderly skated my fingers across the back of his hand, softly turning it palm side up and lacing our fingers together. He tightened his grip three times in quick succession. Our silent gesture of the mutual love we have for each other. Three times for three words. *I love you.*

What started as a childhood secret handshake, one that only we shared, turned into discretely sharing teenage crushes, and eventual adult affection.

In seventeen years of friendship, we'd never crossed the line into anything past the friend zone, except for once. Neither of us was willing to make a move that could ultimately break the sacred bond we'd worked so hard to build.

But seeing him so dejected, and so sad, had me itching to crawl into his lap and kiss away the pain. I'd do anything to take away the torture inside his mind, even if it meant sacrificing my own happiness—but I couldn't lose the best friend I'd ever had.

RAY - 11 YEARS OLD

I PUSHED THROUGH THE WOODS, prickles and brambles snagging on my jeans as I went. I was suddenly glad I had listened and worn jeans instead of the shorts I'd originally planned on wearing.

Daddy told me to make sure I dressed in tough clothes if I planned to venture out into the woods.

I don't think he'd be very happy about how far I had gone from the house, though, right before dinner.

I hadn't meant to walk this far, but I'd honestly gotten a little lost as I tried to remember which way was back to the house and which way was farther into the woods. I heard the gurgle of water, letting me know I was for sure heading the wrong way. Daddy was going to be so mad at me for getting lost out here.

He had told me to stick to the surrounding property, but I just kept walking and walking, relishing the quiet, which was hard to come by at home.

It was almost dark, and I knew soon that he and Mama

would be getting the rest of the kids ready for bed, and I needed to figure out how to make my way back.

I pushed through some very thick branches and on the other side found the water I had been hearing. A pretty stream wound past the trees, so I approached the bank, testing the temperature of the water with my fingers.

Past the sandy water's edge, I felt my sneaker slipping in the mud and braced myself for the inevitable fall that was coming.

Before my butt could hit, a hand reached out and grabbed my elbow.

I tensed, my breath catching in my throat because I hadn't noticed anyone else here. A scream threatened to jump out of my throat.

This was it. I was going to die. An axe murderer was going to kill me, chop my body into bits, and I'd never be seen again.

All because I couldn't just stick to the woods around the house like Mama and Daddy had told me to.

"Whoa. Don't fall," a boy's voice grumbled from behind me. I could hear the old Southern twang in the way he talked, but he sounded young, which took me by surprise.

I took a chance and pried my eyes open to see my attacker, figuring if I got away, I could at least describe the person who assaulted me.

Except it wasn't an attacker at all; it was a boy around my age who looked boyishly charming and nothing like the murderer I'd envisioned.

"You gonna scream? I don't really need my ma and pops thinking I'm out here hurtin' someone."

My voice finally came back as my heart rate slowed. I was still hesitant, but this boy seemed innocent enough.

Actually, now that I got a good look, he was kinda cute. He had scruffy blond hair that reached almost over his ears, curling upward like he'd been wearing a hat all day.

His eyes were dark brown, like chocolate syrup. He had tiny little freckles sprinkled across his cheeks and nose that looked like stars scattered through the night sky.

"No, I'm not going to scream. But please don't kill me," I huffed as he helped steady me before letting go of my arm.

"Kill ya?" he chuckled, snagging a cowboy hat off the ground and plopping it back on his head.

Well, there was the reason his hair looked the way it did, the blond locks curling underneath the wide brim. "Why would I kill ya?"

"I don't know. I just figured it was creepy to be walking through the woods at night. It's something a killer would do." I straightened my shirt and brushed off my pants, hoping to get rid of the sweaty palms that had cropped up after noticing his proximity and relative attractiveness.

Why was this boy suddenly making me nervous?

I took another look at him. He definitely looked familiar, but I couldn't put my finger on where I knew him from, and we were still relatively new to town.

Ignoring my rambling about serial killers, he brushed the dirt from his jeans.

"You're the new girl, right? Just got here last month?" he asked, putting his thumbs in his belt loops.

He looked like a tried-and-true cowboy with his jeans, button-down shirt with pearls on the snaps, and black cowboy hat atop his head, standing with an air of confidence that can't be taught.

"Uh. Yeah." I hummed skeptically. I wasn't about to give

some random stranger in the woods all the intimate details of my life.

"I remember my ma saying something about a new family that moved in next door, but we haven't had a chance to come over and introduce ourselves yet, on account of it being calving season and all." He kicked at the ground around the bank, a small stone tumbling into the water and making a tiny splash. I wondered whether he knew how to skip rocks.

"Do you know how to skip rocks?" I blurted out, not bothering to respond to his previous statement about living next door. Apparently, my mouth had a mind of its own.

"Uh… not really." His brow furrowed in confusion, but it didn't seem like my abrupt change in subject really phased him. He looked at me with an examining stare, like he was trying to figure me out, but there was no judgment in his eyes.

"I know how to skip rocks," I said with an air of confidence, straightening my back and flicking my pigtail braids over my shoulders. I could at least pretend that he wasn't making me nervous.

"That's actually pretty cool." His smile stretched across his face, and little swirly butterflies flapped in my belly. I'd never felt that before.

I wondered if I was coming down with a stomach bug. Izzy had been sick last week, so maybe I'd caught what she had. Hopefully, I didn't puke in front of this guy.

"So.. Are you—"

"Rayna!!" I heard Mama's faint shouting from the back porch. She didn't sound frantic—yet—but I knew if I didn't start moving my butt and quickly, she was going to lose her mind.

"That's my mama. I've gotta go," I said, hiking a thumb over my shoulder in the direction I assumed was my house.

"Do you want me to walk you back?" the boy asked, scratching at the back of his neck with what looked to be a little bit of nervousness. Okay, so I wasn't the only one nervous here.

"Actually, that would be cool. I kinda got lost on the way out here, which is how I ended up by the water."

"The Cove," he corrected. I furrowed my brows in confusion and tilted my head to one side.

"The Cove?" I asked, hoping he would clarify.

"Yeah, this little stream and clearing are called the cove. It's where the town got its name from, or so my ma says," he explained. "It's halfway between my house and yours. We live on the other side, over there."

He pointed toward the thick portion of the forest behind me. It was starting to get dark, so I was honestly thankful he had offered to walk me back to my house.

I wasn't super comfortable walking alone in the dark; plus, I wasn't sure I could figure out which way I needed to go.

"Come on, I'll walk you back; maybe you can tell me the secret to skippin' rocks," he said, gesturing for me to walk toward where we'd heard Mama yellin' from.

We walked side by side, chatting about little things as we went. I learned that his name was Wade Alexander Daniels and that he had a twin. His brother Max and he were fraternal twins, meaning they didn't look alike but were born at the same time.

I also learned that he was a little older than me. He was thirteen, meaning he'd be heading off to high school next year.

For some reason, even in the short time we'd spent talking, that made me a little sad. I enjoyed talking to Wade, and I hadn't really gotten a chance to make many friends since moving here.

Having seven younger siblings meant I was asked to help out a lot at home. It didn't leave much room for hanging out with friends.

I told Wade all about my siblings, easily rattling off all seven of their names and ages. All the way from Isabella, the closest in age to me, to Benedicto, who was still a tiny baby. It was always a challenge for people to remember all of their names, so I normally resorted to just telling them I had three younger sisters and four younger brothers.

Wade talked animatedly about the horses they kept on their ranch, rattling off their names just as easily as I had my siblings.

He told me all about wanting to be a rodeo star when he got older, although he said he wasn't crazy enough to compete as a bronc rider. He wanted to work with cattle and roping. I told him that sounded mean for the cows, but he assured me that it was relatively safe.

There wasn't ever an awkward moment between us, and as the back porch of my house came into view, I started getting a little sad that we weren't going to be able to talk much longer. I couldn't imagine a thirteen-year-old boy really wanting to be seen hanging around with an eleven-year-old girl, outside the comfort of our little bubble in the woods.

"Uh, so, thanks for walking me back to the house. I probably would have gotten lost again had I tried." I chuckled.

Wade was so easy to talk to, and I was glad he'd stumbled upon me in the woods, even if he hadn't quite proven he wasn't a killer yet.

"Ain't no problem, Sunshine," he drawled. A small smile

curved at the corner of his mouth, and I loved the little dimple that popped up as his lips kicked up on one side.

"Oh, we're on a nickname basis now?" I elbowed him playfully as I laughed.

"I mean, you're kinda cool. You don't act like all the rest of the girls I know."

"Yeah, I bet you know a lot of girls." I huffed.

A blind girl could have seen that he was cute. Any girl looking at him would have fallen over themselves to get a peek at those dimples and listen to that Southern twang.

He had an old Western cowboy charm about him, and I was sure he probably had a girlfriend—most cute thirteen-year-old boys did.

"I mean, I know some, but none of them want to skip rocks or talk about horses with me." He adjusted his cowboy hat to cover his eyes, and I kicked it back up with the flick of my wrist.

"Okay, John Wayne," I teased as he adjusted his hat back over his eyes. I could see a faint blush creep over his cheeks, and it made me smile, knowing I made him as nervous as he made me.

"Most of the girls I know are all boy crazy right now. None of them want to be just friends. They're all about kissin' and stuff."

"I'll be your friend." My mouth fired before I even had a chance to think about what was coming out of it. He probably thought I was just as bad as those boy-crazy girls who wanted to kiss and stuff.

"I think I'd like that." His smile was wide as he held out his hand for a handshake. "Shake on it?"

"Well, if we're going to be friends, *best friends*, we should probably have a secret handshake." I tapped my finger to my lips, thinking of a secret handshake on the fly. I didn't want him to think I was some little kid, so it needed to be something short and easy, not something like elementary school kids do on the playground.

"Give me your hand," I said, standing directly beside him and extending my left hand out to my side. To anyone else, it would look like I was trying to hold his hand.

Without hesitation, he put his right hand in mine, his stance rigid beside me. I felt little prickles spread throughout my fingers, but I ignored them as I squeezed my grip three times, one after the other.

"There," I said definitively, releasing his hand. He looked up at me, a confused expression on his face.

"That's it?" he questioned.

"Yep. Three squeezes. One for each word in 'best friends forever,'" I said with an air of confidence. The handshake wasn't elaborate, but it felt natural, and it was subtle enough to be hidden from anyone else. It felt right.

"Okay. Best friends forever," he said, grabbing hold of my hand again and squeezing three times in quick succession just like I had done. He let go as quickly as he'd grabbed it, and I suddenly wished he didn't have to leave. But I could see Mama sitting on the porch waiting for me, a grumpy look on her face.

"I'll see you later," I said as I walked toward the back of my house, waving animatedly over my shoulder.

"See you later, Sunshine," he called after me, and I smiled. I liked it when he called me Sunshine. Those butterflies started flying all around my belly when he did.

When I got about halfway back, I turned around. I saw Wade walking back into the thick brush, and I shouted after him before he disappeared.

"Hey, Wade!" He turned back around, one eyebrow cocked up in question. "Since we're using nicknames now, I'm gonna call you Waddle."

"Waddle?" he asked, his eyes growing wide at the obnoxiously stupid nickname I'd come up with on a whim.

"Your initials are W-A-D, so it seemed better than just calling you Wad."

He shook his head and laughed, clearly amused by my answer. I added a tally in the "win" column of my best friend's playbook.

Without responding, he turned back to the woods to head to his house. I didn't miss the smile that split across his face or the gentle shake of his shoulders in laughter as he turned away from me.

As I reached the top of the stairs, Mama was sitting in her rocking chair with a knowing grin plastered on her face, replacing her earlier scowl.

"¿Quién era esa Princesa?" *Who was that, Princess?* she asked, sipping the lemonade that rested beside her.

"Mi mejor amigo." *My best friend,* I responded, the impish grin never leaving my face.

Mama just shook her head and sighed. She stood and used her gentle fingers to brush a hand across the crown of my head. Leaning over, she placed a tender kiss on my forehead.

"¿Ah, es así?" *Ah, is that so?* She smirked, still shaking her head as she walked back through the sliding glass door into the kitchen.

I sat in the rocking chair on the back porch for another ten minutes, replaying the conversation Wade and I had shared. I don't think the devil himself could wipe the smile from my face if he tried. I was too smitten with my new best friend, the cowboy next door.

WADE

FEELING like a semitruck had run me over, I hauled another bale of hay from the loft above the barn down into the open area below, listening for the heavy thud as it hit the ground.

After leaving Max and Stella's wedding, I'd gone home and continued drinking, attempting to drown out the nightmares that would come when I inevitably closed my eyes. That left me fighting through a massive hangover this morning, and I didn't even get much sleep.

Getting fucked up when you were cresting thirty wasn't exactly my idea of a good time.

I couldn't escape the nightmares. No matter what I drank, how much I drank, who I fucked, or what I did, the images of that night haunted me. They lay in wait until I was on the precipice of sleep, dragging me under as my body finally relaxed. I'd woken up every single night with searing pain scorching its way through my back, the scar beside my spine a physical reminder of all I had sacrificed.

But was it really a valiant sacrifice if I harbored so much animosity toward the person I had done it for?

I hauled the next bale of hay just a little harder, willing my body to wear down enough so that there was no consciousness left for my brain to conjure thoughts of the incident. I channeled my rage, pushing through the pain and exhaustion to get the day's chores done.

"I thought your ma named you Wade, not Hulk," a gruff voice called from down below.

Stripping the hat off my head, I ran the back of my arm across my sweat-slicked forehead before placing it back on. I tugged off my work gloves, tucking them in the back pocket of my jeans before climbing down the ladder from the hayloft to greet Pops.

"Just trying to get this hay moved since Max rode off on his white steed into the sunset with his bride."

I didn't mask my bitterness as the words exited my mouth, but nothing ever phased Pops. He stood firm, much like the enduring branches of the old willow that shaded the earth above my mother's resting place.

He took every ounce of fury I'd given him over the last couple of months and weathered it with unflappable flexibility.

There wasn't much that could break my pops, especially not the wrath I'd been throwing around. After all, he had put up with Ma's smart mouth for over forty years.

"I'd say after the year they've had, they deserve a little bit of happiness," he scolded, shooting a cutting look in my direction.

My scoff echoed through the barn before being swallowed up by the whinnying of horses and stomping of hooves.

"Yeah, well, good for them. Glad they get their happily ever after."

Pops just shook his head, not bothering to feed into the

terrible mood I'd shrouded myself in. I brushed past him, heading toward the stables, shutting down the conversation. I grabbed a hay bale as I went, hefting it onto my shoulder with practiced ease, not bothering with putting on my gloves, hoping the bite of the twine around the straw would quell the raging fire inside me.

There was a frustration in me that grew stronger as I hefted each bale, reminding me that lifting heavy weights was fine, but getting on a horse was forbidden.

The doctors had cleared me for lifting, but the way my spine would compact with each jostle in the saddle was too dangerous to chance.

I could use a drink.

I stomped into the stables, dropping the bale of hay outside the first stall. My horse, Blackjack, slung his head over the gate and whined in protest, stomping his feet at the fact that I hadn't yet given him attention. I stopped to quickly scratch his long, jet-black ears and run my hand down his whiskery snout.

Blackjack had been a present from Ma and Pops on my sixteenth birthday. We had trained hard over the years, and there was a sacred bond between us.

It killed me not to be able to take him out for another ride. I had toyed with the idea of selling him to a rider who could give him the attention he needed, but the selfishness in me wouldn't allow that to happen.

With one last scratch to his neck, I hauled the hay bale into his stall and turned back to grab another.

I'd taken over the daily chores while Max and Stella were on their honeymoon, leaving little free time for anything enjoyable.

They'd opted to take a family vacation to one of the

beaches in South Carolina instead of something more elaborate. Neither Stella nor Max wanted to be without Charlie, and honestly, I couldn't blame them.

But getting up each day at the ass crack of dawn to feed the horses, muck stalls, and then working a full day training wasn't my idea of a good time. Coupled with the fact that I couldn't take the edge off with a ride left me grumpy as fuck.

I felt Pops' presence at my back as I bent down and pulled out a pocketknife, sawing through the twine holding the bale of hay together.

I didn't bother making idle chitchat. Neither of us was very keen to talk about feelings, so we didn't bother discussing what had me slinging hay around like it had done me wrong.

I just needed to get through these chores, get through my training session, and then get back to the house so I could crack open a bottle and wash away the day.

Maybe I'd call up one of the buckle bunnies stored in my phone that lived close enough and get in a quick fuck. Nothing helped quell rage better than fucking out your feelings.

As I stood up straight, tucking the small knife back in the pocket of my jeans, a twinge of pain shot through my back. I hissed through my teeth, clamping them shut to fight off the burning sensation in my scar, as I waited for the fiery tendrils to recede.

It had been six months since the incident, and I still got residual shots of pain if I twisted wrong or stood up too fast. The bullet had nicked my lower lumbar, causing a chip of bone to break off.

During the surgery, they had done their best to remove any fragments left behind, but they said there was a possibility of minuscule pieces causing scar tissue to build, and I'd get little pains here and there.

Essentially, what they'd told me, in layman's terms, was that I'd feel the pain of being shot in the back for the rest of my fucking life. I'd have to deal with debilitating pain no matter how much physical therapy I did, how many surgeries I had, or how much I tried to fight it. I'd have a constant reminder of the night my life had changed and the fact that I wasn't ever going to be able to do the thing I loved most again.

"You okay there, son?" Pops asked from his seat on a wooden bench near the tack room, legs kicked out in front of him in relaxation.

Why he hung around the stables after he'd opted to retire from hard labor made no sense. But, truthfully, not much Pops did made much sense.

"Just fucking peachy," I gritted out, not bothering to look up. I massaged my scar, helping break up the pressure until all that remained was a dull ache.

"You know—"

"Good morning, handsome Daniels men!" a sing-songy voice echoed through the stables. I groaned, not wanting to deal with Ray's sunshiny bullshit this morning, especially hungover.

She waltzed through the barn doors, all spitfire and sass, patting me on the chest as she passed by.

I turned my head skyward and internally counted to ten to keep myself from saying or doing something stupid.

I did my best not to stare at her heart-shaped ass as she walked through the stables toward where the horse she often rode was ready to be tacked up for the day, but the way her jeans curved over her hips and molded to her legs had me adjusting myself discreetly.

Even if my brain kept saying no, my cock kept saying yes, please.

As if she could feel my eyes boring a hole in her back, she looked over her shoulder at me, flicking her hair behind her as she winked.

I rolled my eyes, feigning indifference, but the truth was she could have worn a feed sack and I would have thought she was the most beautiful woman in the room.

Unfortunately for me, Ray knew how to press my buttons, and she loved watching me squirm.

Trailing behind her, her sister Isabella, Izzy for short, stopped to pat me on the shoulder in solidarity.

Izzy was everything Ray wasn't. She was still stunning in her own right, but she was tall, lean, and vicious. She knew the dangerous game that Ray and I had been playing over the years and was highly team "fuck and move on" as she liked to call it.

I had been training Izzy for the greater part of five years now, after I retired from the rodeo circuit.

She was only fourteen months younger than Ray but had been spared the parenting nuances that came along with being the oldest. Ray had taken the brunt of those responsibilities, and it showed in her protectiveness over her siblings.

Izzy was wild, sometimes a little reckless, and it absolutely benefited her when she was competing, but sometimes I wondered if it translated into her personal life a little too much.

She was a champion barrel racer, having numerous buckles and sponsorships to her name. She had trained under another rodeo star previously, but when I'd opened my training business, she had gladly jumped ship to help me get my feet off the ground, and I was thankful to her for believing in me.

She was a natural on her horse, Oakley, and had the winning streak to prove it. She had been on the circuit at the same time as me but was young and still had quite a few years of racing left in her. She rode hard and played harder.

Eventually, that lifestyle would catch up with her, but I hoped that with enough influence from Ray, she wouldn't end up broken like I had.

"When you're done staring at my sister's ass, I'd like to run through some drills in prep for December."

For fuck's sake, that girl had no filter. I was used to barrel racers being a little crazy, but Izzy took it to another level. She could pal around with the best of the guys and never blink an eye at their crudity.

Yep, today was about to be fucking fantastic.

Pops and I made quick work of tacking up Oakley for Izzy and Sunset, one of our more docile mares, for Ray.

She wasn't here every day that Izzy came to train, but when she had a break in clients, she liked to come out and take one of the horses out on the trails for a while. She said it helped clear her head when she was stuck in a design rut to get out in nature. She claimed it helped calm her mind. Half the time, I assumed she came out here just to torture me.

After we got the horses tacked, Izzy led Oakley out to the dirt corral where I'd already set up her barrels for training. She didn't need much coaching, but she liked to have an additional set of eyes on her stance the closer it got to competition time. She often dropped one of her shoulders on turn three and needed constant reminding to keep her core tight.

Instead of watching the younger Cortez sister, my eyes

were glued to Ray as she placed her booted feet in the stirrups and mounted Sunset with ease. She had come a long way in her riding since the first time I'd gotten her on a horse, and a sense of pride flooded through me watching her trot off toward the trails.

"You two ever going to sort your shit out?" Pops grumbled from behind me, dusting the hay off his jeans from spreading it in the empty stalls.

"No shit to sort out," I grumbled back.

It was the same old song and dance around here constantly. Everyone knew Ray and I were head over heels for each other, and they'd been pushing us together for years. Neither Ray nor I had ever crossed that line—well, except once, that neither of us has talked about since.

What if we did, and things didn't work out? I'd lose the best friend I'd ever had, and I don't know that I would survive that. Ray was my center, my true north. She had been there for me through thick and thin, and I couldn't take a chance of losing her.

I looked over at Pops, who was shaking his head and chuckling lightly, muttering something about "stupid fuckin' cowboys."

"Have I ever told you the story of how your ma and I started datin'?" he asked. I could hear the hurt in his voice just mentioning Ma, and it gutted me, but the fact that he was bringing her up willingly had me listening intently.

"Only about fifty times," I responded, not knowing where he was heading with this.

"Your mother…" He cleared his throat, emotion threatening to take over. "Your mother was my saving grace. She walked through hell to pull me from the rubble I called a life. She was kind. She was beautiful. And for some reason, she thought the sun rose and set with me, a rugged ass cowboy without a care in the world."

I didn't dare interrupt his reminiscing. It wasn't often we talked about Ma since she'd passed. She was the glue that held our family together, and without her, we spent a lot of time picking up the pieces to put our lives back together. But here's the thing—no matter how you piece something broken back together, it never quite fits the same again.

"She brought me back to life when all I could see was darkness. She saw something *good* in me that I couldn't see myself. Your ma was the kind of woman who wouldn't ever give up, no matter how many times I pushed her away."

He walked with me out to the dirt corral as I watched Izzy warm Oakley up. We leaned against the thick metal fencing, and I nodded at him to continue.

"Your mother was the *only* one who never gave up on me. When everyone else said I was too much to handle, she kept coming back. One night after your grandpop had lit into me good about getting my life on track, I got to drinking real heavy and almost got behind the wheel of the car. Son, she looked me dead in the eyes and said, 'I'd miss you if you were gone.'" He sniffed, pushing back the tears that threatened to fall. Even though it's said that cowboys don't cry, when it comes to our women, that shit's a lie.

"She saved my life that night. I was ready to risk it all because I felt like everything was falling apart around me. But this spitfire of a woman telling me that she would miss me brought me back from the darkness enough to *try*. After that night, I never let her go."

I kicked my booted foot against the metal bars we were leaning on outside of the corral. I could feel the emotion welling up inside of me, and I pushed it down, forcing it back into the neat little box I had it stored in.

"Son, that girl over there," he subtly pointed to where Ray had ridden off, no longer in view, "that girl sees your darkness and still thinks the sun shines out of your ass, no matter how far up it you have your head shoved."

I groaned, dangling my hands over the top of the fencing and dipping my head between my shoulders. We had been over this so many times, and no one was getting the hint.

"I can't go there, Pops. She's my best friend, and if something ruined that friendship…" I couldn't even vocalize the fear.

Thoughts of a life without Ray had my heart racing as sweat dampened my brow. The very thought of not having her in my life caused such a visceral reaction that I gripped my hands harder on the rungs to keep them from shaking.

"I'm afraid, boy, you're already there, whether or not you want to admit it. You love that girl, and she loves you. The question is, are you going to do something about it, or are you going to let her walk away?"

I sighed as he patted me on the shoulder and walked back toward the stables, whistling, without a care in the world. Acting like he hadn't just set an explosive at my feet and lit the fuse.

I was going to do absolutely nothing about the fact that I was in love with Rayna Cortez because she could do so much better. She deserved better. But would I actually be able to watch her walk away?

RAY

I CAME BACK from my trail ride refreshed and clear-headed. The winding slope through the forest had calmed me in a way that was hard to explain. The steady cadence of Sunset's hooves tamping down the dirt served as a metronome to even out my heartbeat, and with each step farther into the forest, I felt the weight of life lifting off my shoulders.

Pressure like I'd never felt before had been weighing me down over the course of the last month.

Dad had been working overtime, trying to make up for the work he'd gotten behind on while out on administrative leave. That left me as the sole parental figure to three teenagers. I did my best, but I couldn't hold a candle to the woman my mother had been or the man my father was, nor did I want to parent teenagers when I had barely crested out of those years myself.

Life wasn't fair, but I had only one life, and I refused to let my baby siblings grow up too fast, as I had been forced to.

Lucia and Sofia, the twins, kept me on my toes. If they weren't sneaking out, they were blasting pop music from their room or attempting to give me a heart attack with their wardrobe choices.

At least Benny, the other teen occupying the house, was quiet and respectful. At seventeen, he was more responsible than any of the other kids by a long shot, even me at times. Between football, track, and swimming, we barely saw him. When we did, he was eating us out of house and home, growing like a weed and focusing on his endless schoolwork.

Although at fifteen and seventeen, the kids were pretty self-sufficient, they still couldn't be left to their own devices, and with Dad working nonstop, someone had to step in.

Which left me, the oldest, to pick up the slack when Dad needed help.

As Sunset and I trotted our way back to the stables, I felt the prickling sensation of eyes on me. I ignored Wade's gaze, feigning indifference, even though the mere thought of his eyes trailing over the slopes of my body as I used every muscle to stay atop the horse sent sparks straight to my core.

I can only imagine the visual, as I'd seen him in the same scenario time and time again during his rodeo days and riding around the ranch.

Watching him on a horse was sweet torture and an aphrodisiac blended into the form of a powerful cowboy riding a majestic horse in the tightest jeans known to man.

Pulling the reins to stop Sunset, I dismounted with the grace of a manatee. No matter how many times I went out for a ride, I always ended up feeling the effects of it for days.

I wasn't put on a horse as soon as I came out of the womb like the Daniels boys, nor was I a natural like Izzy. I rode occasionally when I could, which often left me sore and waddling around the house for a couple of days as my muscles attempted to heal from the relentless beating they took.

I had somehow ended up with a couple of free hours between clients this afternoon, so I took the opportunity when it presented itself.

I surely hadn't come down to the ranch hoping to catch the eye of a certain broody cowboy who was currently slinging hay like it owed him rent money.

Not. At. All.

"I can feel you staring, Sunshine," he called from the large stable doorway.

With expert ease, he sliced the twine that held together the dry hay, his back to me as he spoke.

I rolled my eyes and walked Sunset over to the wash rack to hose her down. Even though it wasn't extremely hot, Sunset was getting up there in age, and the water helped cool her down, wash her off, and calm any inflammation in her joints that might surface from the walk on uneven terrain.

Just as I was finishing cleaning her off, Izzy brought over Oakley and repeated the routine, cooling down her own horse.

Oakley was much younger than Sunset, but the riders undoubtedly treated championship horses better than they treated themselves.

Izzy and I put the girls out to pasture to graze after they had been cleaned off. We leaned against the metal fencing, watching the majestic gait of the pair as they trotted off happily to munch on grass, and probably roll in dirt directly after their bath.

Izzy turned around, leaning back and propping one booted foot on the rungs of the fencing. Her long dark hair was braided and draped over one shoulder, her head covered with a straw Stetson.

With her dark features and angular lines of her face, she looked menacing, but those close to her knew she was soft under all that rugged exterior. She was all bark and no bite.

"You know, if I wasn't already engaged to a fine fuckin' specimen of a man…" She sighed, nodding her head in Wade's direction. I turned around, mirroring her pose as we watched him work.

Wade was unloading hay from the trailer into the barn, his muscles contracting with each tug and pull on the heavy bales. He wasn't wearing his signature cowboy hat today. Instead, he had a ball cap on to shield his face from the blinding sun. His hair was pulled back into a bun and threaded through the snapback, keeping it off his neck.

The grey T-shirt he was wearing was drenched with sweat, sticking to every line and curve of his muscled torso. The way his jeans clung to his thick thighs and ass was enough to have me nearly panting and my nipples tightening in desire. Every cut of muscle and rope of sinew had been hard earned through rugged manual labor.

"Yeah…" I sighed wistfully.

Sensing an audience, Wade did what he did best and leaned into the show. His eyes met mine in a silent challenge as he brushed his gloved hands over his jeans, dusting off the stray hay remnants.

With his eyes locked on mine, he placed the tip of his gloved pointer finger between his teeth, biting down to tug off the leather, repeating the motion with the other hand. He tucked the set of gloves into the back pocket of his jeans, giving them a little extra tightness around his ass.

He pulled off his ball cap and fisted the back of his shirt. In one swift motion, he tugged it over his head and used the shirt to wipe the sweat from his brow.

Eyes locked back on mine, he tossed his T-shirt to the side and slipped his hat back on— backward.

Fuck.

I watched a drop of sweat trail down his neck and roll across his stomach, settling in the waistband of his boxers that peeked from under his jeans.

I could feel the tingling between my thighs as I watched him work, shamelessly checking out the way his chiseled abs rippled with each tug and pull of the hay bales.

Over the last year, especially, we had fought our feelings for each other tooth and nail. I knew one day they would come to a head, but I wasn't sure I was ready for the impending explosion and destruction that moment would leave in its wake.

Wade and I were playing with fire, and I wasn't sure I was ready to watch the world burn yet.

"Girl, I know I'm your sister," Izzy started, also shamelessly checking him out. "But if you don't ride that…"

"Hush," I scolded, slapping her in the chest with the back of my hand. "I'm sure you'd be changing your tune if Tanner were here." I cut my eyes over at her, and I may have been seeing things, but I could have sworn a flicker of disappointment flashed across her face.

Tanner was her long-term fiancé. They had gotten engaged after her last big rodeo win. He was an attorney in Atlanta, which meant she didn't see him as often as I think she would have liked.

He was nice, clean-cut, and had a respectable job. Honestly, he was a little *too* clean-cut for Izzy's tastes, but she sang his praises any chance she could, and they had been together for years.

She schooled her features quickly, washing away that

fleeting look, a feline smile lazily stretching across her face. I knew that smirk, and it generally meant trouble.

The myth about barrel racers being a little bit crazy? Yeah, it wasn't a myth at all.

"Hey, Cowboy!" she shouted in Wade's direction. He stopped what he was doing to turn around, his hands on his hips, accentuating the muscles in his abs and the sweat-slicked V that trailed down to—*nope, he was my best friend.*

I would not think about what he was packing below the belt. Even if he was giving off broody big-dick energy.

"Yeah, rookie?" he asked, quirking an eyebrow.

"We're all heading down to Jack's this Saturday to celebrate the last free weekend before real training begins. Tanner's got the weekend off from trial prep, Max and Stella will be back and already have a sitter for Charlie, and Ray here needs a dancing partner. You up for it? First round's on me."

I hadn't heard anything about going to Jack's—the dive bar in town—this weekend, so I was sure that Izzy was up to something, but I'd let her meddle just a bit. It wouldn't hurt to have a night out.

Wade's eyes caught mine, questioning if I was thinking the same thing he was. We both could sense that there was an ulterior motive behind Izzy's invitation, but I tipped my head up in a defiant nod, challenging him to a good time.

"I'm sure your sister could have her pick of dancin' partners," he started, and I felt my bravado slowly deflate. "But it's been a while since we've shown the town what the dynamic duo can do."

I could feel the excitement vibrating through my core at not only a night out, but a night out with my best friend and sister. I caught his eye and gave him a smile, but the responding grin he shot back didn't reach his eyes.

The performance he had just put on? It was just that, a performance. He was pretending as if everything was fine, so people would stop questioning if he was okay.

I missed seeing the slight twinkle of mischief that always seemed to sparkle in his gaze and the way his smile lit up his entire face.

Hopefully, a night out was just what we all needed to get our heads on straight.

My mind played back to one of my favorite times we'd gone out dancing together. The only night we tiptoed over the line from friendship into something more.

WADE - 18 YEARS OLD

SENIOR PROM WAS SUPPOSED to be a night to remember—full of beautiful dresses on beautiful girls, flowers, dancing, and sometimes, sex. It was a night out without inhibitions, and I could absolutely use it.

Training for my first rodeo had picked up over the last six months, and I was exhausted.

I truly was only planning on going because Max and I had vowed to live our senior year of high school to the fullest.

I was heading off on the rodeo circuit after graduation, and Max was taking over helping Pops with the farm. As soon as that diploma hit our hands, our lives truly began.

Standing in front of the floor-length mirror in Ma and Pops' bedroom, I adjusted my bowtie and smoothed back my hair. I don't know why I was so nervous; I was only going with Ray.

We had decided that going as friends would be best for both of us. I didn't want to take a date and feed into the idea that I would be available for dating post-graduation.

My focus was solely on making it to the NFR my first year in the circuit, and I couldn't be distracted by tits and ass.

Truthfully, though, I didn't ask anyone to be my date because I didn't want to go to prom with anyone other than Ray. She might have been my best friend, but none of the girls at school held a candle to how beautiful, funny, and strong she was.

Plus, after losing her mom at the beginning of high school, I figured she could use a night off from acting as the additional parent around the house.

I couldn't imagine the stress Mr. Cortez was under, being a single parent to ten kids, but being the sheriff now had its perks, and the town had rallied around their family to help in any way they could.

I knew that Ray's having the night off was going to be tough on him, but she deserved it. She deserved to feel like a teenager, even if she turned back into a pumpkin at midnight.

The doorbell chimed, and I could feel my palms slick with sweat. I brushed them along my pants, trying to dry them off before having to answer the door. I don't know why I was so nervous; it was just Ray.

Thankfully, I didn't have to twist open the knob with my sweaty hands, because Ma had already answered and was gushing in the living room about how beautiful she looked.

I took one last look in the mirror and schooled my nerves enough to head downstairs. As soon as my foot hit the last stair and my eyes lifted to the foyer, my heart stopped.

It was as if someone had turned the volume on the TV from the highest level to complete silence. The only sound was the pounding of my heart as it attempted to return to its normal rhythm. I stood there, unable to speak, completely stunned by the sight before me.

Ray was standing beside the front door, listening intently to whatever Ma was chatting her ear off about. It gave me a few minutes to look my fill uninterrupted. She was a vision in a form-fitting black satin gown that draped beautifully over every inch of her tanned skin.

She hadn't given me any hints as to what her dress looked like, other than the color and that I needed to match.

Her hair was curled and left hanging in thick, dark waves around her shoulders. She had it pinned up on one side with some sort of clip with pearls on it. She looked like a Hollywood starlet, all glitz and glam, ready to take the world by storm.

Somehow, she looked older than the sixteen she actually was.

Ma noticed I was standing awkwardly at the bottom of the stairs and gently tapped Ray's elbow. She turned, and it felt like every ounce of electricity in the room was funneled straight through my system the second her ruby red lips kicked up into her signature smirk.

I knew my best friend was stunning. I had watched each and every one of my friends fall over themselves for a chance to talk to her. She commanded a room with her electric personality and unparalleled charm. But as I stood there looking like a love-struck fool in the foyer of my parents' living room, I realized she wasn't just stunning, funny, and full of life. Ray was everything.

She was perfect, and I wanted her to be *mine*.

The girl I had met five years prior in the middle of the woods, asking to skip rocks and be my best friend, was gone. In her place was this stunning woman who had every hair on my body standing on end and my heart beating overtime.

I don't know how I hadn't seen it before, but my eyes were suddenly open, and I was struck dumb.

I knew at that moment that Rayna Cortez was going to either break my heart or set my soul on fire. But either way, I was royally fucked.

RAY - 16 YEARS OLD

STANDING IN THE DANIELS' living room, trying not to fidget with my dress, I felt every minute of Wade's attention like a brand across my skin.

I watched his eyes take in every feature as if he were seeing me for the first time. His gaze started at the tips of my freshly painted toes and coasted across the draping fabric of my silk gown until his brown eyes met mine.

He looked awestruck, and I preened under his undivided attention. It wasn't every day that a girl got the complete and undivided attention of Wade Daniels.

I had watched as he'd blossomed into the rugged man before me over the last five years. I'd also watched as every girl in our school tripped over themselves to get a sliver of his time.

Wade looked every bit the rugged cowboy he was trying to portray, except he'd cleaned up for the evening and put on a well-tailored suit. His sandy-blond hair was long, hanging half up, half down, in his signature "man bun." He was wearing a solid black tux and patent leather shoes, the perfect complement to my gown.

I had given Ma explicit instructions that Wade was not to know what my dress looked like. I wanted to surprise him. By the way he was struck dumb in the middle of his living room, I knew I had made the right choice.

He shook his head as if pulling himself from a daze and stumbled forward awkwardly. I'd never seen Wade awkward a day in his life, but right now, he was fumbling over his feet to right himself.

I could hear Ma and Pops chuckling from the kitchen as they watched from behind the archway. Ma had made herself scarce, citing the need to get my corsage from the fridge, but I knew she and Pops wanted to watch this shitshow unfold.

"Uhm… Hi," Wade said, clearing his throat and scrubbing a hand over the back of his neck.

"Hey," I replied, attempting to quell the nervous butterflies that had taken flight in my stomach.

Wade always gave me butterflies, but it seemed lately that we were doing a lot of dancing around our feelings for each other, and my butterflies were at a rave.

As we'd grown older, it seemed that our childhood friendship had started blossoming into something more.

"You look…" he started and cleared his throat again, standing up straighter, almost as if he was slipping on a mask of confidence.

I chuckled and reached out to grab his hand. I squeezed it three times, our signature handshake, and I saw his body visibly relax.

"You look good yourself, Waddle."

He groaned, rolling his eyes, and I chuckled. We needed something to break the stifling tension in the room, and I knew calling him by his childhood nickname would do the trick. We had been best friends for almost so long, so there was no need for either of us to be nervous around one another.

Ma popped her head through the archway from the kitchen, a big smile on her face. Wade's twin brother, Max, and his girlfriend, Shannon, sauntered into the room behind her.

Max and Wade stood off to the side, and Shannon reluctantly stood beside me.

I wasn't her biggest fan, but she and Max had been together since they were in their early teens, and I knew he was head over heels in love with her.

Honestly, she was always a bitch to me, but I kept the peace because Max was almost as much my best friend as Wade was… almost. I figured that one day, karma would rear its head, and she would get what was coming to her. I just hoped that Max was smart enough to have kicked her to the curb before that happened.

"Okay, kids, let's get some pictures," Penny Daniels, a.k.a. Ma, chimed as she ushered us in front of the living room fireplace and staged us in pairs.

We all groaned, but we knew it was a rite of passage for every prom to get the quintessential pictures before heading off to the dance.

Ma handed Max and Wade the corsages for Shannon and me, and I snagged the flowers I'd gotten to pin to Wade's suit from where I'd set them on the couch.

I turned toward Wade and smiled as if his general presence wasn't throwing my world completely out of orbit. He looked so damn good in his suit that I found it hard to focus, and my hands started to shake.

I removed the pearl-tipped pin from the stem of the

boutonniere and held the small bouquet on the satin lapel of his suit jacket.

With Herculean effort, I managed to pin on the flowers, thankfully without poking myself or Wade in the process. I could hear the snapping of the shutter as Ma took pictures, forever cementing the moment in time.

Wade grabbed the corsage from its plastic container as I raised my hand in front of him with a flourish and a smile. His warm fingers took hold of mine, steadying my hand as he slipped the elastic band over my wrist.

A tingle of electricity coasted across my skin at such a simple touch, and he jolted back as if it had been an electric shock. I tried my best to keep my features neutral, but his dismissal stung.

After enduring almost an hour of picture taking, we'd finally made our way to the dance.

If there was one thing Wade and I loved more than riding horses together, it was dancing. The awkwardness from earlier had faded, and we were back to our normal playful selves, getting down low on the dance floor and breaking a sweat.

The laughter had been abundant, and by the time the dance was over, I was ready to get out of my dress and into my bed.

At the end of the night, we separated from Max and Shannon, who I'm sure were heading out to the cove to check off another prom night stereotype.

Wade drove me back to my house, as I'd walked over earlier in the evening so we didn't have to take multiple cars. As he pulled into the driveway, I could see that all the lights in the house were off.

It wasn't surprising, seeing as how having three-year-old

twins who still didn't sleep well kept most of us up at odd hours. We slept when we could.

"Thanks for a great night," I said, looking down at the beautiful flowers that adorned my wrist, fingering the soft petals.

It was quiet in the cab of Wade's truck, and I felt the same electric current floating through the air that had been present in the living room before the dance. Something was shifting between us, and I wasn't sure whether it was heading in a good direction or not.

"Anytime, Sunshine," he responded, not bothering to avert his gaze from the front door of the house or loosen his white-knuckle grip on the steering wheel. I wasn't sure what he was looking for, but he seemed at war with himself, so I kept quiet.

"I guess I'll see you to—" I reached for the door handle but was cut off as Wade's hand reached out and grabbed hold of my wrist. It was such a striking move that my breath caught in my throat, and I could feel my heart pounding in my chest.

"Can I ask you a question?" he said as he traced the veins in my wrist, almost as if memorizing their pathways. I was sure that he could feel my pulse racing at the simplest of touches.

"Anything." My words came out breathy as I fought for control of my emotions.

The air around us felt thick with tension, and I knew that this moment in time would forever change our friendship—for better or worse.

"Do you feel it, too?"

I wasn't sure my heart could beat any faster as I looked up from where our hands were connected and met his gaze. He seemed conflicted, and I was sure that my face mirrored his.

I nodded softly and watched as his fingers trailed from my wrist up the crook of my elbow, brushing tenderly across my shoulder until they rested on the side of my throat. His touch was gentle, almost reverent, and I leaned into his warm palm.

His eyes met mine, and a moment of recognition passed across his face. We were about to do this. We were about to cross a line we couldn't come back from. The trajectory of our friendship was about to shift, and neither of us was stopping it.

I'm not sure who leaned in first, but before I knew it, Wade's lips were on me. They were gentle, almost hesitant, as they pressed softly against mine. It felt as if time stopped and everything faded away. But as soon as the moment happened, it was over, and we were left staring breathlessly at each other across the dimly lit front seat of his truck.

Breaking the tense moment, Wade retreated to his side and scratched at the stubble that had formed across his chin.

Neither of us uttered a word for a good ten minutes, afraid to break the spell of the kiss. The reality was, though, that this couldn't happen again.

Wade and I were best friends. If we crossed that line into something more, we could lose every single thing we held dear about each other. We had only kissed. That was just a tiptoe over the line. Anything more would have been disastrous.

We could pretend it hadn't happened, couldn't we?

"Um, so…" he mumbled, unsure of what to say.

"I'll see you tomorrow?" I asked nonchalantly, taking control of the situation.

Someone was going to have to make a move to get out of the car, and, seeing as how he had driven, I made the executive decision to erase the last five minutes of my life from my brain, choosing to ignore everything that had happened.

Wade looked at me, confusion crossing his face, but I could also see the realization of what we had just done coasting across his features, and the silent resignation that it shouldn't happen again. Even wordlessly, we were both on the same page.

Neither of us wanted to sacrifice our friendship to see if what had just transpired could blossom into something more.

We stood to lose too much, and we weren't sure that leaning into passing feelings was worth breaking down everything we had built together.

So, we did what any other teenagers would do; we never talked about it again.

RAY

LEANING IN, I expertly applied my favorite berry-red lipstick, "Berry Burning Love," my reflection staring back at me in the mirror. I spritzed some setting spray across my makeup before doing a quick fit check.

Wade would be here any minute to pick me up, and I didn't want to start my night with Sir Grumps-A-Lot on the wrong foot.

I had put a little more effort into tonight's look than I usually would for a night down at the dive bar in town.

A strange energy hung in the air, making tonight feel different from all the other times Wade and I had gone out with friends. I felt as if I were donning armor and heading out onto the battlefield.

After the stunt he had pulled earlier in the week—throwing around hay and sexual frustration—it seemed we were on the losing end of our years-long war of fighting our feelings.

I often felt the heat of his gaze like a brand on my skin

when he thought I didn't notice, his stare like the lick of flames edging across my flesh.

The thing was, I didn't need to see Wade's eyes on me to know he was looking. When he walked into a room that I was already in, it was as if someone turned on an electrical current and was coasting the live wire tortuously slow across my skin.

Although I found myself watching him just as often as I sensed him watching me. Time and puberty had been so good to the lanky boy I had fallen in love with at eleven years old. He exuded sex appeal, and I was no stranger to the way that women threw themselves at him.

The difference was that lately I'd started to despise those other women. They could have him untethered, no threat of ruining a decades-long friendship clouding their advances.

Recently, I started to seriously wonder what it would feel like to be the center of his attention and know that he was *mine*.

We had been there once, at the precipice of falling over the edge of our proverbial cliff. We chose to ignore it, spending years dodging the heated glances, accidental touches, and pressure from our friend group.

I wasn't sure what had shifted in the last year or so; all I knew was that I wanted to show Wade Daniels that I was more than just his best friend.

I was the woman standing beside him as he burned the world to the ground, handing him the match and gasoline to set things ablaze.

I wanted to fight his demons alongside him and bring back the fire to his haunted eyes. I wanted to be the one he turned to when everything felt heavy and he couldn't find his way out.

Most importantly, I wanted to be *his,* in every way I could be, and I wasn't going to back down from the challenge ahead.

Standing in front of the floor-length mirror on the back of my bedroom door, I fluffed my thick, dark hair and smudged a rogue spot of eyeliner from under my eye.

Hoping to make Wade swoon over me this evening, I went for a more seductive makeup style, different from what I usually wore. A dramatic smoky eye and winged eyeliner framed my hazel eyes, while the berry lipstick I'd chosen accentuated my full lips. I felt confident, sexy, and fierce—perfect for the battle I was about to face.

I smoothed my hands over my black dress, the hem barely hitting mid-thigh. It was shorter than I normally would have worn, but I liked the way it hugged every curve on my body and accentuated my small waist. The back was a lace-up corset, and the thin straps led to a balconette-style bodice that made my boobs look fantastic.

Stella had helped me pick it out when Charlie and I went on our weekly walk down Main Street. She worked at a local boutique, curating collections of styles to showcase. The fact that they focused on a mid-twenties to early thirties clientele was perfect for finding a special outfit for a night on the town.

The doorbell rang, and my heart nearly leaped out of my chest. This was it. It was now or never. I looked at myself in the mirror, meeting the reflection of my hazel gaze.

Pushing my shoulders back, I repeated the words my mom had always told me growing up. "Eres fuerte. Eres hermosa. Eres amado. Yo creo en ti." *You are strong. You are beautiful. You are loved. I believe in you.*

I missed her more and more each day as I navigated adulthood without her sage words of wisdom. The only solace I took from her passing was the knowledge that I would see her again one day, and it would be the sweetest reunion I could imagine.

Bringing my fingers to my lips, I pressed a soft kiss to the pads and then pressed them to the picture of my mom I had taped on the frame of the mirror.

She would have been so proud of the woman I had turned into in her absence, and she was probably laughing from the great beyond that it took me this long to accept whatever feelings these were for my best friend.

She was always a sucker for a good love story, and she was always convinced that Wade and I were meant to be together. No matter how many times I insisted we were *just friends*.

"Te amo, Mama," I crooned softly as I turned to head toward the front door.

I slid my feet into my trusty brown cowboy boots that were nearly buried under a pile of the twins' discarded shoes. I made a mental note to remind them to bring their shoes up to their room so no one tripped over them trying to get out of the house.

The doorbell rang again, Wade clearly growing impatient on the other side. "I'm coming!" I called, twisting the knob and pulling it open as I attempted to tug my boots on, hopping from one foot to the other.

The moment the door opened, the air crackled with a familiar energy, and my skin tingled as the feeling of an electrical current wafted over my skin, raking its way from my head to my boots.

Wade's gaze tracked a slow trail down my body, cataloging every inch of skin visible. His eyes held an unrestrained hunger, like a predator sizing up its prey.

I stood in front of him, unashamed and basking in his

attention. I liked the way I felt when I had Wade's undivided attention.

Granted, I had been the sole recipient of most of his attention since we were in our early teens, but this was different. He wasn't looking at me like I was the loudmouthed girl next door who had declared him her best friend.

He was looking at me with an unrestrained lust that could only be described as unfiltered desire. It was a sensation unlike any other, and I wasn't ashamed to admit that I wanted more of it.

Snapping out of his haze, Wade cleared his throat awkwardly and ran his hand across the back of his neck, dropping his head and breaking our stare. I swore I saw a hint of blush crest over his cheeks, but it was dark, and I couldn't be sure.

"You ready?" he asked, refusing to meet my eyes.

Sure, it stung a little that he had felt the same connection I did yet chose to ignore it. But tonight, things were going to change.

I was tired of the same old song and dance, and we were either going to turn it up or cut the music before the night was through.

WADE

FUCK ME SIDEWAYS.

It took every ounce of strength in my body to rip my eyes from the vision of Ray bent over in the doorframe, tugging on her boots. Her tits were barely restrained in the low neckline of her dress, and when she bent over to pull her boot on?

Fuck me.

I was sure one of them was going to fall out, and I silently prayed to whoever was listening for it to happen.

Once she stood up, I raked my eyes over her entire body. She was stunning. Actually, stunning is too simple a word for the knockout standing in front of me. She was all curves and softness, yet her gaze was sharp as a knife.

As if the curtain had been pulled back and my eyes were seeing her for the first time, I couldn't get enough. She was all silky tanned skin, thick, dark hair, and those lips… *fuck.*

When her eyes caught mine, her signature smirk kicked up on one side of her mouth. The things I'd do to that mou—

Nope. Not going there.

This was my best friend, for Christ's sake. I had known this girl since we were preteens.

But the thing about growing up? Rayna Cortez wasn't a girl anymore. She was an incredibly intelligent, hardworking, and caring woman. Not to mention, sexy as all fucking get out.

The self-deprecating thoughts started creeping in, a black cloud over the bright light that surrounded Ray.

She could do better than me. She deserved better than me. I wasn't the type of man who deserved *her*. She needed someone who could make her happy, who was stable, a man who knew what he wanted out of life and wasn't afraid to go after it.

Six months ago, I probably could have been that man. Now? I can barely get out of bed without a stiff drink in my hand and a whirlwind of thoughts about how useless I am.

I wouldn't ever be able to deserve Ray, as much as I wanted to. I wasn't that carefree man anymore.

Clearing my throat of the tightness of anxiety that threatened to cut off my breathing, I brought myself back to reality.

"You ready?" I asked her, stepping off the front porch and waiting for her to follow.

Ray didn't reply, but I saw a quick flicker of sadness wash across her features. She schooled it back into neutrality, but I had seen it, and the gut punch of realization hit me like a ton of bricks. She was dressed up tonight, and it was far from her normal look. Had she dressed up for me? There was no way.

I pushed the thought from my mind as I climbed in the truck and turned the key, the engine roaring to life.

The entire drive to Jack's was spent in awkward silence, something neither of us was familiar with. It was unnerving to watch the town roll by without the constant commentary of what was happening at Ray's house.

With ten kids, there was always a story to tell. But she sat silent, her hands clasped in front of her, watching out the window as if anything was more interesting than the inside of my truck cab.

It was unnatural to see her so docile. There hadn't been a time since I'd met her in the cove that summer evening when Ray had been silent.

One of two things was happening: she was either upset about something and didn't want to talk, or she was coming up with a plan. Neither was an inherently good option.

Pulling into the parking lot, her demeanor changed. A mask seemed to fall into place, arranging her features into her customary cheerful facade.

She looked over in my direction, her gaze full of fire as she smiled. Despite the dance of flames in her eyes, an unrelenting icy dread consumed me.

Something about the look on her face had my balls involuntarily shriveling and my dick rock hard with desire.

Ray was scary when she was mad, but this look? It was sheer determination, and I was sitting in the driver's seat, an uncomfortable mix of deathly afraid and undeniably turned on.

RAY

JACK'S WAS a hustle and bustle of activity as we pulled open the heavy wooden doors and stepped inside.

Every corner of the run-down bar was filled with cowboys and cowgirls celebrating their last weekend of freedom before they needed to buckle down on training for the December National Finals Rodeo in Las Vegas.

I didn't wait for Wade to follow me, my footsteps echoing across the sticky floors. I walked with confident strides, the polished wood of the bar cool beneath my hands as I leaned over to catch Hayes, the longtime bartender's, attention.

I felt the stares of drunken cowboys on my skin, their shameless perusal of my body a welcome distraction from the one person's stare I wanted and didn't have.

Wade had acted like I didn't exist from the moment we stepped out of the truck. If I was donning a mask of enjoyment, he was donning a mask of indifference.

I leaned over the bar, holding down the back of my dress, and grinned at the rugged bartender pouring shots.

"No funny business tonight, Ray," he grumbled in my

direction, pouring what looked like bourbon into a rocks glass and adding two small ice cubes.

He slid the glass across the bar to the patron, a tall man with a fitted grey tee, black cowboy hat, and a thick but neatly trimmed chestnut-brown beard.

I raked my eyes over the tattoos that trailed across his arms, swirling over every inch of visible skin.

The man nodded his thanks and headed over to a four-top table that was occupied by a few other men of his same stature.

He looked familiar, but I couldn't put my finger on where I knew him from. I knew he must have been part of the rodeo circuit because Wade walked right up and slapped him on the shoulder, garnering a firm handshake and a nod.

I turned back to Hayes, grinning as he waited for me to order.

"Oh, Hayes-y baby. I never cause funny business," I drawled sweetly, slipping into a thick Southern accent. "I'm just a lowly Southern belle looking for a strong cowboy to sweep me off my feet."

Hayes rolled his eyes and grabbed a bottle of Jose Cuervo, my drink of choice. He poured two shots and slid one my way, picking the other up in a simple toast.

I tipped my head back and brought the cool edge of the shot glass to my lips, drinking it down as if it were nothing more than a glass of water.

Tequila and I had a volatile relationship, but the liquid courage coursed through my system, creating a warmth across my body that was welcome and relaxing.

I set the shot glass back on the bar top, signaling Hayes to pour me another. He grumbled something that sounded oddly like "fucking tequila" under his breath, but reluctantly filled the small glass to the brim.

I brazenly reached across the bar to grab a lime and a salt-shaker, much to Hayes's dismay. Righting myself back on the sticky floor of the bar, I winked in his direction and blew him an exaggerated kiss.

I laughed when he placed his fists on his hips and tilted his head back in exasperation as he did his best to act affronted.

Hayes had been the sole bartender at Jack's for as long as I could remember. He was in his early fifties and had seen his fair share of Cortez and Daniels shenanigans over the years.

There may have been a few instances where Hayes threatened to call my father after one too many shots. Subsequently, there may also have been a night that included a weaponized pool stick, Coyote Ugly-style tabletop dancing, and bucket loads of puke all over the floor.

I twirled around and leaned against the bar top, scanning the room for our group of friends.

The bar was packed, but I couldn't mistake Stella's bright blonde hair and frantically waving arm flapping animatedly from across the room. My smile spread wide as I made my way over to where they had commandeered a large table for our ever-growing group.

Stella was expertly perched on Max's lap, even though a perfectly good chair sat directly beside him. I couldn't blame her, though; if my husband looked like he did, I'd want to touch him any chance I could get, too.

Although the conversation was loud around them, I watched as Max stared at his wife with rapt attention. It was as if the words coming out of her mouth were something profound, instead of her chatter about the latest runway looks she was scouring for the boutique. He looked at her with a reverence that can only be described as sheer awe and love.

A pang of jealousy coursed through my chest as I watched them, silently wishing I had what they did.

I wanted someone to look at me like their world would end if I were gone. I wanted to be the center of someone's attention and the star of every thought in their head.

Truthfully, all I wanted was to be *wanted.*

Wade unceremoniously plopped down next to me; his cologne, a mix of something earthy and warm, mingled with the scent of bourbon, hung heavy in the air. I resisted leaning in to wrap myself in the intoxicating scent that was pure Wade Daniels.

His wide hand gripped a rocks glass as he lifted his drink to his plush lips. I watched from the corner of my eye as he tipped it back and took a small sip of the amber liquid, reveling in the way his throat constricted as he swallowed.

A drop remained suspended on his bottom lip, and I watched as he expertly swiped out his tongue and whisked it away. My eyes trailed from his lips up the strong bridge of his nose, slightly crooked from too many breaks falling off the back of a horse, to the chocolate-brown eyes that stared directly into mine.

Shit.

I shot up from my seat, wiped my sweaty palms down my dress, and grabbed hold of Stella's hand, pulling her from Max's lap.

"Shots?" I asked, my voice an octave higher than normal. I cleared my throat and schooled my features back into neutrality as I nearly dragged Stella back to the bar.

No matter that I'd only been there a few minutes prior, I needed more alcohol to deal with the ever-growing ache thrumming through my core at the sight of the sexy cowboy I wanted to mount like a saddled bronc.

"You okay, girl? You seem a little…on edge," Stella asked as we sidled up to the bar, and I waved in Hayes's direction again.

He cut his eyes at me in exasperation but didn't hesitate to pour two more shots and slide them my way.

"Yep! I'm fine, all good, nothing going on here," I replied, the words coming far too quickly to be anything *but* okay as I shot back the tequila with practiced ease.

I caught the quirk of Stella's eyebrow as she leaned her hip against the bar and kicked back her own shot.

"Cool… so, we're going to try that again, and this time, try to pretend just a little harder."

Hanging my head forward, I stretched myself exasperatedly over the bar, again much to Hayes's dismay.

The tequila was starting to take effect, leaving my inhibitions and emotions on the fraying end of a very long rope. I dropped my head onto my arms and felt Stella's warm hand as it coasted gently over my back.

It felt nice to be "mothered" in a sense and to have someone to vent to. Stella and I had fallen into an easy friendship when she arrived in Firefly Cove, but opening up about my feelings would always be somewhat foreign to me.

"Ray, I'm serious." I turned my head, meeting her emerald gaze. Her face was a canvas of worry and concern.

I didn't want to worry her; I just didn't know how to explain so many years of unrequited longing to someone who hadn't experienced it.

"I'm fine. Just dealing with some…" I struggled to find the right word for what I was experiencing.

"Emotions?" she finished for me, her lips curling into a teasing grin as she playfully bumped my shoulder.

"Yeah, those things," I chuckled, standing upright and feeling the swirly warmth that came along with three shots of tequila in the span of about twenty minutes.

"Does it have something to do with the broody cowboy staring daggers in your direction, acting like everyone in this bar needs to scrub their eyes after they just got a good look under your dress?"

I felt my cheeks heat with embarrassment as I realized quickly that I'd been doubled over the bar, and my dress was barely cresting the bottom of my ass. I turned around, putting my back to the bar as I surveyed the crowd.

A couple of younger guys stared unabashedly over in my direction, one even giving me an exaggerated wink. I rolled my eyes and sighed.

The last thing I needed was some young saddle bronc rider thinking I was a buckle bunny looking for a good time. My glare was enough to send him the message that I was not interested.

"You wanna talk about it?" Stella asked softly, sliding a fresh shot of tequila my way. This girl knew the key to my heart and how to loosen my lips.

"I'm just..." I started, attempting to find the right words for the emotions that were swirling through my head. I was a jumbled mix of angry, frustrated, and incomprehensibly turned on.

"Frustrated," I settled on, not bothering to elaborate on which type. I twirled the shot of tequila around, running my finger across the rim.

"I know I haven't been here as long as some of the other guys who saw you and Wade grow up together, but I'm sure even a blind man could see how you guys look at each other." She chuckled.

"That's the thing. We've grown up together. He's my best friend. How do I throw away seventeen years of friendship for a relationship that will undoubtedly fail?" The words came out in a jumbled mess, flowing like a rushing stream from my lips.

Trying to suck some of the words back in, I took my shot and placed it face down on the bar, signaling to Hayes that I was done drinking. Tequila was obviously the enemy tonight, as it left me feeling far from happy or energized.

I felt Stella's hand reach down beside me and her slender fingers interlace with mine. The sign of solidarity was warm and much needed as I grappled with the torrent of emotions flooding through me.

"I don't think you'd be throwing anything away," she said softly, neither of us looking anywhere but out into the crowd.

Anyone watching would just see two drunk girls standing next to a bar holding hands. They wouldn't see or feel the raw emotion bleeding from my pores as I struggled to maintain my composure under the weight of "what ifs."

"You and Wade have known each other since you were teens. You've seen each other through every stage of each other's lives as you've grown, and neither of you has managed to break the bond you share. If it were going to happen, don't you think it would have already happened? There's something raw and special there, Ray. How do you *know* it's destined to fail?"

Like a crashing wave of interrogation, her words drowned me as I struggled to find a reply.

How *did* I know we would fail? Was I just expecting the

worst to happen, or was there tried-and-true evidence that Wade and I would never work out as a couple?

"Your silence speaks volumes, Ray. Just remember that nothing worth having comes easy."

She was right. I didn't know that Wade and I wouldn't work out, and I could either sit back and let myself wonder, or I could do something about it and see where it goes.

With that emotional bomb detonated, Stella and I made our way back to the table and sat down. She plopped herself back down on Max's lap like she owned it, although she did, and snagged his Stetson off his head, depositing it on her own.

I swore I heard a light growl as he leaned forward, nuzzling the space where her shoulder met her neck, and the peal of laughter that Stella let out hit me right in the chest.

I wanted that.

WADE

I DON'T KNOW what was pissing me off more, the fact that my brother and his new wife couldn't be bothered to stop mauling each other for five seconds, or that Ray had bent her tiny ass over the bar top and damn near flashed everyone her lacy red panties.

Not that I was looking. If one thing was certain, neither of those situations was helping my mood.

I sipped my bourbon, making every valiant effort to keep my eyes from drifting to the swell of Ray's tits that were nearly falling out of her dress each time she leaned forward to laugh at something Stella or Max said. It was as if the dress that was expertly painted on her body was done with the intention of sending me to an early grave.

"So, tell us about the honeymoon!" Ray crooned with a wistful sigh, her cheek resting dreamily against her hand.

"It was so nice," Stella remarked, gazing longingly back at my brother.

I took another sip of my drink, fighting down the current of emotion that threatened to make its way up my throat.

Watching them make heart eyes at each other was almost enough to make me sick.

"We did a lot of relaxing on the beach. Charlie hadn't ever seen the ocean, so it was nice to be able to experience that as a family."

Max twirled one of Stella's blonde locks around his finger as he kissed her tenderly on the neck.

Never had I felt such an all-consuming anger coupled with the craving for what my brother had. The ease with which he and Stella interacted was something I had only dreamed about with one girl.

I hadn't ever really been the relationship type. Getting onto the rodeo circuit meant lots of training that wore you down physically and mentally.

At the end of a long training session, the only thing I wanted was a shower and a nap. I'm not going to say I was exactly celibate through the last twelve years, but I sure as hell didn't let them stay over, and I generally never called them again.

Buckle bunnies were a dime a dozen, and I generally didn't meet the same one twice.

The only girl I had ever imagined coming home to at the end of a long day of training was my best friend. Until recently, I hadn't ever imagined anything outside of a platonic relationship, but the desire for something more hit me straight in the gut tonight as I watched the happiness radiate from my twin.

I wanted someone to look at me the way Stella looked at Max. The idea of coasting my fingers across bare skin, a simple touch only for us two, felt like heaven.

I wanted someone to come home to at the end of a long day and decompress with a warm shower and a stupid TV show. Someone who knew me and wouldn't blink an eye at the long hours that training and ranching required.

I needed someone I could confide in without judgment and who would pick me up when I was feeling low. I needed my best friend.

The anger simmered beneath my skin as I listened to Max and Stella recount all the fun they had on their honeymoon. I knew I shouldn't have been jealous; they surely deserved every ounce of happiness they had. Yet still, I felt the rage rise, as if the world was intentionally flaunting their happiness just to torment me.

"We even got to ride horses on the beach. It was a dream come true." Stella's wistful sigh grated on my nerves, and I didn't bother hiding my scoff.

Max's eyes shot over to me, and I could see the anger coursing through him that matched mine.

"You got something to say?" he spat, an eyebrow hiking up in question.

I shook my head with a sardonic chuckle, the heat from the bourbon I'd been sipping lowering my inhibitions and loosening my tongue.

"Just that it must be nice to be able to pick up, leave all your responsibilities behind, and ride off into the fucking sunset," I huffed.

"What the fuck is wrong with you?" Max stood angrily, setting Stella gently beside him. She placed her hand on his chest in an effort to calm him, but if there was anything I knew about my twin, it was how to rile him up.

Maybe if he got in a good right hook, it would make him feel better and make me feel anything other than the choking anger I was currently fighting.

"Besides the fact that your *wife* got me shot in the back,

and I lost everything in this world that's fucking important to me? Nothing." I spat the word "wife" with enough venom to have Stella inching backward, her eyes filling with tears.

Where I should have felt bad for making Stella upset, I just felt numb. She was the reason I was in the position I was in. She was the reason I hated waking up every single morning and every single second I closed my eyes to sleep.

If she hadn't shown up in Firefly Cove, everything would have been different.

"Wade…" Ray's soft voice echoed through the red-tinged haze that was my vision, her slender fingers softly gripping my forearm.

I shook her off, violently throwing my arm to the side as I pulled my wallet from my pocket and tossed a fifty-dollar bill unceremoniously on the table.

"No, it's fine," I spat. "I was just leaving anyway."

I didn't bother glancing back at the table as I stormed out of the bar, shoving the wooden door so hard it bounced against the opposite wall.

The warm and muggy air hit me like an invisible barrier, making my shirt cling to me uncomfortably. I didn't care what people in this godforsaken town thought of me or my outburst. I honestly couldn't give a fuck about *myself,* much less the court of public opinion.

Seeing as I wasn't sober enough to drive back to the ranch, I edged my way down the side of the bar, resting against the coarse brick wall.

The smell of the trash in the dumpster overpowered the calming scent of the night air, and I let out a loud growl of frustration. I couldn't even have one thing to help ground me; everything was trash. Literally and figuratively.

The door to the bar opened with a whoosh, and I could sense the impending rage before it edged into my vision.

It felt like the moment before they opened the gate for a bronc rider at a rodeo. You know you're about to be thrown around, but you willingly put yourself on the back of that horse.

I knew riling Max up and spitting the venom I did at Stella wouldn't end well, yet I did it anyway. Maybe it was my subconscious playing with fire, hoping to get burned.

Max stomped his way over, standing directly in front of me, his arms crossed across his chest.

"I don't want to hear it," I spat, not bothering to hide the hurt and anguish in my words.

"No, you're going to stand there and fucking listen," he spat back. "This is not her fucking fault, Wade. She didn't hold your hand and drag your stubborn ass into that building. We went in as a family because families stick together. Or have you forgotten that while you've been planning the world's most extravagant fucking pity party? Get your head out of your ass, brother, and look at the facts. The only person you get to blame here is that stupid motherfucker who pulled the trigger and shot you in the back. Not me, not God, and sure as hell not my fucking wife."

I watched as his chest rose and fell with ragged breaths, his eyes ablaze with the fire of protection. At his core, Max was a fierce protector, and I had taken a low blow at Stella with what I had said. I wasn't immune to the fact that what I had said would have been hurtful. I just didn't have the capacity to care.

"Wade, we all know you're hurting," he said, his voice barely audible, the initial rage now replaced by a controlled fury.

"YOU DON'T KNOW SHIT," I yelled, my fists clenching in frustration. No one could ever understand the pain I was dealing with, nor did I ever want them to experience it first-hand. It was all-consuming.

There were days I woke up, having gotten a fitful night's sleep, and dreaded the day ahead, knowing what lay on the other side. Nights when I wished that when I closed my eyes, they wouldn't reopen. Moments when, in the silence, all I can hear is the crack of that gun as it stripped me of the one thing I held closest to my heart.

I wouldn't wish this life on anyone because it wasn't a life. It was a death sentence, and I was a walking, talking corpse.

"You don't know shit," I repeated, softening my words until they were almost a whisper.

"I may not know how you're feeling, but I know *you*. And this version, standing in front of me? That's not the brother I know and love. Above all else, that's not the brother Ma and Pops raised."

His words hit home, and I dropped my head in defeat. Ma would have killed me for talking to Stella the way I had. She had always taught us the importance of respecting women.

"Here's the problem, Max—that man, the man you all knew and loved? I don't think he exists anymore."

I could feel the wetness dripping off my chin, and I avoided wiping it away. I didn't lift my head and give Max the satisfaction of knowing how his words had affected me, but he knew. We always knew.

He stepped closer, extending a finger and pointing it at my chest. The sharp jab was enough to push me backward against the wall. He flicked up the brim of my hat, forcing me to meet his gaze as his words decimated me.

"You may not think he exists here," he said, tapping his finger on my temple. "But he sure as hell still exists here."

His finger poked me square in the heart, a direct shot to my emotions. I hung my head in shame, adjusting my hat back over my brow.

With the final blow having been dealt and me properly chastised, he sauntered back into the bar like he hadn't just served me my ass on a silver platter.

RAY

SHORTLY AFTER MAX came back in, with a wild look of fury etched onto his face, he and Stella said their goodbyes. She hugged me tightly and promised to bring Charlie by over the weekend since I hadn't seen her since the wedding. Max gave me a one-armed side hug that was tense and stilted, but I commended him for trying.

I paid my tab and walked outside in search of the buzzkill who had made a fool of himself on what was supposed to be a fun night out.

Wade's outburst had sobered us up quickly, and no one could find it in themselves to continue on with the night. He had effectively doused the entire outing with a bucket of ice-cold water.

I popped by the table my sister was sitting at, hanging out with a bunch of her rodeo friends, and placed a quick kiss on her cheek. She barely acknowledged me, lost in a heated conversation with some of the guys seated around her.

Walking out the door, it didn't take me long to find him. He was sitting on the ground, leaning back against the brick wall on the side of the bar. His Stetson was pulled down low, shielding everyone from seeing his face. He had his knees bent and was resting his elbows on top of them, his head hung forward in a clear posture of defeat.

Instead of sitting down next to him, knowing I wasn't properly dressed for anything that required bending, I leaned against the wall beside him, standing in silent companionship.

The night was cooling off, with the sounds of chirping crickets the soundtrack of the season. Even though we were in the main part of town, it was quiet.

Neither of us said anything for what felt like forever, just listening to the sounds around us and reveling in the cool evening air as it washed over our skin.

"I can't do this, Ray." His soft voice was barely perceptible over the sounds of the night, but I heard him.

The words coming from his mouth felt like an icy trail of dread coursing through my veins, freezing me to the spot.

The fact that he had called me Ray instead of his usual Sunshine spoke volumes about the pain and anguish swirling around his mind. I felt tears well up on my lashes, threatening to fall.

I didn't bother responding, letting him work out the kinks of his emotions in his mind. Neither of us was good at vocalizing the hard things, but somehow, we understood each other in our times of need.

He stood, dusting his jeans of the tiny pebbles of dirt and concrete that clung to them. He took off his hat, setting it on the tailgate of his truck. I didn't get why we were sitting on the grimy ground instead of in his truck, which was parked right there, but I didn't dare question him.

His long hair fell in gentle waves, skimming the strong

lines of his jaw. I stopped myself from reaching out and brushing my fingers through the dark blond strands.

Wade paced the length of the side alley of Jack's, almost as if the rage that was building inside of him prevented him from staying still. He gave the impression of a caged animal, stuck inside the confines of his mind.

"I'm just so fucking *angry*!" He snapped, causing me to flinch at his sudden outburst.

He punctuated his words by kicking the gravel with his booted foot and threading his fingers through his hair, pulling tightly on the strands.

I didn't need him to tell me in words that he was angry; I could feel it in the way he moved, breathed, and existed. He was wound tight, his movements stiff and stilted as he continued his relentless pacing.

"I'm so—" I started.

"You're what, sorry? You're sorry that I got shot?" His laugh was mirthless as it bubbled from his lips. "Poor Wade Daniels, the retired rodeo star who won't ever ride again. I was already washed up, so why not make me completely fucking useless?"

"You're not useless, and I'm not sorry," I spat, finally finding my voice amid the storm that was this new and unimproved version of my best friend.

He stopped pacing, edging closer to me like a predator stalking its prey. I could feel the heat of his gaze as he backed me against the wall, mere inches separating our bodies.

The way his eyes tracked mine, an unrestrained hunger thrumming through him, had my heart fluttering wildly in my chest.

"You deserve better," he whispered, leaning in so his

breath coasted across the shell of my ear. He braced his hands on either side of my head, bracketing me in.

I wasn't afraid. No matter what Wade did, said, or threw my way, I wouldn't ever be scared of him. I knew that the boy I had fallen in love with was hidden deep inside this raging shell of a man.

"I deserve to have my best friend back," I responded fiercely, my head held high.

His chuckle was sardonic as he skated his nose across my jaw, his lips just a tease as he feathered them across my throat. My eyelids fluttered closed at the sensation.

The air crackled with electricity as he removed one of his hands from the brick wall beside me and coasted his thick fingers across the skin of my thigh where the hem of my dress was riding up.

I could feel my core tightening as he ran the fabric of my dress through his fingers, teasing and testing how far I was willing to let him go.

Feeling brave due to the tequila still pumping through my veins, I grabbed his wrist and edged his palm around until it was resting on the swell of my ass.

He growled low in his throat as he hung his head against the arm still propping him up. I could feel the dampness pooling in my core as we played this relentless game of tug-of-war. But what Wade wasn't prepared for was the fact that I was ready to play dirty.

He squeezed my ass in a punishing grip, edging me forward until our bodies were flush. I could feel the thick evidence of his arousal pressing into my belly, and I stifled a moan.

I hadn't ever allowed myself to imagine Wade's dick, but I'm sure even my fantasies couldn't live up to the hype. I could feel the hard heat of him, even through the thick barrier of his jeans.

"I don't think your best friend is supposed to be thinking about how much he wants to turn you against this wall, flip up this skimpy dress, pull down those little red panties, and fuck you until you scream." He groaned against my throat, once again trailing his lips across my fluttering pulse point.

This time, I didn't hold back as an involuntary moan crested up my throat and across my plush lips, causing Wade to groan in response.

I raised my eyes to his as I crested my hand across the hard planes of his chest, heading down toward his belt buckle.

My deft fingers slid over the front of his jeans, cupping his dick through the thick denim. He let out a hiss and bucked his hips involuntarily into my hand.

"I don't think your best friend is supposed to be thinking about how much the thought of that turns her on."

I had barely finished my sentence when Wade's mouth crashed over mine. The kiss was demanding, a rough clash of tongue and teeth. His plush lips expertly glided their way across mine as if we had been kissing for years, not seconds.

We melted together in a way that was unexplainable but felt so right. My arms involuntarily snaked their way around his neck as he grabbed a fistful of my thick hair and tugged my head back, allowing himself to delve deeper.

There was nothing soft or loving in the way we kissed. This was a battle of wills, a tango of emotion, and a tidal wave that had finally crashed against the shore.

Releasing my hair, Wade reached behind me, grabbing a handful of ass in each palm, and lifted me against the brick wall.

My legs found their way around his trim waist as I struggled to find purchase. The roughness of the brick scratched into my bare skin, adding to the sensation of being utterly and wholly ravaged.

His fingers teased the edge of my panties, and I was suddenly very thankful I had opted for something better than my usual boy shorts.

Without breaking our embrace, Wade leaned back, watching my expression for any signs of wanting to stop. He trailed his middle finger over the damp center of my thong, teasing my clit through the thin lace.

I bucked my hips into his hand, seeking more pressure, my eyes never straying from his. He broke our gaze, trailing his lips across my throat as he laid sloppy kisses along my skin. He pressed a kiss to the pulse point below my ear, and a shiver snaked its way through my body.

"I need your words, Sunshine," he teased, nipping my earlobe as he coasted his lips back down my throat and across the tops of my breasts.

I gripped the long strands of his hair, forcing his head back and his gaze eye level.

"I need you to fuck me, Wade Daniels," I said, a devilish smirk stretching across my face. "Clear enough?"

The resounding growl that crested from his throat was enough to have me unabashedly grinding against him as he trailed kisses over my neck and back to my tits. He reached down, gripping the top of my dress, ready to yank, when a tall figure let out an awkward cough to signal their approach.

Wade turned his head slightly to see who had interrupted and lowered his head into the crook of my neck, groaning in frustration.

"What the fuck do you want, Sterling?"

WADE

"UM, I'm really sorry to have to break up whatever the fuck this is," Sterling said, a sly, cocky smirk on his face as he signaled between Ray and me. "But Izzy Cortez is one of your riders, right?"

I used my large frame to block his view of Ray until I knew she was sufficiently covered. She stiffened beneath me, hearing her sister's name.

After glancing down to make sure she was decent, I guided her to step in front of me, concealing the massive erection I was going to be sporting for a while.

"That's my sister," she declared, a wild look of concern marring her face.

I was sure that whatever Izzy had gotten up to, Sterling wouldn't have interrupted me if it wasn't serious. Especially if he had known it was Ray I was mauling against the side of the building.

Sterling and I had been buddies for as long as I'd been circling the rodeo. He was intimately familiar with my hang-up about Rayna Cortez after my lips got loose one too many drunken post-win nights.

"Well, she's currently three button presses away from Hayes calling the sheriff."

I could sense the tension radiating from Sterling, and I wasn't quite sure how to place it. I hadn't known that he even knew who Izzy was, much less that she was one of the riders I trained. Odd, since I would consider him one of my closest friends.

"What the fuck happened?" Ray pressed, already high-tailing it toward the door in search of her sister.

"Something about stupid fucking lawyers, she could drink anyone under the table, and barrel racers are crazy?"

The look of concern that floated across his vision was enough to have both Ray and me moving double time to get back inside the bar.

What we hadn't expected stepping back into Jack's was to see Izzy standing at the dartboards, pressing a young buck bronc rider against the wall with a pool cue, cutting off his windpipe, and his buddies standing around laughing, cheering her on.

Ray and I shared a look of concern before both muttering "fucking tequila" under our breath and heading in Izzy's direction.

"I bet your pansy ass couldn't ride a horse, much less a woman. Can you even see your small-ass dick? You stupid ass motherfu—"

"Ooookay." Ray halted her sister, putting a hand gently on her arm, encouraging her to loosen her grip on the pool stick and release the guy she had pinned. "Izzy, let's go. He's not worth getting arrested for," she added softly.

It felt like watching a trainer tame a wild horse. The soft

way Ray spoke to her eased the tension in her muscles, instantly relaxing her rigid stature.

Izzy's head fell in defeat as she dropped the pool cue, the thin wooden stick clattering to the ground with a loud clack.

The guy she'd pinned had the decency to look a little frightened as he scrambled back to his group of friends, who were still doubled over in laughter. He snatched up his sparkling-clean cowboy hat and hightailed it toward the exit, mumbling about crazy fucking barrel racers as he went.

Izzy struggled against Ray's hold, but she didn't have much fight behind her resistance. She knew that whatever the guy had said wasn't worth losing her sponsorships or her career over.

Young bucks like that guy liked to run their mouths, and nothing she could say or do would keep him from thinking his shit didn't stink.

"I'm fine," Izzy spat toward Ray, punctuating her words with a flick of her arm, throwing off her sister's grasp.

"Why don't we drive you home?" I asked, clearly having sobered up after my own rage-filled incident and subsequent hot and heavy episode out back.

I made a mental note to talk to Ray about that whole incident later. It was a conversation long overdue, and I wanted to know where it left us—if there was an "us."

Without uttering a word, Izzy stomped out of the bar, the heavy wooden door thudding against the wall for the second time that night.

Ray went over to Hayes to make sure her tab had been paid and apologized for all the drama we had brought with us this evening.

Hayes brushed her off, having dealt with his fair share of bar fights in his day. If there was one thing you could guarantee about a small town, it sure came with a healthy dose of drama.

I walked out to the truck to check on Izzy while Ray settled things up inside. She was leaning against the tailgate, one of her boots propped up on the rear tire. There was a tightness in her posture that I hadn't seen in her before tonight.

Granted, I didn't see much of Izzy outside of training and the occasional rodeo event I was able to make it to, but I'd known her as long as I'd known Ray. She was normally an easygoing, albeit wild at heart, woman. Something had to have set her off tonight to get her that riled up, and it wasn't just the tequila.

"Wanna tell me what the fuck that was about?" I asked, hiking a thumb over my shoulder in the direction of the bar.

"Not particularly," was her curt response. Giving her the quiet space to stew, I watched as she edged a rock around the gravel parking lot with the toe of her boot. She was focused, lost in thought, and I could tell something was eating at her.

"You know your sister is going to want to know what's going on."

I could feel the rage simmering in her, even though we were at least ten feet apart. It was something akin to the rage that simmered within me. She was nearly vibrating against my truck, holding back the venomous words she really wanted to say.

"How about this? You've got approximately thirty—make that twenty-nine—seconds until your sister comes out here and chews you a new one for that stunt you just pulled. Wanna cut the bullshit and tell me what's really going on?"

Hanging her head in defeat, Izzy resumed kicking at the

gravel around her feet. She looked exhausted, mentally and physically. I felt for her because I knew that pain all too well.

"I just thought that maybe this time, things would be different." Her deep sigh cut through the warm air with a twinge of sadness. "Tanner was supposed to meet us out tonight to celebrate the start of the heavy training season, but he couldn't be bothered to put his own shit aside to do something for me for once. I was heading to the bar for another drink, and the guy got handsy. I snapped."

Tanner was Izzy's fiancé. He didn't live in Firefly Cove, but he and Izzy had been doing the long-distance thing for a couple of years now.

I didn't know much about their relationship, other than what I heard from Ray. She wasn't the guy's biggest fan, but she was Izzy's big sister, and I always brushed her hatred of him off as her being overprotective.

"He said he had a work event with the partners at his firm. Drinks and dinner at some fancy-schmancy bar in Atlanta. He *promised* that he was going to make it out here tonight."

The hurt in her voice was almost palpable, and I watched as tears welled up on her lower lashes. It took a lot to make a cowgirl cry, and it was at that moment that I surmised that this wasn't the first time she'd been stood up by him.

Clearly, this was a habit of his, and I could see how much it was hurting her.

"Tab's all paid, let's go." Ray's tense voice cut through the emotional fog surrounding Izzy and me. I could hear the sniffles of someone holding back tears as Izzy turned away from her sister and stepped toward the back door of my truck.

I clicked the unlock button, and Izzy immediately flung open the door and, with graceful ease, scaled her way into my lifted truck. I stopped Ray with a hand on her arm before she had a chance to berate her sister.

"Go easy on her," I said softly, running my fingers down to tangle with hers. I squeezed her hand three times in quick succession and rolled my lips inward in a tense smile.

It seemed Izzy had enough on her plate. If there was one thing I was intimately familiar with, it was anger and pain, and Izzy Cortez was plagued with both.

RAY

WADE'S SENTIMENT TO go easy on Izzy told me she'd been more forthcoming with him over what was bothering her than she ever would have been with me.

I had a feeling her outburst hadn't just stemmed from some first-year bronc rider getting handsy, like Hayes had said when I asked if he knew what had set her off.

The ride back to Izzy's place was quiet. She lived on the outskirts of town in a duplex she and Tanner had bought together. Although he was rarely there, leaving her to take care of the house alone after long stints on the road. Tension hung heavily in the air, blanketing everything in a haze that felt oppressive.

As her big sister, I wanted to heal whatever was hurting her, but I knew Izzy wasn't a child anymore and could fend for herself.

Realistically, she hadn't been a child at all when Mom had died, and we'd all been forced to grow up before our time. Although we were only a little over a year apart, there was a weighted expectation thrust upon me that she'd been spared.

The difference between eleven and thirteen hadn't been any clearer when she got to choose her life path. Being the oldest meant I didn't get to choose.

As we pulled up to the duplex, Wade had barely stopped the truck when Izzy was launching the door open and stepping out. I watched her stumble toward the front door, pulling her keys out of her pocket as she swayed from side to side on the thin sidewalk.

It gutted me to see her so dejected. She was drunk off her ass, which wasn't common for my straitlaced sister. Whatever had set her off tonight must have been major enough to warrant the chance of throwing her entire career away.

I turned in my seat, facing Wade, a look of pure apology on my face. I knew we needed to talk about what had happened outside of Jack's, but at this moment, my sister needed me more.

"Go," he commanded, hiking his chin toward Izzy's door as we both watched her feeble attempt at shoving her key in the lock. It was almost painful to watch her struggle with such a mundane task.

I reached across the center console and gently squeezed his muscled forearm. "Thank you," I sighed.

I warred within myself on whether I should lean over and kiss him, but without knowing where we stood, I didn't want to cross that line and make things more awkward than they already were.

As soon as I closed the door to his truck, he was speeding away toward the ranch. I felt torn between the man that I had grown up loving and the girl I had grown up raising. But right now, my sister needed me, and Wade would have to understand.

We had been dancing around our feelings for the better

part of fifteen years, so what was one more night of ignoring the inevitable?

Somehow, Izzy had managed to find the right key and fit it into the lock, letting herself inside. She hadn't bothered closing the door behind her, probably knowing I wasn't going to let her off without talking about whatever had happened at Jack's.

I followed behind her, letting myself in and closing the door behind me with a soft click. I flipped the deadbolt, since it was evident that neither of us was going anywhere this evening.

I found my sister stomping around the kitchen, attempting to get her boots off but failing miserably as she ping-ponged from one set of cabinets to the other. With each thud against the wooden doors, I wondered how many hits they could take before they broke.

Heaving one last valiant tug and an animalistic grunt, she gave up attempting to get her boots off, sinking to the floor in defeat. I watched as all the fight and bravado she'd been hiding behind drained out of her in the form of two rivers of tears tracking down her cheeks.

I sank down across from her; me propped up against the island and her against the cabinets. The space between us felt like an uncrossable canyon.

Looking at the broken and defeated woman sitting opposite me, I was met with the image of the little girl I'd tried so hard to shield from the harsh realities of the world.

Without speaking, I grabbed one of her feet and tugged off her boots one by one, setting them upright beside me. I let her pull her legs back up toward her body and wrap her arms around them. The vibrant and fearless cowgirl I so admired was nowhere to be found.

"¿Quieres hablar de ello?" *Do you want to talk about it?* I asked softly, knowing that Izzy would understand, as she was one of the few siblings who could fluently converse with me in Spanish.

It often felt like a special bond between us, having grown up completely bilingual. It wasn't something we shared with most of the other siblings and was exceptionally special after our mom died, as she had been the one pushing us all to learn.

"En realidad no." *Not really.*

The war between giving her the space I knew she wanted and trying to fix whatever was eating her up was overwhelming.

I wanted to know who I could hunt down and bury for turning my sister into this shell of the girl sitting before me, but also, I knew she was old enough and scrappy enough to fight her own battles.

We sat in silence for a few beats before either of us found the voice to speak.

Barely perceptible, I heard my sister whisper, "It's exhausting."

"What is?" I asked, confused. I wasn't sure if the alcohol was catching up and she was getting tired, or if she was making the moves to open up to me. I truly hoped it was the latter but expected the former.

"Living in your shadow."

Her words hit me like a knife to the chest, and I fought for a response as my mouth gaped open and closed. It was as if my brain had malfunctioned, and I couldn't formulate any semblance of a response.

Living in *my* shadow? How could she possibly think that? She was the one making it big in the rodeo. She was the one with a big-wig fiancé who was one test away from becoming a practicing attorney. If anyone was living in anyone's shadow, it was me living in hers.

"Good talk," she spat as she pushed to stand, taking my silence as an adequate response, wobbling even as she held onto the counter.

Having finally found my voice, I stopped her with a hand on her wrist. "Now, wait a damn minute." She turned to face me, and I could practically see the flames flickering at the edge of her vision, itching for a fight.

I had a feeling that the hate and anger she was feeling had more to do with a culmination of things, but if she needed to get something off her chest, now was as good a time as any. I had already prepared myself for a battle tonight. I'd just expected it to be with a broody, six-foot-two cowboy instead of my little sister.

She flung her arm from my grasp, turning to face me fully, standing to her full height. I hadn't been blessed with the tall genes in our family, but Izzy sure had. She stood at a whopping five feet nine and towered over my five-foot-four frame. She did her best to look intimidating, but all I could see was my sister—scared, hurt, and in obvious mental anguish.

"No, *you* wait a damn minute. You don't get to talk to me like you're my mother. *YOU ARE NOT HER.*"

"I'm not trying to mother you, Izzy. I'm just concerned."

"Oh, now you're concerned? Daddy's little golden child isn't the center of fucking attention anymore, so you need to make this all about you."

I reared back, her words striking as she spat them. "That's not fair."

Even though she stood opposite me, I felt each of her words hit like a punch. She had clearly been building up for an emotional release, and whatever had set her off this evening acted as the catalyst.

The one thing family knew how to do better than anyone else? Hurt you.

I steeled my spine in preparation for a screaming match. It wouldn't have been our first and probably wouldn't be our last.

I knew that at her core, Izzy didn't mean the hateful words that were spewing from her mouth unchecked. The alcohol had taken away her filter, and she was using me as her verbal punching bag. If that's what she needed, I'd take every hit and jab ten times over to spare her the pain of feeling things so deeply.

Deep down, I knew her contempt for me wasn't the reason she had started that fight at Jack's, but if she needed to hash this out, I was here and ready to take it.

"You've got it all. The job, the free rent, the freedom, Dad's attention, the guy, everything I've ever wanted. Meanwhile, I've had to work for every single ounce of everything I've got. I threw myself into the rodeo, hoping he would see me. I moved out in hopes that he would visit. I even settled down with a respectable guy in hopes that he would finally see me as more than just the wild child with a wayward heart. But no, I'm still here, fighting through my daddy issues while you get everything handed to you."

The fact that she thought I'd had everything handed to me led me to believe I'd sheltered my sister more than I probably should have.

I'd spent the last fifteen years making sure she had the ability to chase her dreams, no matter how far-fetched they seemed. What I'd done instead was make it seem as if she needed to work harder, train longer, and do better to be respected and loved by the men in her life.

What she failed to remember were all the times I'd spent late nights reading bedtime stories to the twins, hoping they would fall asleep quickly so I could log onto my online community college and work on my degree. The time I skipped partying with my friends for my twenty-first birthday because Benny had come home from school with a stomach bug, when Dad had to be on duty. She didn't see that I was the one moving money around accounts to make sure the lights stayed on, the water ran hot, and the kids' sports fees were paid for because our dad worked so much, he'd forget.

If anyone should have been angry, it should have been me. But Izzy was right. This wasn't about me, and nothing I could say tonight would change the way she felt—especially as the tequila worked its way through her system.

She didn't bother waiting for a response. She knew there was nothing that I could have said to make all the pain she was feeling go away. Turning toward the stairs leading up to her room, she stopped and said softly over her shoulder, "I'm sorry."

I knew she meant it more for the fact that she had just verbally assaulted me, throwing around years of harbored anger, but there was a tinge of sadness that laced the words, and I knew there was a double meaning behind the sentiment. Nodding, I watched her back as she retreated, making sure she got herself up the stairs without incident.

Content that Izzy could fend for herself for the night, I grabbed a weathered quilt from the hall closet and padded my way over to the sofa. I lay down on the lumpy cushions, trying my best to get comfortable.

Finally, finding a suitable spot, I looked up at the ceiling, the idea of Izzy's sleeping form snuggled up in her bed above me, floating across my vision.

Closing my eyes, I softly whispered, "Yo también lo siento." *I'm sorry, too.*

I let the cool dampness of years of pent-up sadness lull me off to sleep, the trickle of tears a soft reminder that sometimes life isn't pretty, but it's sure as hell worth the pain.

WADE

THE WEATHERED EDGES of the worn business card felt soft against my fingers as I flipped it through them for the hundredth time.

I woke up this morning to find the card slipped between my door and its frame. Someone must have shoved it in there after I'd gone to bed. I had my suspicions as to who the culprit might be, but it didn't matter. The sentiment was still the same—do better.

I'd turned the card over in my palm enough times so that I could read the embossed letters with my eyes closed: Ember Ridge Recovery Center.

I hadn't looked into the facility further than what was written on this now-worn piece of cardstock, but the phrases "healing" and "PTSD" had me itching with unease.

I didn't have PTSD; what I had was anger at anything and everything for the shitty hand life had dealt me in the last year.

PTSD was for soldiers returning from war. I didn't have flashbacks that took me out of reality and into a war zone. I wasn't hypervigilant about my surroundings. I was just fucking *angry* and rightfully so.

I slipped the card into the back pocket of my Wranglers, resigning myself to the fact that this was either Stella's or Max's way of saying they cared. I knew I needed to get a grip, especially for Charlie's sake.

It had been over a month since I'd spent any time with my niece, and that hurt. She wasn't going to be little for long, and did I really want all of her memories from her childhood to be of an angry version of me? She already had a dead dad and enough trauma to last a lifetime; she didn't need me adding to it.

Pushing down the thoughts and focusing back on my work, I trudged into the office attached to the barn. It was a pathetic excuse for an office, but I wasn't in there often enough to care.

The only things housed there were my training logs, notes on riders, boarding information, and a couple of belt buckles from my rodeo days I'd half-ass attempted to decorate with to appease Ray, who had said the room was boring and sad.

I thumbed through a folder on top of my desk, checking that each of the horses being boarded for the week was accounted for and that their riders were set for training.

Instead of the trainees having to load and haul their horses to and from the facility each time they had lessons, we offered to board them in our stables for an additional fee. Most of them took the opportunity and left them in our care.

We could take a maximum of ten horses at a time, and that included the four we kept around for ourselves. Anything more than that, and it was more than Max and I could handle on our own.

Having the horses housed here allowed us the opportunity

to keep an eye on them for changes in gait, any shoeing issues, or signs that they may need veterinary care before their issues became unfixable.

Truthfully, the horses of rodeo riders were taken better care of than the riders themselves.

As I was checking one last thing, a soft knock came from the doorway. I expected to see Ray standing there after the night we had shared, but instead I was greeted with the soft features and emerald eyes of my new sister-in-law.

"Got a sec?" Stella asked hesitantly, refusing to step foot into the office without implicit permission. I held out a hand, signaling for her to sit in the one chair I kept on the opposite side of my desk.

It seemed formal, but I truthfully didn't know how to act around her since the incident or my subsequent freak-out at Jack's.

"Max was going to come down here and invite you, but I thought it would be better for us to chat a bit without an audience."

Stella wasn't meek by nature. The woman was a godforsaken tornado in human form and had barreled into our lives without an ounce of remorse. Seeing the dejected look on her face should have made me feel bad.

As much as I wanted to feel some semblance of remorse for the wedge that had been thrust into our relationship, I couldn't find any response other than seething hatred for the woman.

Getting the hint that I wasn't too keen on talking, she continued. "Max and I are having dinner and a game night on Friday. I know you technically live in the house and don't need to be invited, but—"

"I don't *technically* live there. I live there, point-blank."

Though my harsh tone made her wince, she didn't let it stop her from saying what she felt we needed to discuss. "We wanted to make sure you were aware that we *wanted* you to be there for dinner at the least. You don't have to stay and play games; I know that's not really your speed, but it would mean a lot to your brother if you were there."

I mulled over the invite, not missing the fact that she hadn't said it would mean a lot to *her* if I were there.

Things between Max and me had been strained since he and Stella had announced their quick engagement and wedding, but he was still my brother, and I needed to make an effort to be present in his life.

I stuck my hands in my back pockets, continuing to process Stella's words. When my fingers touched the crumpled business card I'd slid in there earlier, I knew I could do this.

How hard could it be to have dinner with my brother, his new wife, and my adorable niece?

WADE

I SEVERELY UNDERESTIMATED HOW hard it would be to sit down and have a civil dinner with my brother, Stella, and Charlie. They had also invited Pops and Ray, so it was a bona fide family fucking dinner—trauma, resentment, and all.

Ray and I hadn't had a chance to talk all week. She had taken on a couple of new clients at her virtual design firm and was in and out of meetings in the evenings when I was available after training sessions.

Working virtually meant that she was at the mercy of whatever time zone her client was in, and that often left her working late since we were on the East Coast.

During the day, when she didn't have client meetings, she watched Charlie so Stella and Max could go to work, and I could bust my ass to keep the ranch running.

Sitting around the dinner table, everyone except me laughing at something Pops said, I couldn't have felt more out of place. It seemed as though all of their lives had moved on, but I was still stuck in the same rut of anger and exhaustion I had been in since the moment I was shot.

I picked at my chicken and moved the mashed potatoes around my plate to make it look like I had eaten. I didn't miss the side-eyes I was getting from Ray, who seemingly never missed a beat. I swear, sometimes that woman scared me straight more times than my own mother had.

She didn't need words to convey the disappointment coursing through her at my lack of enthusiasm for this dinner; I could feel her staring into my soul from across the table.

As everyone started to clear the plates from the table, I noticed the way Max gently took Stella's hand beneath it, their fingers laced together tenderly.

The pair looked nervous as they darted their eyes around at each of us. Like a storm brewing in the distance, I could feel the pressure shifting, and I knew that something big was about to happen.

Max cleared his throat, a subtle signal for everyone to give him their attention, and looked lovingly down at Stella before addressing the rest of us. "Thank you, guys, so much for coming tonight. Stella and I wanted to get all of our family together for a little announcement."

I watched as he slowly slid his hand from where it was tangled with hers and rested it on the barely perceptible swell of her lower belly. As if all the air had been sucked out of the room, I suddenly felt like I couldn't breathe.

"Stella and I are promoting Charlie to big sister in the new year. It's still early, but we wanted everyone to know, and keeping it a secret when she's been constantly puking her guts up has been a challenge."

Ray's squeal of excitement could have been heard four counties over as she pushed out of her chair and rushed to Stella, pulling her in for a big hug. I could hear her gushing over all the baby things she was going to buy for their new little one and how amazing a big sister Charlie was going to be.

Pops stood, shaking Max's hand and pulling him in for a back-slapping hug, congratulating him as well. I felt as if I had melted directly into my dining room chair.

My limbs felt heavy and the air thick as all the surrounding voices started fading into muddled whispers. The loud rush of blood pumping through my fast-beating heart was a persistent whoosh in my ears.

Just like at their wedding, I wanted to be happy for them, but my mind wouldn't let me feel anything other than the burning fire of oppressive rage. That could have been me. Years down the road, sure, but it still could have been me.

Max would get his happily ever after with the woman who had brought pain and suffering to the life of his twin brother, while I got the shit sandwich called life.

I pushed back my chair; the legs scraped against the floor in a loud screech, breaking everyone's happy trance and forcing all their attention in my direction.

I felt like I was suffocating as I pushed out of my seat and stumbled toward the front door, acting blindly on impulse.

I didn't bother with showering them with empty platitudes and congratulations. They didn't need my support or well-wishes; they were doing just fine on their own.

As I threw open the front door, the thick humidity hung like a velvet curtain in the air, surrounding me and further weighing down the darkness of my mind.

Without thinking, I started running. I ran past the stables, past the dimly lit bunkhouse, and through the brambles and bushes of the woods.

Even though it was dark, I knew exactly where I was

going as if an invisible string was pulling me toward a place where I could quiet my mind and slow my racing heart.

My feet pounded on the damp earth in time with my racing heartbeat, propelling me further from the house and the trauma I didn't want to face.

Pushing through the thick brush, I stumbled into the cove, doubling over with my hands braced on my knees. As the damp, cool air surrounded me, I was able to suck in a shallow, shuddering breath. Each inhale was painful as my lungs struggled to catch up. My stomach retched, lurching with emptiness and leaving me gasping through each heave.

What felt like hours—but was probably only minutes—ticked by as I struggled to draw in each breath. Thoughts swirled around my head that scared me, and I struggled to hold back a torrent of tears as one or two traitorous droplets coasted down my cheeks.

My mind swirled with thoughts of how much easier everyone's lives would be without me and how much pain I was putting them through. It begged me for silence, a reprieve from the daily onslaught of fury.

A true testament of how far into my mind I had retreated, I didn't hear or feel her approach until Ray's slender fingers rubbed gentle circles across my back.

"Just breathe," she whispered, as if her words were floating softly through the wind. Timing my breaths with the gentle cadence of her soft caresses across my skin, I was able to regulate my breathing and slow my heart rate.

My mind was still a depraved mix of thoughts, and the tightness in my chest refused to release, but something about Ray's touch was calming me enough for the darkness to retreat to where it had come.

"Sit," she commanded, guiding me softly to the creek's

edge and helping me sit gently on the bank. Any other time, I would have given her shit for treating me like a child, but right now I could barely focus on a steady heartbeat, much less ribbing her.

"I'm—"

She stopped me with a quiet shush from her plump lips as she looked out into the quiet forest around us, closing her eyes. "Just listen."

I didn't dare argue with her as I closed my eyes, surrounding myself with the sounds of the cove.

In the distance, I heard the soft hooting of an owl, calling out into the wind. Crickets chirped a steady cadence, their soft song a timed metronome, further slowing my heart rate. A trickle of water flowing at our feet softened the edges of the red haze clouding my vision. With each cataloged sound, I felt the tension release from my frame and my shoulders inch away from my ears.

"I'm sorry." I tried again, needing to apologize to someone for the way I had acted.

"I'm not the one you need to be apologizing to," she said softly, her eyes still closed, a quiet contentment flowing through her features. The serenity wafting off her was enviable, but she looked so soft and unmarred by my grizzly mood.

"Want to tell me what happened?" Her hazel eyes opened, turning in my direction, a look of "no bullshit" accented by her arched brow.

I pulled my knees to my chest and wrapped my arms around them, hoping that if I made myself small, it would physically hold me together. Everything felt like it was falling apart around me when, in reality, life couldn't have been better for everyone else. Somehow, I had been stuck in this twilight zone of reliving that night—day in and day out, destined to be reminded of it at every turn.

"As soon as the words left Max's mouth about Stella being pregnant again, my vision turned red, and I couldn't breathe. Everything felt like it was closing in, and I couldn't find a way out. I should be happy for them, but all I can think about is all that I've lost in the face of all that they've gained."

Seemingly sensing my ratcheting heart rate, Ray's hand reached out, and her fingers laced with mine—a silent reminder that I wasn't alone, and this was a safe space to unload if I wanted to.

"It felt like my heart was beating out of my chest, and I couldn't take a breath. I had to get out of there before I absolutely lost it."

Admitting my freak-out to Ray felt uncomfortable, but I knew in my heart that, no matter what, she wasn't going to judge me.

"Wade," she said softly, using the same voice I'd heard her use on Izzy at the bar. The one that felt like she was placating you but was soft and serene because she was afraid you'd fight back. "I think you had a panic attack."

Brushing her off, I released her hand and stood up, pacing the length of the small cove, my hands running through the long strands of my hair.

"I've been doing some research—"

"Research? You've been looking up my form of crazy, Sunshine?"

"You're not crazy. I think you may have a form of PTSD. It's—"

The moment she insinuated I was suffering from PTSD,

she obliterated all the work we had just done to calm my breathing and my racing heart.

There was no fucking way I was being shoved into a box with America's heroes. Nothing I did warranted being on the same playing field, or even in the same realm as the people who valiantly served our country.

"I don't have PTSD! What is it with everyone trying to shove that diagnosis down my fucking throat?" I shouted, standing toe-to-toe with her, my fists tightening by my sides. True to her nature, she didn't so much as flinch.

"Okay, so you don't have PTSD. What do you think this is?" Waving her hand from top to bottom, she gestured at my body, currently vibrating with rage. I took a step back and resumed my pacing.

Being close to Rayna Cortez in the mindset I was in was dangerous. I knew in my heart that I wouldn't hurt her, but I might make decisions that couldn't be taken back. Ones that might push us over the edge and past the point of no return.

Stepping up behind me, I felt her slender arms wrap around my waist, holding me tightly as she rested her cheek in the center of my back.

"Tell me what you need," she whispered into the cotton of my shirt. Her words vibrated through me as the thrumming need to lose myself in her took over.

Turning around so we were face-to-face, I placed both hands on the sides of her throat, using my thumbs to lift her chin.

"You, Sunshine. I need you."

RAY

WORDS I never thought I'd hear coasted from his lips as if he'd been saying them his entire life. In a way, it felt like we had. The stolen glances, tender moments of silence, playful banter, all of it leading us to this very moment.

We were standing on the edge of a cliff, both of us content to jump but not knowing if we were going to be jumping alone. Except this time, Wade reached out a hand and asked me to jump with him.

"You, Sunshine, I need you."

Five simple words set me ablaze faster than dry kindling and the spark of an ember. I gripped his wrists, which were holding tightly on either side of my neck, and used them as leverage to pull myself toward him.

I had to stand on my tiptoes to be able to reach his mouth, but nothing was going to stop me from putting my lips on his.

Just like it had been outside Jack's, there was nothing gentle about the way Wade and I kissed. There was a potent hunger that had been building for almost fifteen years, desperate to claw its way out through our touches. Each brush of our lips sent shivers down my spine and tingles of desire straight to my core.

Like a man possessed, Wade held my jaw, using his thumb to open me up to him as his tongue coasted across my bottom lip, requesting entrance.

With a soft moan, I opened for him and melted into his strong embrace. One of his hands coasted down my side and came to rest on my hip. His grip was punishing as he tugged me closer, erasing any semblance of space between us.

With an agonizing groan, he tore his lips from mine and coasted them down the slope of my neck. Where each open-mouthed kiss had been placed, the cool air coasted across it, bringing goosebumps to my skin.

"Fuck, baby," he rasped as his hands trailed over every inch of skin they could.

I felt the rough calluses of his hands as they brushed along my waist, hitching up my T-shirt in their wake. The undiluted need in his groan, blended with his words, caused my nipples to tighten beneath my thin cotton bra and my core to ache with need.

Wade had always been so put together, albeit a joker, but he was always responsible and wise beyond his years. Seeing him so uninhibited and possessing the knowledge that it was me who caused his undoing gave me a heady sense of power.

"I need you, Wade Daniels," I moaned, cupping his growing erection through his jeans. He sucked in a hiss between clenched teeth as I slowly added pressure and continued rubbing against his length.

He gripped my wrist to stop me, and I held back the whimper of disappointment that threatened to spill past my lips. A wicked grin spread across his face as he let go of my wrist and trailed his hand up the center of my chest, avoiding exactly where I wanted him to touch me.

He gripped my neck, adding slight pressure on the sides, and I nodded in approval at his questioning gaze. Yep, I sure as fuck liked that.

I had only been with a couple of guys through the years, and none of them made me feel as powerful and sexy as Wade did.

Even if we were just friends, I knew I held a sense of control over him that he wouldn't find with any other woman, and it was the most rewarding feeling knowing I could bring him to his knees.

Dipping his head to whisper in my ear, his warm breath deepened my desire as he crooned, "You want this, Sunshine?" He pushed one of his knees between my legs, and I could feel his rigid desire as it pressed into my thigh.

Yes, I sure as fuck wanted that.

I nodded, suddenly unable to speak as I reached my slender fingers down to the buckle of his belt and started pulling the leather through the metal clasp and loosening its hold on the starched denim. I unbuttoned them and slid down the zipper torturously slow, teasing him with every inch it descended.

Once his pants were undone, I slowly sank to my knees at his feet, gripping the sides of his jeans and boxer briefs in each of my hands. I looked up at him through my lashes, a sly smile playing upon my lips.

Tugging the fabric concealing him from his hips, I dropped them just enough for his cock to spring free.

He was hard as steel, bobbing in front of my face, begging for my touch. I could see a small bead of pre-cum glistening from the crown, and I leaned down, swiping it away with the tip of my tongue.

Wade's sharp intake of breath was enough to spur me on as I wrapped my fingers around his length and sat back on my heels, ready and waiting.

He looked down at me reverently, brushing a strand of hair tenderly from my face and tucking it behind my ear.

"Are you going to look at me all night, or are you going to let me suck your cock?" I asked playfully, batting my lashes at him with practiced innocence.

With a loud chuckle, he reached down and gripped my chin, tipping my gaze up to his.

"I could look at you from sunup to sundown, Rayna Cortez, but I'm sure there's not a prettier sight in this world than you on your knees, begging for my cock in that filthy fucking mouth."

WADE

I HAVE SEEN my fair share of beautiful things in this world. Cotton candy skies painted over the fields of D&D Ranch from horseback, the way the stars shone on clear summer nights as if each one painted with expert precision, the utter freedom of a rescue horse when it meets grass for the first time after spending its life in confinement.

All of these things paled in comparison to the sight of Ray, on her knees, hand on my cock, ready and waiting to take me in her mouth.

It was dark, but the way the sliver of moonlight coasting through the cove shone off her thick raven hair as she swept it over her shoulder left me speechless. The way her hazel eyes shone with undiluted passion and desire as she looked up at me made me weak in the knees.

There was inexplicable beauty in the way that she held me captive, completely at her mercy.

There wasn't a single thing I wouldn't do for Rayna Cortez in the light of day, but under the darkness of night, with only the moonlight to guide us and all our inhibitions washed away, I was a goner.

"You are so fucking beautiful," I drawled as my fingers danced along her jaw. Her eyes fluttered closed as she leaned her cheek into my palm, feeling the power in my words.

"So are you." Her soft whisper coasted across my skin as she leaned forward and tenderly kissed the tip of my silky crown. Softly stroking my length with her fist, she swirled her tongue around the head and across the slit, gathering the remnants of pre-cum as she went.

If she didn't quit teasing me, this wasn't going to last long. I'd waited at least ten years to be inside of Ray; another second might break me.

"Sunshine," I hissed as she swirled the head of my cock again with that skillful tongue.

"Mmm?" she hummed, sending tingling vibrations through me, causing a low moan to escape my lips.

"As much as I'm enjoying this little show, I've waited ten fucking years to either have my cock in your mouth or the pussy of my dreams. If you don't stop teasing the fuck out of—"

My words were cut short as she dropped her head forward, taking my entire length to the back of her throat, gagging lightly.

I swear, in that moment I saw stars. With each pull of her mouth and swirl of her tongue, she brought me closer and closer to the edge as she bobbed her head up and down, relentlessly swallowing my cock.

"Fuuuuuuuuuck," I groaned, feeling the pressure of release building in my spine. I gripped Ray's chin as I tensed. "Baby, I'm about to blow. Slow down unless you want to swallow every drop of me like the good girl you are."

I watched as she tightened her thighs together, seeking friction to ease the ache I knew was growing between them. She doubled down on her efforts, hollowing her cheeks and taking me to the back of her throat again, as my release crashed over me and I spilled into her warm, silky mouth.

I watched in awe as she took every last drop and pulled back, releasing me with an audible pop.

Using her thumb to wipe the corner of her lips, she sat back on her heels and smiled up at me innocently.

"Good girl, you say? I think I like the sound of that," she teased, coasting her hand down the front of her shirt and under the waistband of her shorts.

I watched as her eyes fluttered closed the second her fingers came into contact with her aching clit.

Tucking my dick back into my pants, I stepped closer and bracketed her throat in my hand, tilting her chin up to look at me. She licked her lips as she continued swirling her fingers around her core, taunting and teasing me.

After that show she just put on, I wanted nothing more than to return the favor.

"We've got two options," I stated, using the pad of my thumb to drag her bottom lip from where she'd been biting it between her teeth. "I can either fuck you right here on the ground, which wouldn't be my preference seeing as how I've been waiting a long fucking time to be inside you, and I'd like to do it right, or I can taste that sweet pussy I've been dreaming about and put you out of your misery until we can find a more suitable place to continue tomorrow."

As if she were mulling it over, she brought her fingers up from out of her waistband, tapping them on her lips in contemplation. I grew painfully hard watching her paint the remnants of her desire along her lips. "Or, I could put *you* out of your misery and tell you that my house is completely empty all weekend."

The words barely left her throat before I hauled her up, threw her over my shoulder like a caveman and started running as fast as my legs would allow.

Her peals of laughter probably could have been heard all the way back at the ranch, but I didn't give a fuck.

I didn't even care that I was trying to keep my pants up as I ran, having forgotten to button and buckle them after that mind-blowing blow job. I was about to fulfill a fantasy that eighteen-year-old me would die over.

It only took us five minutes to get to the Cortez house, and true to her word, there wasn't a car in the driveway or a single light on in the house. I set Ray down on the porch, sliding her body slowly down mine, and caging her against the front door, my hands on either side of her head.

This was it. The moment everything was about to change.

Yes, one could argue that getting my dick sucked in the middle of the woods by my best friend had crossed the line into something more than friendship, but this?

This was it. There wouldn't be any going back after I sank deep inside Rayna Cortez.

Looking down at her standing beneath me, her breathing wild and her cheeks flushed, I cataloged every one of her beautiful features up close. The soft sprinkling of freckles that brushed across the apples of her cheeks that got darker each summer she spent basking in the sunny days on the ranch. The plushness of her kiss-swollen lips that I couldn't wait to taste again. I could see her pulse fluttering wildly on the slender column of her throat, begging for me to trail my lips across it.

"Are you sure this is what you want?" I whispered, suddenly unsure and second-guessing every moment from this evening. She had been so willing at the cove, and there was clear verbal consent, but the little voice inside my head planted doubts quicker than I could will them away.

"There are three things in life I am certain of." She held up a single finger between our bodies. "One, the sun will rise and set each day like clockwork." She raised another finger. "Two, there isn't anything better than my dad's authentic Mexican home cooking."

A deep chuckle left my lips. She was right; Emmanuel's home cooking was the best Mexican food I'd ever tasted.

She reached out with the hand that had been counting and slid it up my neck, cupping my cheek tenderly. "And three, I have been in love with you since the day you kept me from falling on my ass in the mud at eleven years old. You are my best friend in the entire world, Wade Daniels, and I couldn't imagine anyone else I'd rather do this crazy thing called life with. So, the answer is yes, I would like you to take me inside and fuck me on every surface you can before the sun comes up."

RAY

WE WERE an uncoordinated tangle of limbs as I did my best to navigate our bodies through the dark house. We managed to only knock over one thing in our haste to make it to my bedroom, but we ping-ponged our way down the hallway, stopping to kiss each other breathless every few feet against the nearest wall.

Once the floodgates had been opened, there was no stopping the relentless passion between us. We were feral with need for each other, and as we stepped into my bedroom and the door shut behind us with a soft snick, the finality of the situation sank in.

Wade stood across the room, leaning his back against my door, his chest heaving with ragged breaths as he held himself back. I flicked on one of the bedside lamps, bathing my small bedroom in a warm, sensual glow.

"I'm only going to ask one more time. Are you sure?" Wade panted, clearly at war with himself for wanting to cross this invisible line from friendship into something more.

Boldly, I took a step toward him, still ten feet or more

between us. I reached for the hem of my cotton T-shirt, pulling it over my head and tossing it toward the laundry hamper in the corner. I could see his pupils dilate with need as he took in my lace-covered breasts, nipples pebbled and begging to be touched.

Taking another step forward, I unbuttoned my shorts and slid the zipper down before sliding them off my legs and kicking them over to where I'd just thrown my shirt.

I wasn't worried about whether they had made it in the laundry basket; that was tomorrow's problem.

Right now, my focus was getting underneath Wade Daniels and finally taking what I so desperately craved.

His breathing had been reduced to shuddering pants as I took another step closer to him, now only about an arm's length away.

I reached behind me, undoing the clasp on my bra and sliding the straps from my shoulders slowly, tossing it among the growing pile of clothes.

His eyes tracked down from my eyes to gaze upon my breasts. There were many things I loved about my body, but my tits and ass topped that list. Coupled with the hungry way that Wade was licking his lips, I was preening under his gaze.

I noticed his fingers twitching, itching to touch me, but I wasn't done teasing him.

Taking one last step forward, I slid my panties from my waist and twirled them around my finger as I tossed them too into the pile, a feline smile on my lips.

Standing naked, in all my feminine glory, in front of the man I loved was a potent drug. His eyes trailed over every inch of my skin, cataloging the way my body was begging for his touch.

I reached down and tenderly laced my fingers with his, squeezing three times before speaking.

"You asked me if I'm sure," I said, raising my chin to look him directly in the eye. I guided his hand to my core, slowly sliding his fingers through the wetness that had been pooling between my thighs. A low growl left his throat as he came into contact with the evidence of my arousal.

Gliding his fingers upward, he swirled his thumb against my clit, causing me to close my eyes and a wanton moan to escape my lips.

I opened my eyes and was met with the look of a desperate man. His eyes were hooded, pupils dilated with desire, and I could tell he was holding himself back from breaking past that final barrier.

"Does that feel like I'm sure?" I asked, stepping forward until our bodies were flush, his hand trapped against my pulsing core, fingers slowly teasing my aching clit.

"Now, I'm not going to ask you again. Please fuck me, Wade."

As if the leash on his restraint had snapped, he tugged me toward him, crashing his mouth down on firmly mine. I moaned, opening myself up to the feral way he was ravaging me. He broke the kiss long enough to tug his shirt over his head and shove his jeans and boxers off his hips.

Since he hadn't fully redressed after that stellar blow job I'd given him in the cove, it didn't take long until we were both naked, and he was guiding me backward toward my bed.

The back of my legs hit the edge of my mattress as I sat, and I watched with rapt attention as Wade stroked the rigid length of his cock, spreading his pre-cum across the head with each stroke.

Even though I'd just had his cock in my mouth, I

marveled at the beauty that was Wade Daniels in all his masculine glory.

He was lean, toned from long days of manual labor around the ranch, and his skin was effortlessly sun-kissed as he hated working with his shirt on. He had a light dusting of sandy blonde hair that trailed from his belly button to where he was currently stroking himself.

Unsurprisingly, his cock was just as beautiful as the rest of him. He wasn't huge, which was absolutely fine by me, but he was large enough that it had been a struggle to take him down my throat without gagging.

"Like what you see?" he asked with a cocky grin as he stepped between my knees, spreading them to accommodate his wide frame. His fingers tangled in the hair at the nape of my neck as he gripped gently, tugging my head backward.

My eyes fluttered closed at the pinpricks of pressure that glittered across my scalp. I hummed a pleasant response as he tightened his grip, almost enough to be borderline painful.

If there was one thing I was certain of, it was that Wade could match me toe-to-toe for roughness. I didn't want to be treated like a porcelain doll. Sure, I was small, but I wasn't breakable—I liked it a little rough.

"You're going to be the death of me, Sunshine," he crooned as he released my hair and sank to his knees between my thighs. He gently pushed between my breasts, instructing me to lie back, and I rolled my eyes at him petulantly.

His breath was warm against my core as he spoke. "Now, lie there like a good girl and let me taste this pretty fucking pussy I've been dreaming about."

And with that declaration, he did just that, feasting on me as if I were his last meal and he was a man starved.

WADE

I KNEW beyond any shadow of a doubt that the sweetness of Ray's pussy was the best thing my tongue had ever tasted. I alternated between licking through the length of her and focusing on the swollen bud at the apex of her thighs.

I cataloged each breathy moan and sharp intake of breath as I learned each and every way she liked to be touched. There was no way any other man was going to touch this woman after tonight; she was *mine*. Mine to taste, mine to tease, mine to fuck, mine to *love*.

I brought one of my fingers to her core and slid it through her wetness, pushing into her and curling up to hit that perfect spot. She threw her head back in ecstasy, letting out a loud, unrestrained moan.

I couldn't have been more grateful that we were the only ones in the house because I couldn't imagine trying to keep this woman quiet. I wanted to hear every beautiful cry uttered from her lips as I brought her closer and closer to the edge of her release.

I felt her core tightening around my finger, and I focused

my efforts directly on her clit as I used the tip of my tongue to flick relentlessly over the swollen bud.

"Oh, God, yes. Right there. Don't you dare fucking stop," she chanted, writhing beneath my grasp. I hooked both of my arms around her thighs, holding her sweet pussy to my mouth as I wrapped my lips around her and sucked.

She rocked her core against my lips, using me exactly how she wanted to take her over that edge. Her body went rigid, spine bowing off the mattress as I held her in place and wrung out each wave of her orgasm, lapping up her release.

Before she had a chance to recover, I crawled up the bed and hovered over her, my cock lined up perfectly with her entrance. I bracketed my arms on each side of her head and brushed a sweaty tendril of hair from her face.

She radiated a satiated glow that could only be described as pure bliss as she looked up into my eyes and smiled lazily. Even though I could tell she was wrung out and spent, I wasn't close to done with her.

Leaning down, I pressed a tender kiss to her lips, letting her taste the evidence of her release on my tongue. She moaned softly as I palmed one of her breasts, pinching her nipple between my thumb and index finger.

I placed a reverent kiss on the corner of her mouth and continued trailing kisses down her throat. She ran her fingers through my hair, gently tugging out the hair elastic that held it back, feathering her nails across my scalp. I swear, if I were a cat, I would have purred at the sensation.

There was nothing rushed about that moment. Each of us had taken our pleasure, and we both clearly wanted to savor the feel of something we had waited so long for.

I placed soft kisses across her collarbone, making my way

back to her ear, where I placed one last kiss on the pulse point right below it.

"Te amo, Sol," I whispered against the shell of her ear, pouring all of my emotions from the last fifteen years into three simple words.

Leaning back to look into her eyes, I saw tears pooling across her lower lash line at my tender sentiment.

"Please don't cry," I begged, using the pad of my thumb to swipe the wetness before it could fall.

"They're happy tears," she said softly, sniffling and bringing her hand up to interlock her fingers with mine. "I love you, too."

Hearing those words coming from her lips broke my chest wide open, my heart swelling with pride. I had been so unbelievably in love with Rayna Cortez for so long that hearing words I'd only fantasized about left me soaring.

Placing my hand on the side of her neck, I angled her head up to meet me in a tender kiss. I poured every ounce of passion I'd been harboring over the last fifteen years into how my lips tangled with hers. Our tongues danced fervently against each other as our passion heightened.

I felt Ray reach between us and wrap her fingers around my cock, lining it up with her entrance.

I paused and pulled back before things went too far. "Hold on, let me grab a condom."

I rolled off her bed, reaching for my pants and opening my wallet. I sent up a silent prayer that the condom I kept there hadn't expired.

I knew it was risky keeping it in my wallet, but I rarely had the damn thing on me anyway. Verifying that it was in fact still in date, I turned around, holding it up like the prize-winning ribbon at the county fair.

Ray was a timeless vision, lying splayed out across the top of her bed, ready and waiting for me. She was propped up on her elbows, watching me with raw hunger as I slowly stepped toward the edge of the bed, slowly stalking my prey.

When I got close enough to touch her, I spread her thighs and placed my knee on the bed between them. I leaned over and placed a scorching kiss on her beautiful lips, leaving her panting and breathless.

Grabbing her hand, I turned it over and placed the condom in the center of her palm. "Will you do the honors?" I asked with one eyebrow raised.

She smirked and wasted no time before tearing open the foil packet with her teeth and tossing the wrapper on the floor beside us. I straightened as she wrapped her hand around my length and rolled the condom down with acing slowness.

She leaned back, pulling me by the neck down with her until our foreheads pressed together. The ferocity of our need for each other was still present, but this moment felt different. It felt life-changing. I brushed my fingers down the side of her face as she lined me up with her center.

Her eyes met mine as I slowly eased the head of my cock inside her. I didn't have a huge dick, but I took it slow, letting her body adjust and feel every inch of me connecting with her core. I felt her pussy clench around me like a vise grip, and I caught the hint of a smile across her lips.

Oh, she wanted to play like that?

Getting the hint, I slammed home until our hips were flush. She threw her head back in a loud moan, and I gritted my teeth at how good it felt to finally be fully seated inside her.

She wrapped her arms around my neck tightly as she met me thrust for thrust. Our bodies fit perfectly against each other as I pumped into her wet heat. I could feel her core tightening around me, the flutters of her building release pulsing against my cock.

"That's it, baby, I can feel your body begging for me. Let go. Let me hear how beautiful you sound coming all over my cock," I whispered in her ear as I reached between us to press the pad of my thumb against her clit.

"Oh, God," she moaned, throwing her head back as she writhed beneath me.

"No, Sunshine. My name is Wade. If you need to scream something, it's going to be my name from those pretty lips."

I drove into her harder, the headboard smacking against the wall. She chanted my name over and over again as I felt her tightening and the pressure of release building at my spine.

My thrusts became erratic as her pussy gripped me in an iron fist, and we both crested over the hill of our orgasms in tandem.

It felt like our release was never-ending as we continued to writhe against each other, wringing out the last droplets of our pleasure. After the waves of release relinquished their hold on us, I rolled over beside her, throwing an arm over my face in exhaustion.

I needed to deal with the condom, but I didn't think I had an ounce of energy left in my body after that. I felt Ray reach between us and intertwine our hands, squeezing three times.

I smiled behind my arm and removed it to look down at her. She had the most beautiful smile on her face, and the sweetest blush from her orgasm painted across her cheeks.

I rolled over and kissed her softly on the mouth before getting up and padding my way to her en suite bathroom to throw away the condom. I grabbed a rag off the shelf next to the sink and wet it with warm water.

Heading back into her room, Ray was still sprawled out naked across the top of her covers, her eyes closed in contented bliss.

I ran my hand softly across one of her thighs before spreading her legs and using the warm rag to clean her up.

When I brushed across her clit, she hissed and let out a soft moan, making me chuckle. I could see that neither of us was going to be satisfied doing this just once tonight.

Tossing the rag onto her growing laundry pile, I rounded the side of her bed and pulled back the covers, throwing them back enough for her to get under them, too.

She shimmied under the blankets, curled into my side, and let out a loud sigh as she lay her head on my chest. I wrapped my arms around her, tugging her close and resting my chin on top of her head.

Nothing felt more right than being in her arms, knowing this is what our forever would look like.

"Next time, I'm on top," she said, breaking the silence. I could feel her smile against my skin, and I pressed a gentle kiss to the top of her head.

"Is that so, Sunshine?"

She tilted her head up and grinned, her eyes twinkling with mischief. "Gotta show my cowboy how well I ride."

I growled and rolled her over, pressing fervent kisses to her neck and chest. It looked like neither of us was going to be sleeping anytime soon.

WADE

AFTER SUCCESSFULLY FUCKING Ray on nearly every flat surface in her room, the bathroom counter, and against the tiled wall of her shower, we both crawled into bed, wrung out and exhausted.

With the lights out and the curtains drawn, I relished the feel of her body pressed against mine. She wore my T-shirt and nothing else, leaving me in just my black boxer briefs.

Ray's warm breath coasted across my chest, where she had her head resting in the divot of my shoulder, her leg slung over my thigh as she softly snored beside me.

She looked so serene, her eyelashes fluttering against her tan cheeks. She had pulled her hair up into a messy bun, and I brushed a tendril that had fallen out, tucking it behind her ear. Stirring softly, she hummed a contented sigh as she snuggled in closer to my side.

Knowing that Ray and I had watched each other grow up, side by side and hand in hand, made this moment even sweeter. Life had a way of bringing things around full circle, and I softly chuckled to myself, thinking about what eighteen-year-old me would have thought about this moment.

So many fond memories with the beautiful woman tucked in close to my side floated through the highlight reel of my mind.

Eighteen-year-old me, a senior in high school, on the precipice of real life beginning, kissing Ray in the front seat of my truck on prom night.

In my early twenties, during countless nights on the rodeo circuit, ending up balls deep in some no-name buckle bunny, always wishing it was Ray.

When she pretended to be my fiancée one time to kick a buckle bunny out of my hotel room when she overstayed her welcome.

So many stolen glances where I took in the sight of her, uninhibited and free, basking in the sunny days at the ranch.

Even in the hard moments, there was comfort between us, as we held each other from falling apart when life felt too heavy to carry alone.

Ray was my rock, my savior, my guiding light.

As my eyes drifted shut and sleep threatened to take me under, I vowed that I would do whatever it took to become the best man I could be for the woman beside me, who deserved the world.

She could do better than me by a long shot, but for some ungodly reason, she believed there was good inside me, and I was determined to find it for her.

"BRO, *we need to get out of here,*" *I called toward my brother and his girlfriend, Stella, as I stood in the warehouse opening. I didn't want to linger inside this hellhole any longer than need be, but for some fucking reason, Max chose now, in the middle of a crime scene, to hold and console his woman after she shot a man and he rescued her daughter.*

I wanted to get out of here, get back to my bed, and pretend the last twenty-four hours never happened. Hearing that Charlie, my soon-to-be niece, had been kidnapped had gutted me. She and Stella hadn't been in our lives long, but they had cemented a place in each of our hearts. They were family, no matter if they didn't carry the Daniels name yet.

This whole building smelled of mold and something pungently vile. It had clearly been sitting vacant for a long time before the crazy fuckers who kidnapped Charlie, and subsequently Stella, started using it to stash their drugs.

POP

What the fuck?!

Fuck, why am I on the ground? Why can't I move my legs? Why does everything feel like it's on fire?

POP POP POP

Turning my head to the side, still stunned and confused as to why I couldn't fucking stand up, I saw Emmanuel, Ray's dad, standing off to the side with his pistol pointed at something or someone behind me. Everything had happened so fast, and I was trying to put the pieces together as everything unfolded around me.

Max knelt down next to me, taking my hand. Why did he look so frantic?

"Shh, it's okay. We've got paramedics on the way. Don't move," he scolded.

Excuse me, I was the older twin here; I would do the bossing around.

I tried to move, but nothing seemed to work as it was supposed to. I pushed off the ground with my hands but immediately fell back down as agonizing pain shot through every single fiber of my core, radiating down my legs. How could I feel the pain coursing through my limbs but not lift the lifeless appendages to move?

"Max..." I started, but even my lungs hurt. Every breath felt like it was tearing my chest in two. There was no other way to describe it than a searing and scorching pain that felt like fire was consuming every piece of me and burning me from the inside out.

"No. No, you're not giving me some lame-ass speech that I need to take care of things if you die." Die? I was just going to ask him to help me up. "You're not going to fucking die, do you hear me?"

"Fuck...you..." I gritted out, ready to lay into him for bossing me around but losing the steam to argue.

"It's gonna be okay." His promises hung heavily in the air as reality dawned on me. The pop, a gunshot, my legs... Fuck, my legs. I couldn't move my fucking legs. What was happening?

Tears welled in my eyes, blurring my vision, as the pain—physical and emotional—gripped hold of me. A choked sob crested my lips, and it felt as if it stole every ounce of breath I had left.

"Max..." I sobbed, not caring if I looked like a whiny ass bitch. Suddenly, I was terrified, point-blank. "I can't feel my legs."

Fear like I'd never experienced before flooded my veins. I fought for every ragged intake of breath as my heart beat wildly in my chest. I'd been shot, and I couldn't feel my fucking legs.

"WADE."

The sweetest voice called to me in the haze of my dream, a frantic lilt to the words.

Was I dreaming? The nightmares had become so vivid and frequent that I sometimes had trouble deciphering whether I was actually lying on the musty floor of that warehouse or if I was snug at home in my bed.

"Wade, baby, wake up." I could feel someone shaking me, but the pain was overwhelming. Sweat dotted my brow, and I struggled to catch my breath.

My chest was on fire, my back felt like someone had poked a cattle brand directly on it, and the screaming… Fuck, why was someone screaming?

"WADE!"

At the terrified sound of her voice, I felt my senses snap back to reality. Ray stood beside the bed, tears streaming down her face, and her arms clutched tightly around her body, my shirt dwarfing her small frame.

She looked terrified, and the idea that I'd done something to cause that look gutted me.

Blinking away the haze of the nightmare, I took in my surroundings. The bedside lamp lay shattered on the floor, shards of porcelain scattered across the rug.

Sheets were strewn about as if they'd been balled up and tossed haphazardly back on the bed, tangled around my waist.

The spot where I had been lying was damp with the sweat that I could feel beading down my neck and soaking the hair at the nape.

Ray stood on the opposite side of the room now, her hands now by her sides. I didn't miss the subtle shake in them as she warred with how to approach, and it hit me. I was the one scaring her. The screaming had been me.

"Sunshine…" I whispered, afraid to scare her further.

"How long?" Her words came out breathless, and the shake clearly wasn't only in her hands as I heard the tremor radiate through her voice.

I hung my head, ashamed to admit how long I'd been fighting these demons alone. I didn't want her pity. I finally had the woman of my dreams, and I didn't need her realizing how truly broken a man I was.

"How long, Wade?" she repeated, anger replacing terror as she took a fortified step forward, her shoulders back and chin lifted as she fought to put her mask of bravery in place.

"Since a month or so after coming home from the hospital." The words felt like acid on my tongue as I shared the darkest parts of me with the only thing that brought me light. "They started out mild, but lately they've gotten worse. They've gotten harder to snap out of and more vivid. Sometimes I can't tell the difference between a dream and reality." Seeing her flinch, I backpedaled, scared that things had gone too far and I'd done something I couldn't take back.

"I promise I won't hurt you."

"Hurt me?" she scoffed, tears pouring down her cheeks, leaving damp rivers of betrayal in their wake. She brushed them away with the back of her hand and turned her head away to speak softly. "I'm not scared of you. I'm scared *for* you."

"I'm fine. It's just nightmares. Anyone who'd been through the hell I have would have nightmares."

"Just nightmares?!" she screeched, her voice rising and breaking with a sob at the tail end of her words. Her carefully placed armor was cracking, and I could see the scared and hurt woman beneath. "You call that just a nightmare?"

She took another step closer, and I threw back the covers, turning so my legs dangled off the edge of the bed. She stepped between my knees and pressed her hand to my cheek. I leaned into her caress as I felt the hot tears drip off her chin onto my sweat-slicked skin.

"Wade, just nightmares would be seeing yourself in a classroom full of your friends while you gave a presentation in your underwear. Just nightmares would be missing a deadline, your teeth falling out, being chased by snakes. This was not just a nightmare. That empty look of pure terror in your eyes will haunt me." Her touch was a brand against my clammy skin as she tilted my chin up to look at her.

"I think you're having flashbacks."

Her soft words hit like daggers to my chest as I fought for each ragged breath, the weight of anxiety threatening to close my throat. Flashbacks meant PTSD. Flashbacks meant I was broken. Flashbacks meant I needed help.

Fuck.

For so long, I'd been fighting this battle alone, not realizing how it was affecting everyone around me, even when I tried my hardest to keep them away from it.

Seeing the hurt in Ray's eyes as I fought to control my breathing, soaking in the warm comfort of her touch, I realized I couldn't do this anymore. I couldn't stand back and push this to the side, letting it eat away at the goodness left inside of me.

The nightmares were getting worse; I was angry all the damn time, and before long, I was going to burn bridges with the people most important to me that wouldn't be able to be repaired.

"I think I need help, Sunshine," I whispered into the darkness, leaning forward and pressing my forehead to her belly.

She hugged me to her and rubbed my back as I let the tears I'd been holding fall, soaking her shirt with all the pain and anger I'd been trying to hide.

"It's okay. We will do this together."

I didn't deserve this woman, but I was damn sure determined to prove that I could be a better man. She deserved to be loved by the man I was before the incident. She deserved to be loved wholly and without reservations.

As she held me softly under the glow of moonlight, I vowed within myself that I would do what it took to be a better man for her, even if it meant facing the demons I didn't want to acknowledge.

RAY

THE MORNING after Wade's nightmare and emotional purge was tense. Neither of us knew what to say in the light of day, but we both knew that something needed to be done to help him heal the broken parts of himself he was so desperate to hide.

Days passed, and we didn't talk much, outside of the occasional text or funny meme sent back and forth. It was as if the events of that night hadn't happened.

Wade was busy getting the ranch ready for the next influx of riders and their horses, while I threw myself into designs for an upscale office building in Atlanta, a small-town hair salon across the pond in Ember Ridge, and a couple of party plans for various functions.

Over the course of the last year, business had doubled, and I was looking into finally hiring some part-time help.

Even though the majority of my job was virtual, going out to the different thrift stores during the day took me away from more important work that needed to be done in the office, and vice versa.

I wanted to get back to the root of the things that I enjoyed about my business, and if that meant handing off the boring stuff like paperwork to someone else, I was finally in a place where I could afford to do it.

I was enjoying my day off, spending it with the cutest kid on the planet. Stella's daughter, Charlie, came over at least once a week to spend time with me while her mama went to work down at the boutique on Main Street.

There was nothing I loved more than getting to spend time with that sweet little chunk.

The plan was to head over to the ranch for a little bit. One of the heifers had just given birth to her first calf, and it was getting the VIP treatment and staying in one of the barns due to it being small and mama not taking to nursing well.

While it would have made logistical sense for me to just head over to the ranch and watch Charlie over at the big house all day, Stella had brought her by early because inventory was arriving, and I knew that we would be in the way of daily ranch operations if we got over there at the ass crack of dawn.

Especially since Charlie had endless energy that wasn't bound within the constraints of what most people deemed an acceptable wake-up time.

I looked down at my watch, checking the time, and then darted my eyes over to the baby monitor on the coffee table.

Charlie had gone down for an early morning nap, and I could see her squirming around in the portable crib in my room, waking up.

After she'd been kidnapped right under our noses at her first birthday party, it had taken all of us a long time to get comfortable with her being out of our sight, even if just to take a nap. She'd been taken from her crib while we were busy setting up her party, and I don't think any of us will ever get over the fear and anxiety that moment created.

Stella's screams when she realized Charlie's crib was empty would haunt me for the rest of my life. Much in the same way Wade's screams of terror from his flashback would.

"Wayyyy!" Charlie screamed from my room, demanding I come get her out of the prison conditions she was so clearly trapped in. Silently rolling my eyes, I set my laptop on the sofa and padded back to my room.

Opening the door, I was greeted with the happiest smile and excited giggles. There was nothing better than the unfiltered joy of a child. Their world was so small compared to an adult's, and even the tiniest of things could make them the happiest humans on the planet.

"Hiya, cupcake," I cooed, extricating her from baby jail and placing her on the ground.

At almost two, the girl was growing like a weed and refused to be carried by anyone other than Max, or Mass Da, as she liked to call him.

As a wedding present to Max, Stella had consulted with an attorney and had adoption papers drawn up, asking him to officially be Charlie's dad.

Her biological father had been killed during a drug dispute, which was ultimately what had Stella running to Firefly Cove and into Max's arms and all of our hearts.

Without so much as acknowledging my existence, Charlie ran to the living room as fast as her chubby little legs would take her. I sighed in mock annoyance as I dutifully followed.

It was Charlie's world, and the rest of us were just living in it.

"Way!" she hollered from the kitchen, pushing a dining room chair across the floor and over to the counter to reach something on top of it. I clocked the plate of chocolate chip cookies before she could grab hold of one and snatched her off the chair, spinning her around.

"I don't think so, little lady," I chided playfully. She squirmed in my grasp and let out a long string of giggles as I feathered my fingers gently over her ribs.

"Down! Down!" she hollered through each fit of giggles. I smacked a loud and wet kiss on her cheek as I set her gently on the ground.

She brushed off her dress as if I'd messed up her pristine outfit and stood with her tiny hands on her hips and a deep furrow in her brow. I knew that look well, and it was the spitting image of the broody cowboy she so affectionately called "dad."

Rolling my lips inward to fight a chuckle, I reached my hand out in offering. She placed her tiny hand in mine, and I gave it three quick squeezes to which she returned, even if they were like tiny little squishes against my palm.

"Where goin'?" she asked as we walked into the living room and I picked her up, depositing her on the sofa.

Snagging her boots from where she'd haphazardly taken them off next to the door, I fitted them on her feet and helped her stand.

"We've got a date with some cowboys, horses, and a cute baby cow," I told her. Her smile could have lit up the room at the idea of getting to see a baby cow, and I chuckled as she scrambled happily toward the door, grabbing her tiny cowboy hat along the way.

It had been so long since we'd had little ones in the house, and it was nice to have some extra energy to siphon from when life seemed all too heavy.

Charlie was the balm to anyone's weary soul, especially

mine. Secretly, I hoped that should an emotionally closed-off cowboy she called an uncle make an appearance, she could turn on that cuteness charm and act as my wingman.

Instead of loading Charlie up and driving all the way around to the ranch, I figured it was a nice enough day that we could take a little walk through the woods.

True to her wild cowgirl nature, Charlie was untamable as we made our way down the well-worn path between my house and the Daniels' property.

She hopped from one spot to the next, marveling at how many different kinds of bugs she could see, how high the trees were, asking about all the chirping and cooing sounds, and so much more. Her curiosity about the world around her was a fire I hoped she'd never lose.

As we crested the clearing of the woods and the big red barn came into view, Charlie took off at a dead sprint.

There was no way I could catch up with her, even if I weren't pushing thirty and feeling every bit of it. That girl was faster than the wind and knew exactly where she was going to get what she wanted.

Just as she neared the barn doors, I saw a large man step out, his straw cowboy hat shielding him from the sun. Charlie ran straight into his arms, not bothering to slow down as she launched herself upward, expecting him to catch her.

True to Max's nature, he caught her with ease, twirling her around and propping her on his hip. I finally made my way close enough to the two of them, and the sight had me tearing up.

Even though Charlie was growing up and asserting her independence, there seemed to be a special bond between her and Max.

Charlie had only ever known Max as the father figure in

her life. Stella had arrived in Firefly Cove when the little girl was only ten months old. Max had swooped in and easily taken on the fatherly role. But I think the fact that Max was the one who rescued her when she'd been kidnapped solidified their bond the most.

Amid all the chaos, the only familiar face she saw was his. That day forever changed all of us, but observing from the outside, I could see the subtle changes in the way Max and Charlie interacted.

She looked at him as if he hung the moon, and he looked at her as if he'd rope every star in the galaxy just to see her smile.

She lay her head gently on his shoulder as she filled him in on all the things we had done during the day, even my refusal to give in and give her a chocolate chip cookie.

"I'm sure Ray would have given you a cookie had you asked nicely, little one." Max's words were soft as he brushed the wayward curls from Charlie's forehead and placed a tender kiss above her brow.

Charlie nodded, then wiggled in his hold to be put down again. Like I said, she wasn't able to be contained for long.

"Mass Da, can I see cow?" she asked, tilting to the side to look around his large frame into the barn, as if the cow was going to appear out of thin air.

"Ah, I see. You don't come down here to see your ol' dad. You came down here to see the baby cow." He teased her, picking up her hat and ruffling her mess of curls before setting it back down crooked.

She huffed, righting herself and standing with her hands on her hips in annoyance. That face? All Stella.

"I lub yew, Dad, but I wanna see cow."

I couldn't hold back the laughter as Max tipped his head

back and sighed up at the sky, as if some higher power was going to grant him the patience to deal with his tiny tornado he called a daughter.

I walked up beside him, clapping him on the shoulder as a sign of solidarity. "Yeah, good luck with that one in her teenage years."

"Fu—"

"Mass Da, bad word!" Charlie scolded, shaking her little finger in his direction. He reluctantly pulled out his wallet and handed her a dollar.

A couple of months ago, we started putting money in a swear jar to go toward Charlie's college fund. She'd caught on and had started scolding anyone and everyone who uttered a curse when she was around.

We knew she didn't understand the importance of money yet, but she knew that it kept us all in line, and that girl loved nothing more than bossing us around.

Let's just say the kid was going to have enough in the jar to afford the Ivy League school of her dreams, should she want to.

"And on that note," I chuckled, walking backward toward the stables, "I've gotta see a man about a horse. You got this?"

Max picked Charlie up, tossing her over his shoulder as she held on tightly to her hat so it wouldn't fall. "Yep, go on. He's just finishing cleaning up the tack room. I've got the little hellion."

"Mass Da! BAD WORD," she shrieked as he tickled her ribs.

"Come on, cowgirl. Let's go see the baby cow."

And with that one sentence, her shrieks became excited giggles as she kicked against Max's hold, and they took off into the barn.

I took a deep, fortifying breath and pushed my shoulders back, readying myself for battle as I made my way toward the stables.

Pushing open the large wooden door, I was greeted with the sound of stomping hooves and the smell of damp hay swirling through the space. One by one, each of the horses leaned their heads out of their stalls, trying to get a look at who was coming in and if there was a possibility of treats being doled out.

Stopping in front of Oakley, Izzy's horse, I ran my hand down her soft nose as she nodded her head in greeting. Her whiskery lips nuzzled my hand, looking for a treat.

"I'm sorry, old girl, I'm fresh out of mints," I said softly, scratching behind her long ears.

"Rookie mistake 'round these parts," a gruff voice echoed behind me, and I felt the tingles of awareness prickle my skin as I turned and regarded him with a raised eyebrow.

Wade stood across the alleyway, his arms crossed over his broad chest. His Wranglers cupped his muscular thighs in all the right places, and his boots stomped with heavy thuds as he prowled closer.

With the brim of his Stetson pulled low, I could only make out the lazy grin that spread across his face at his notice of my blatant perusal.

I turned back to Oakley, pretending to be unaffected, but he was sex, sin, and a Southern girl's wet dream all wrapped up and tied with a cowboy-shaped bow.

WADE

I KNEW that ignoring Ray for the last week made me a coward, but I needed the space and time to think about my next moves.

If I was going to get help, I needed to do it right, and I couldn't just up and leave the ranch in the middle of training season.

Riders relied on me to help get them ready for some of the biggest events of their careers, and I couldn't be dicking off into a treatment center, no matter how badly I needed to.

Ray refused to meet my eyes as she continued stroking Oakley's forehead. It was clear that I'd hurt her in my sudden absence, but given the circumstances, I knew she'd forgive me.

"Looks like you're mad at me, Sunshine," I crooned, taking a step closer, my body only a couple of inches from pressing against hers.

I didn't need to press my fingers to her pulse to know it was racing; I could see the thrumming of her heartbeat in the tender slope of her neck.

"What makes you think that?" she huffed.

I took a chance of catching her wrath and laid my hand on the dip of her waist. As if struck with a live wire, all the nerve endings of my body sang when I grazed my fingers over the little sliver of skin that peeked out between her crop top and jean shorts.

There was no doubt that this woman was made for me as she softened her resolve and melted into my touch. She responded so well to every little brush of my skin on hers, and after seeing how her body reacted to mine under the cover of darkness, I wanted to claim her in the afternoon light.

"Well, let's see," I whispered, inching my body closer to hers so that the lush roundness of her ass fit against my front. She didn't hesitate to shift on her feet, brushing herself against my quickly hardening cock.

Stifling a groan, I splayed my hand on her belly, inching my index finger toward the hem of her tee and teasing it under the fabric, caressing the edge of her bra.

"You won't look at me, but I don't need your eyes to tell me how much you want me. Do I, Sunshine?" Coasting my lips across the shell of her ear, she let out a little whimper as she leaned more of her weight back, our bodies now flush.

"You might think you're mad, but I bet if I stuck my hand down these sweet little shorts and ran my fingers through that pretty pussy, she'd be dripping for me."

Her sharp intake of breath was all the confirmation I needed. She may have wanted to be mad at me for not being available, but she wouldn't ever stay mad at me for long.

At the end of the day, even if we'd crossed the line into whatever weird territory this was, she was my best friend, and I knew every single facet of her like the back of my hand.

I brushed one of my hands up the front of her chest, using

the other to hold her against me by her hip. I settled my fingers across her throat as I tipped her head back onto my shoulder.

I hoped to God that all the ranch hands kept themselves busy for another couple of minutes because if one of them walked in and saw the sight I was looking at right now, I'd carve out their eyes and feed them to the horses for looking at what was mine.

I ran my nose down the column of her throat, halting my lips right over her fluttering pulse. I placed a soft kiss on the sensitive spot, and she rewarded me with a soft moan.

My cock was aching behind my zipper, but it was broad daylight, and I wasn't risking someone walking in while I was balls deep inside of her, no matter how hard I wanted to be.

"Sorry, Sunshine. You'll just have to wait until later," I said, releasing her quickly and taking a step back. With a sharp gasp, she turned around and pushed my chest with both of her hands.

"You—"

With a hearty chuckle, I stepped forward, pulling her body flush to mine. Her mouth was still primed to speak as I lowered my lips to hers, teasing her bottom lip for entrance.

She softened in my arms and matched me stroke for stroke as she wound her arms around my neck.

I backed her up against one of the pillars and nestled myself between her thighs. She moaned into my mouth as she ground against me, seeking friction to quell the ache I'd built, but I didn't give her the satisfaction.

She'd have to wait until later, and how sweet it would be when I finally got my hands on her.

Breaking the kiss, I trailed soft kisses down her throat as she panted and writhed beneath me. I was so close to giving in and bending her over in one of the empty horse stalls, but I had work that needed to get done by the end of the week, and I couldn't let myself get distracted by the beautiful Latina currently grinding herself on my thigh.

"Later, baby. I promise I'll make it worth your while."

She huffed in annoyance as she toyed with the hair at the nape of my neck. She rested her head in the center of my chest, fighting to regain a normal breathing pattern, and I kissed her crown with tenderness.

"I hate you, Wade Daniels."

"Sure, you do, Sunshine. Remember that later when my head's between those pretty thighs making you scream my—"

A throat clearing behind us had our attention shooting toward the barn doors. We had been so lost in each other that we hadn't heard them slide open.

Clearly, Pops was the world's biggest cockblock as he stood, arms crossed, with a huge shit-eating grin plastered across his face. I'm sure he loved the sight of me and Ray together.

Our entire family had been rooting for the two of us to finally shit or get off the pot for as long as I can remember.

"As much as I'm sure Miss Cortez would love to hear you finish that sentence, your last trainee of the day just got here, and Sterling called," he announced gruffly.

Pops sounded and acted like the weathered cowboy who couldn't give a damn, but I'd never seen anyone with a bigger heart, except for Ma.

"Thanks, Pops, I'll be out in a second."

"If it only takes a second, son, you ain't doin' it right," he called over his shoulder as he retreated from the barn. I groaned and rested my head on Ray's as she chuckled. She wrapped her arms around my waist and kissed the side of my neck gently.

"I'm sorry, baby. This week has been a lot, and I've been running myself ragged trying to get things lined up," I said as I peered down at her. She smiled gently and cupped my cheek, her thumb coasting across my lips.

I nipped at the pad of her finger, and she yelped lightly and then laughed.

Making Ray smile and laugh was the best medicine for a tough week.

"Wanna talk about it?" she asked.

I didn't want to jinx anything or talk myself out of my plan, but since it affected her just as much, I figured I needed to fill her in. I looked down at my watch, checking to make sure I had a little bit of time before my next session.

I had about twenty minutes to spare, and I could call Sterling back later, so I took a step back and reached out my hand to take hers.

"Walk with me?" I asked, a small smile kicking up one edge of my mouth.

"Anywhere," she responded.

If there was ever a second of doubt between us, she could wash it away with a single word. I knew that no matter what happened, where I went, or what I did, Ray would selflessly put herself second to my happiness. Which is why I needed to put her first and do this for the both of us.

Walking past the stables and out to the far reaches of the main section of the ranch only took a couple of minutes. We weren't far enough away to avoid all the hustle and bustle of ranch activity, but there was a small outcropping of trees that could provide a little shade and a quiet place to talk.

Once we were under the shade of the large oak trees, I sat

down, leaning my back against the time-weathered trunk. I spread my legs and patted the dirt in front of me for Ray to sit with her back against my chest.

Once she was settled, I wrapped my arms around her and nestled my chin on her shoulder.

"I'm going to be leaving for a little bit," I said, choosing to just cut to the chase. Neither Ray nor I ever minced words when it came to tough news, but we especially didn't pussy-foot around when it came to each other's feelings. We were always open and honest with each other, even if we were closed off to everyone else.

"Okay…" she remarked hesitantly, waiting for me to continue.

There was something so calming about the way she didn't press me for more information. She didn't jump to conclusions or expect me to say something; she just gave me the space I needed to process the thoughts and emotions swirling around in my fucked-up mind.

"There's a treatment facility in Ember Ridge that I've been looking into." I pulled out the now barely decipherable business card from my back pocket and placed it in her palm.

She turned it over, squinting to read the information. I didn't need the card to recite every word that had once been printed there. I'd turned it over time and time again, willing myself to reach out a hand like I so desperately wanted to, needing to grab hold of something to pull me from the depths of this darkness.

Ray threaded her fingers with mine as I continued. "It's an inpatient treatment facility that specializes in trauma, addiction, and rehab. They have a dedicated treatment course that focuses on PTSD. It's a thirty-day program, and they're holding a spot for me."

A heavy sigh crested my lips as I felt the weight of sharing this float off my shoulders. Needing help and accepting it were two completely different beasts. I knew I needed help but reaching out to ask for it had been excruciating. It had taken me three hours, four hang-ups, and a shot of whiskey just to call and inquire about a space.

Originally, they hadn't had an opening and were going to email me some other resources for places to look into, but they called back a couple of hours later and said if I could get there by week's end, they'd hold a slot open for me. Hence why my week had already been so busy.

Pops was the first person I had let in on my plan of going to the treatment facility. He had clapped me on the shoulder and said, "I'm proud of you, son," with a softness to his words I hadn't heard before. That was as sentimental as I'd seen the man get in the years since Ma's passing.

The second call I made was to Sterling Morgen, the buddy we had run into down at Jack's the night Ray and I had stopped fighting our feelings.

Sterling was still circling the rodeo circuit but was slowing down to take on some more stable responsibilities at his own family's ranch. He actually lived on the outskirts of Ember Ridge and was more than happy to help out after I'd explained the situation.

He'd grown up learning to rope and ride; his dad had been a big rodeo star back in his day. He knew what my training seminars entailed, how important they were to me, and how I ran them. After all, his dad had been the one to train me when I first expressed interest in roping.

Sterling was going to come and stay in one of the smaller empty bunkhouses and run my training sessions in my absence.

Pops said he would make all the calls to let the trainees know they would be having a substitute for a little bit, and if they wanted to reschedule their sessions until my return, he would take care of it.

The fact that everyone had pitched in to help filled me with warmth, but a niggling tendril of dread kept tugging at the back of my mind. I hated putting them in a position of needing to step up. Everyone had their own lives to attend to. They didn't need to be taking over mine, but I knew if I didn't do this, I'd lose everything—more than I already had.

"I'm proud of you," Ray whispered, bringing our still intertwined hands to her lips and pressing a soft kiss to my knuckles.

"I'm just trying to be the best man for you, and I can't do that when I'm so broken." The pain behind my words was evident, and Ray twisted around so that she straddled my thighs.

She took my face in her hands, and I could see my reflection in her hazel eyes. I looked worn down. If this was the man she saw daily, I don't know why she stuck around at all.

"Do this for you, not for me. Get better for *you* because *you* deserve the best version of yourself. I'll love you in any version, but will you love yourself if you don't do this?"

I turned my head, pressing a kiss to her palm as I rested my head in her hands. Her touch was soft, but strong as she poured the strength and faith she held for the both of us into my body.

"I don't deserve you," I remarked softly.

"You do. I promise you, Wade Daniels, we deserve each other."

WADE

AFTER ONE HELL OF A WEEK, Friday rolled around like a storm cloud hovering over the ranch, threatening to break at any moment. Gnawing anxiety ate at my chest as I thought of all the people who were going to be stepping up in my absence.

No matter how many times my family had reassured me they could handle things for the time I'd be gone and how proud they were that I was prioritizing my mental health, I felt terrible for leaving them behind.

Telling Max and Stella I was heading to an inpatient treatment facility to get help with the aftermath of the incident had been overwhelmingly emotional.

Stella had burst out in tears, hugging me tightly as she sobbed. I'm sure pregnancy hormones were playing a part, but the raw emotion behind her tears gutted me.

I had been terrible to her over the last six months as I fought tooth and nail to place the blame on someone other than myself. I knew in my heart that she hadn't deserved it, and once I got my head on straight, I'd make it up to her.

Max had given me a tight, back-slapping, brotherly hug, but I didn't miss the streams of tears that tracked down his cheeks as he whispered how proud of me he was. Not a single person in the room stood a chance against the tears as they fell.

Thankfully, Charlie had already been asleep when I'd come over because after seeing her mom and dad cry, I didn't think I could handle explaining my leaving to her in a way she would understand. I would leave that torture up to Max and Stella.

There was only one person left I needed to talk to before I could leave. I had already loaded my bags into my truck under the cover of darkness. I wanted this to be as painless as possible, so leaving in the middle of the night seemed like the best option.

Ray and I had said our goodbyes earlier in the day in a way that made sense for both of us, with our bodies and endless "I love you's."

There had been no rushing, no tears, just slow and meaningful sex that expressed all the words we couldn't voice out loud.

We had poured our love into each caress and touch, promising each other in the silence that we would make it through this and come out stronger on the other side.

Shutting the door to the big house, I stood on the front porch, marveling at the view of the ranch at night.

It was still muggy, the air sticking to my skin like glue, but it had cooled down significantly as the sun retreated. Stars dotted the horizon, blinking in time with the crickets' chirps, as if they were dancing to their nighttime song.

I leaned against one of the whitewashed posts of the porch, breathing in deeply, the warm air acting as a calming balm for my rising anxiety. I could do this—I needed to do this.

A gentle breeze rustled the leaves of the trees on the outskirts of the property, and a quiet creak sounded from beside me.

Looking to my right, I noticed the soft sway of Ma's porch swing floating in the wind. Tendrils of breeze coasted across my skin, leaving goosebumps in its wake, pushing me toward the direction I knew I needed to go.

I stepped off the front porch, avoiding the creaky last step —a force of habit I don't think Max or I will ever break.

I walked along the well-worn dirt path that led to the barn. Before getting to the doors, I veered left, my boots knowing the way, even if I was struggling to see in the inky darkness.

To the side of the barn, there was a small pond, its edges overgrown with brush. But beside the pond stood a tall willow tree, shading a small bench with its long-reaching branches. The grass around the bench was meticulously maintained, and the brush directly in front of it had been cut back, allowing for a clear view across the water.

I lowered myself onto the weathered wooden slats of the bench seat, placing my hands in my lap and closing my eyes. I listened to the soft splashes of fish cresting the surface of the pond and the frogs croaking loudly, enjoying the cooler night air; the rustle of the branches of the sturdy willow provided a space of solace from the world.

Softly, as if the universe was listening, I spoke out toward the water. "Hey, Ma."

Looking down beside the bench, I took in the small wooden cross Pops had placed to mark where we'd laid Ma to rest.

Technically, we had scattered her ashes as she'd requested

in her will, something we didn't think we'd be using so early, but she and Pops had drawn up as a precaution many years ago.

The air had been warm and muggy just like tonight, the mood just as somber. Pops had turned one of her favorite spots on the entire property into a place of quiet reflection for all of us to have a place to remember her.

It had been a long time since I'd felt the need to come and be where I felt closest to her. Max always said the cove was where he went when he needed to be surrounded by thoughts of Ma.

This spot here, among the evening stars, the quiet breeze, and the rustling of willow branches, was where I felt like I was being wrapped in Ma's comforting embrace.

The cove had somehow morphed from somewhere I only shared with my mom to something special to Ray and me. This spot was untainted by anyone's memory but Ma's.

I looked down at my hands, resting gently in my lap, and picked at the skin around my nails. It felt weird to be talking to the air, but if there was any chance she could hear me, I wanted her to know that I was thinking about her and that I carried her with me every single day.

Huffing a little laugh at how ridiculous this all seemed, I propped my elbows on my knees, letting my hands dangle limp between them. I hung my head and sighed, gathering the words to explain why, after so long, I'd finally come to visit.

"Honestly, I'm not sure what I'm even supposed to say. If I'm supposed to say anything at all." Silence was the only response I got, but I didn't let it deter me from saying what I needed to get off my chest.

"You always taught me to be a good man, a respectable man, a man people could rely on. Lately, Ma, I've been none of those men. I'm so fucking angry all the time." Another humorless chuckle left my lips, thinking of how much she'd hated my dirty mouth.

"I know you're probably up there scowling down at me for my language, but sorry, Ma, ya raised a cowboy, and it comes with the job." I paused, gathering my thoughts and strength to continue.

"I'm gonna be going away for a little bit." I looked out at the serene water, moonlight shining on the silver ripples as the wind flowed across its surface. "I found a really nice treatment facility in Ember Ridge. They specialize in trauma and PTSD. They've got doctors, therapists, and even an equine center to focus on healing after life-altering events."

The breeze coasted across the back of my neck, as if nestling me into its embrace.

"I need help, Ma. I can't keep living with all of this anger. I'm lashing out at Stella, Ray, Max, even Pops. I hate myself every second of every day for the way I've treated them."

I lifted my eyes to look over at the cross, wishing it was actually Ma who was seated beside me, instead of two thin wooden boards nailed together, standing stoically in the dirt.

"You raised me to be better. You raised me to be strong. Somehow along the way, I've forgotten what that's like. I know you wouldn't be ashamed of the man I've become because that's just not you, but I can *feel* your disappointment and desire for me to do better. That idea hurts more than anything else ever could."

Twin trails of tears coasted down my cheeks as I continued. I didn't bother to wipe them away. I needed to feel them as a reminder that there *was* still emotion inside of me.

"I'm gonna get better. I'm going to deal with these

demons, and I'm going to come back whole. I'm going to come back as a man you can be proud of."

As if she herself were wrapping me in a hug, the wind coasted along my arms, and the world around me seemingly ceased to exist.

"I miss you… so fucking much. You've missed out on some of the biggest parts of our lives, and I can't help but be angry that you didn't get to experience them with us. You missed Max meeting Stella, their wedding, Charlie's adoption, my retirement from rodeo, opening my training center, Ray and me finally telling each other we're head over heels in love. You would love everything about the life we have created here."

Finally, I used the back of my hand to wipe the tears that had fallen from my chin as I looked up toward the night sky.

"She's been with you every step of the way." A soft voice spoke from the shadows. I chuckled, shaking my head and turning around, taking in the sight of Ray in her sleep shorts and oversized T-shirt standing at the edge of the space.

"Sunshine, I didn't take you for a stalker," I joked.

She rolled her eyes as she came to stand between my knees, taking my hands tightly in hers.

"I came over here because I had a feeling you were going to try to leave without a proper goodbye."

"I said my goodbyes yesterday. I'm trying to make this as painless as possible for everyone involved."

She released one of my hands, tilting my chin up to look at her. The moon highlighted her raven hair, and I didn't miss the tears streaming down her cheeks that mirrored my own.

"Wade, nothing about this is going to be painless. It's going to hurt like hell. But sometimes you need to walk through fire to come out the other side."

Her thumb traced over the scruff on my chin before she softly leaned down, pulling my head to rest between her breasts and resting her cheek on top of my head. She wound her arms around my shoulders and held me gently against her, letting her strength pour into me.

"She'd be proud of you. No matter how much you tell yourself that you're not the man she raised. You are. It takes a strong man, especially a cowboy, to admit that he needs help. Penny Daniels raised two of the strongest men I know, and she would be damn proud of you if she were standing here today."

I could feel the tears soaking through her shirt as her words hit their mark. She held me to her until the tear tracks dried, leaving a tightness across my cheeks.

When my breathing had finally evened out, I leaned back and pulled her down for a soft kiss.

"Walk me to the truck?" I asked against her soft lips, and I could feel the small tilt of a smile as she rewarded me with another gentle kiss.

We walked hand in hand back to the big house, the silence neither oppressive nor stilted as we both prepared for the goodbye we didn't want but knew needed to happen. I knew that neither of us wanted to make a scene, so as I opened the door to my truck, readying myself to take off, I turned around and gathered her into a tight hug.

I felt the tension in her shoulders relax as she melted into my embrace. Pulling back slightly, I cupped the side of her neck and pulled her in for a deep kiss. There was nothing hurried about the languid strokes of our tongues as we poured our emotions into each other.

Ray was the first to pull back, pressing one last soft kiss to my swollen lips as she pushed on my chest to extricate herself from my hold. I stole one last peck and shot her a small smile as I climbed up into the truck.

My engine roared to life as I turned the key, putting the address of the treatment center into the navigation. Two hours. It would take two hours to get to where I was hopeful my new beginning waited.

As I backed out of the makeshift parking lot beside the house and turned toward the exit of the ranch, I chanced a glance in the rearview mirror. Ray stood on the porch, leaning against the same post I had been earlier, as she raised a hand in a soft wave, tears shining on her cheeks.

I heaved one gigantic sigh as I crossed under the D&D Ranch sign and headed toward healing the parts of me that were so heavily broken.

RAY

WATCHING Wade drive away from the ranch nearly broke me.

I knew how important it was for him to get the help he so desperately needed, and I was so proud of him for accepting the spot the treatment center had available. But even knowing that it was what was best for him, and in the long run for me, didn't make it hurt any less.

There had been very few times over the seventeen years of our friendship that we had spent long stints apart. Even when he was making it big on the rodeo circuit, he made time to send me a text or get in a quick call after the event. Most of the time, if I could swing it, I would travel with him in support.

Max and Pops were both busy trying to keep the ranch going, and taking off a weekend to go watch a small-town rodeo qualifier wasn't something they had the luxury of being able to do.

I dutifully stood in many sets of bleachers, screaming until my throat was raw and my voice was gone, cheering enough for him to feel the love of every single person who couldn't be beside me. I did my best to make sure he never felt the loss of those who hadn't been able to be there in person.

As I watched him drive away, I let the tears fall for all the moments we'd had to hold each other up. I let the tears fall for the broken man who had done everything in his power to be everything for everybody, often to his own detriment. I cried for the boy whose mother was taken far too soon, even if he had been well into adulthood when it had happened, knowing personally how painful that loss is.

The rickety porch swing on the side of the wraparound porch creaked in the gentle breeze, and I chuckled softly to myself. The memory of when Ma begged Pops to put that swing up played through my mind.

She had wanted somewhere she could sit and watch as the ranch life passed by around her. He had been willing to do anything and everything for that woman.

Every single night, without fail, she could be found sitting on that porch swing, a cup of chai tea in one hand and a book in the other.

I remember the first time Wade brought me over to the house and I met Penny Daniels. She'd been sitting right there on that same porch swing as she so easily folded me into their family, no questions asked.

WADE *and I walked toward the big house, heading to grab something before we tacked up the horses for our ride. We had spent the afternoon skipping rocks out at the cove and were*

going to the stables for our weekly trail time. Wade had been teaching me all the ins and outs of being a cowboy and, unfortunately for my butt, that included riding a horse. I hadn't quite gotten my horse legs yet and still ended up hurting for a couple of days after each ride. Honestly, I wasn't much good at anything cowboy-related, but it gave me uninterrupted time with Wade.

"I'll be right back. I've just gotta grab a couple of things, and we'll be good to go," he called behind him as we neared the steps of the wraparound front porch.

I stood awkwardly at the bottom of the stairs with my hands pushed into the back pockets of my jeans. Kicking at the dirt, I waited patiently while Wade took forever grabbing whatever was so important that he had to stop at the house before our ride.

"You don't have to stand there. You can come sit," a woman's warm voice called from the top of the stairs. I craned my neck looking for where the voice had come from, coming up empty. I couldn't see the whole porch from my vantage point, and for a second I wondered if I'd made the voice up inside my head.

"Over here," the woman called from the side of the porch. I stepped onto the first step, listening to the weathered boards creak beneath my feet. Afraid the step would give and I'd fall through, I stepped up a couple more and onto the top of the wooden deck.

Sitting on a white porch swing on the far side was a woman rocking softly back and forth, a purple quilt draped across her lap, and a book nestled beside her.

It was evident from the sandy blonde of her hair and the sharp edges of her face that she was somehow related to Wade. I assumed she was more than likely his mom.

"You don't have to stand all the way over there," she chuckled, scooting the quilt off her lap onto one of the empty rocking chairs beside the porch swing. She patted the space beside her, and I dutifully walked over, sitting down softly, trying my hardest not to rock the swing too hard.

For what felt like the longest couple of minutes of my life, we sat in silence, neither of us sure of what to say.

"So, you must be the infamous Rayna my son won't stop talking about."

"Yes, ma'am." Manners were something that had been drilled into me relentlessly throughout my childhood. My dad was the current sheriff of Firefly Cove, and I knew there was a standard I had to uphold as his oldest child.

"It's nice to finally meet you, sweetheart. I'm Penny, but the boys call me Ma. You're welcome to do the same."

The softness of her voice and the welcoming lilt to her words eased my anxiety. I don't know why I was so nervous, but something about meeting Wade's parents made our friendship more real.

Inside the cove, we were in our own little bubble. No one questioned why a thirteen-year-old boy was hanging out with an eleven-year-old girl, skipping rocks and riding horses. Between the branches of the wide oak trees that shaded our spot, we could be anyone, or no one at all.

"It's nice to meet you, too. Wade has said nothing but wonderful things about both you and Pops."

"I'm sure. That boy has a hard time seeing anything but sunshine, even on a rainy day," she said wistfully. You could see the evidence of her love for her family in the soft smile that played upon her lips and the tiny laugh lines that fanned out from her eyes.

"He's definitely something." I laughed softly, thinking of

all the times Wade had so easily made me laugh, even when I felt like nothing made sense.

Speaking of the devil, he pushed out the screen door, his hands full and pockets bulging. He seemed to have cleaned out the pantry, filled water bottles, and grabbed a can of bug spray during his absence. I shook my head with a slight chuckle at his over-preparedness.

"Don't laugh. I'm a growing boy," he smirked as he adjusted his spoils in his arms and turned toward his mother, who sat shaking her head at him.

"You two have fun; be back before supper and don't spoil your appetite, Wade Alexander," she chided as she reached for the quilt and her book.

"It was a pleasure to meet you, Ray." Her smile was warm as I stood, making my way over to where Wade was standing, noisily crunching on some chips like he hadn't eaten in a week.

"You too, Ma," I responded politely with a gentle wave back in her direction.

"Ready, Sunshine?" Wade asked as he stomped down the porch steps, taking great care to step around the creaky step, clearly out of habit.

Looking back at Penny, I saw a soft smile on her face and those little laugh lines making their appearance as she pretended to be interested in her book. Her eyes caught mine, and I didn't miss the little wink she sent my way as Wade tugged me toward the barn.

PENNY HAD SO EASILY WELCOMED me into their family, never once making me feel like an outsider. In a house that often felt cramped, chaotic, and oppressive, it was nice to be able to come to the Daniels' residence and step into a little bit of calm. Something about her presence had always brought me such a sense of peace.

Every single person she had the pleasure of meeting felt her absence in the wake of her death.

As I stood here on the porch, watching the love of my life drive away toward a better future for himself, I felt the breeze wrap around me as if Penny were here, giving me a much-needed hug.

"You okay?" I heard a voice whisper from behind me. I turned around and was surprised to see Stella standing in the shadows, accented by the soft light of the foyer shining through the open door.

"I'm not sure," I answered honestly as I hung my head and felt the tears drip down my chin.

"Do you want to talk about it?"

"Not really,"

"I've got a bottle of wine that I can't drink and some chocolate that I can surely share," she coaxed, pushing the front door wide and stepping back into the house in invitation.

I let out a small chuckle as I stepped into the big house, trying my best not to buckle under the weight of my feelings.

As Stella shut the front door and turned off the foyer light, I felt her arms come around me in a tight hug. I leaned on my friend as I let the tears flow, not bothering to hold back the emotion that was weighing me down.

I knew this was what both Wade and I needed, but it didn't mean it wasn't going to be the hardest thing we'd ever gone through.

"It's going to be okay," Stella crooned, rubbing soft circles on my back and letting me purge every pent-up feeling in the form of tears soaking through her nightshirt.

After a couple of minutes of mental breakdown, I took a step back and wiped the still-flowing tears from below my eyes.

"Thank you," I said softly, sniffling and using the sleeve of my shirt to wipe away my snot. I couldn't find it in myself to care about my appearance when half of my heart was gone.

"That's what best friends are for," she responded as she grabbed my hand and gently squeezed three times. I squeezed back, feeling the sentiment to my core. "Now, let's crack open that wine, and I'll live vicariously through you until I'm able to drink again."

WADE

EMBER RIDGE SAT to the north of Firefly Cove, hidden among the sprawling landscape of the Georgia coast. It was another small town with nosy neighbors, few amenities, and a couple of hidden gems.

My buddy Sterling lived on the outskirts of the small town, having been raised on one of the largest ranches in the state. His father was a big-time bronc rider who had retired after a one-night stand dropped Sterling on his doorstep.

He went from riding broncs to roping a toddler in eight seconds, flat.

Their ranch, passed down from one generation to the next, embodied old money. They had state-of-the-art facilities, plenty of hired help, and one of the most successful breeding programs in the state.

Unfortunately, I wasn't there to hang out and shoot the shit around a bonfire at the Morgen Ranch.

After a little over two hours of driving, I pulled into the parking lot of the Ember Ridge Recovery Center, idling my truck in one of the empty spaces near the back of the lot.

I'd made it this far, and I couldn't back down now. I checked the clock, the LED lights glaring in the dark cab: two in the morning.

When I'd spoken to the intake coordinator on the phone, she had said they are open twenty-four hours a day, seven days a week. They knew that walking through those sliding glass doors was half the battle, so they made themselves available whenever the need arose.

With a heavy sigh, I cut the engine and unbuckled my seatbelt. One step at a time. I could do this if I took it one fucking baby step at a time.

I snagged my duffel bag from the back seat, slinging it over my shoulder as I locked the truck and walked slowly toward the front doors of the building.

It was quiet out. The same peaceful feeling of being on the ranch washed over my skin, giving me an added edge of confidence.

A stone walkway led to a massive overhang that shielded the front doors. Wooden benches lined its edges alongside planters filled with flowers.

I had expected it to feel more sterile, seeing how it was a medical treatment facility, but nothing about this building stood out as clinical. It felt oddly welcoming with each measured step I took closer to the entrance.

A large part of me was looking for something to be wrong with this situation. Each step of the way, I'd been met with perfect timing, calm surroundings, and an easy cadence to my breathing. I wanted a reason for me to get back in my truck and drive back to Firefly Cove, losing myself in Ray.

Yet, as if the stars were aligning, and Ma was whispering in my ear, I kept walking toward hopeful healing and growth.

I couldn't go back to Ray the same broken man I was when I left.

The automatic doors opened with a whoosh, and I stepped into the brightly lit foyer. It smelled like cinnamon and vanilla, a warm and welcoming hug of fragrance as I eased my way toward the front desk.

The middle-aged woman sitting behind the desk looked up with a wide smile, adjusting her glasses up on the bridge of her nose and standing to greet me.

"Welcome to Ember Ridge. You must be Wade," she said sweetly as she rounded the edge of the desk with her hand outstretched. "I'm Lydia, one of the intake coordinators here. We're happy to have you."

I didn't trust myself to speak, afraid of what might come out, but I took her small hand in mine and gave it a brief shake.

"Why don't we head back to my office and go over a few things? Do you have everything with you that you'll need?"

I nodded again, clearing my throat of the emotion that was bubbling up. "Yes, ma'am."

Everything about this was beginning to feel real, and I could feel the tightness of anxiety clawing at my chest with each step we took away from the front doors.

She led me down a series of hallways, stopping outside of a wooden door while she found the key and unlocked it.

She motioned for me to enter; I stepped around her and placed my duffel bag down on one of the plush chairs in the corner. I lowered myself into one of the chairs in front of her desk but was surprised when she didn't take the seat opposite me. Instead, she sat down in the chair beside me and crossed one of her legs over the other.

"I'm sure this has to be exceptionally overwhelming," she

said, grabbing a notebook and pen off the top of her desk and setting them in her lap. "We try to make the process here at ERRC as painless as possible, but unfortunately, healing isn't linear, and I can't promise that any part of your journey will be easy."

I scrubbed my sweaty palms down the thighs of my jeans, once again clearing my throat before speaking. "Yes, ma'am. I understand."

She nodded once, uncapped the pen, and opened the notebook to a blank page.

"I want to start with gathering some basic information about you, Wade. I'm going to be writing things down so that I can input them after we get you settled. We try to keep things as nonclinical as possible because we've seen that it helps with a patient's trust in us. This whole facility is built on a high level of trust. We aren't here to lock you in, take away all of your rights to the outside world, and beat happiness back into your body."

Somehow, a chuckle passed my lips, and I watched as the corners of Lydia's mouth turned up in another gentle smile.

"So, Wade. In your own words, why are you here?"

I thought about the anger, the snippiness, the nightmares, the pain. All of that paled in comparison to the shame I felt when I looked in the mirror and saw the pathetic man looking back at me.

"I look in the mirror, and I hate the man I see." I watched as Lydia wrote down what I said, a look of determination marring her features.

"And when did this start, or has it been a constant feeling?"

A rush of anxious adrenaline coursed through my body, and I felt my hands begin to shake. I tried to avoid thinking about the incident in the light of day. It could stay in the recesses of my mind, coming out to haunt me in my dreams, but thinking about it when the world was moving around me made it feel too real. I wished more than anything that I could just forget it had happened.

"I can tell that this is a sensitive topic for you. So, please take your time."

I leaned forward to rest my elbows on my knees, running my fingers through my hair and bringing my hands to the back of my neck, lacing my fingers together. Looking down at my boots, I sighed.

"I wasn't always this way." I picked at the skin around my nails, not able to look the coordinator in the eyes. "I used to laugh, joke, and live life to its fullest. I was the fun one in our group. Last year, my brother's girlfriend and her daughter were kidnapped. Well, I guess Charlie was kidnapped, and Stella couldn't wait for the damn police to do their jobs, so she went after her.

My brother, Max, and I went into the warehouse after we realized Stella had run after Charlie. When we arrived at the building, we heard gunshots. Stella had managed to shoot the guy holding her hostage, and Max went on to rescue her daughter from the tweaked-out crackhead keeping her locked up in another room. As Stella and I were leaving, the stupid fucker—" I paused. "Sorry about my language, ma'am."

Lydia laughed, putting her pen down to rest on top of her notebook. "Wade, I've seen and heard the worst demons in people's lives. A little brash language isn't going to scare me. You say what you need to say, in whatever way you need to say it. I'm here to listen, not to judge."

Nodding, I continued, "As Stella and I were leaving, the guy who had been holding her hostage, the one she'd managed to shoot in the leg, hobbled his way out behind us. He was able to fire one shot from his handgun before the sheriff shot back. Unfortunately, that fucking bullet went right in my back.

I know I should feel grateful that I'm alive, and don't get me wrong, I am. But the bullet managed to graze my spine, missing my spinal cord and nicking some of the bone. According to the doctors, because of a previous rodeo injury, I'm at greater risk for paralysis if I were to go back to riding."

"Were you able to get a second opinion about that diagnosis?" she asked, scribbling furiously to keep up with my rambling. "That's a very drastic change to your lifestyle; I can only imagine how hard that must have been for you."

I thought about that question for a second. I *hadn't* sought a second opinion on what the surgeon had said. I'd taken what he'd said at face value and changed the course of my entire life.

What if there were a chance I could ride again? Hope flooded my system as I sat straighter, thoughts and plans swirling around in my head.

"I'm going to take that as a no, you didn't get a second opinion." Lydia chuckled, setting the pen and notebook down on her desk.

"Here's what I think, Wade." She turned toward me, giving me her full attention. "I think you've been through something exceptionally traumatic that changed the trajectory of your entire life, causing you to question who you are at your core. I think you're a man who puts everyone else's needs above his own, often to your own detriment. But I also think that with some group and individual therapy and maybe a second opinion on your medical diagnosis, we can work together to focus on healing and getting that spark of joy back. What do you think?"

An overwhelming surge of emotion caused prickles to erupt along my skin, and I felt the pressure of tears threatening to fall from my lower lashes. Afraid to speak for fear of completely breaking down, I nodded.

"The man looking back at you in the mirror is the same man, regardless of how your mind tricks you into thinking he's not. You are still *you* at the end of the day."

I continued nodding, the dam holding the tears back breaking as they coasted down my cheeks.

"Welcome to Ember Ridge Recovery Center, Wade Daniels. I am proud of you for making the choice to become the best version of yourself, and I can't wait to see the true man underneath the weight of all of this pain you're holding onto."

RAY

SITTING at the messy kitchen table, surrounded by magazine clippings, mood boards, and color swatches, I brushed the loose strands of hair that had fallen from my bun into some semblance of submission.

Wade had been gone seven days, and I was feeling restless already. Sure, over the years, we had times where we went a week or two without talking, but this was different. We had opened the threshold of our feelings for each other, and shoving them back into the tiny box we had kept them stored in for so long just wouldn't happen.

Instead of sitting around twiddling my thumbs, I'd poured myself into work, needing some sort of release for the pent-up energy that raged inside of me.

My client list was constantly growing, and I knew it was almost time to add a team member or two to the books. But for now, I was a one-woman show who was very thankful to be busy.

I was currently combing through online catalogs of thrift

stores in surrounding counties, looking for the perfect accent piece for a new high-end salon in Atlanta.

They wanted a shabby-chic vibe with a heavy dose of upscale class. I had a vision of thrifting a large armoire that could double as storage, purposefully mismatched stylist chairs, and a statement chandelier hanging above the entryway to bring everything together.

Earlier in the week, I sent over color swatches for paint, and the client had loved everything I'd suggested.

Projects like this gave me butterflies and reminded me of why I loved doing what I did. I could find beauty in broken things, taking something that otherwise would have been trash and sprucing it up with a little sanding and paint to create a beautiful accent to a space.

In my world, there was no such thing as trash. Everything had a discoverable treasure hidden inside of it; you just had to take the time to uncover all the layers to find it.

The front door opened, and the jangling of keys echoed through the small space. Judging by the heavy footfalls of work boots, Dad must have just gotten off his shift. He strode into the kitchen, where I was haphazardly working, and plopped into one of the dining room chairs with a heavy sigh.

No one on this earth worked harder than my father. Even though his position wasn't physically taxing, the emotional toll it took on him was excruciating at times.

Not only was he responsible for keeping the town safe, but he was also responsible for an entire team of deputies who put their lives on the line every single day to protect our community. The weight of so many people relying on him was a heavy burden to carry.

I could argue that Firefly Cove was one of the safest places to live, but after what transpired last year with Stella and Charlie, the town had understandably been a little on edge. Even though the incident had technically happened outside of city limits, closer to Atlanta, the residents of our small town had started being more vigilant.

People dead bolted doors they had previously left unlocked, bumps in the night that had once been brushed off as the wind were called in to the police station, and residents stopped walking past the cover of darkness. Our sleepy little town was suddenly wide awake, and it kept the sheriff's office quite busy.

"Long day?" I asked, brushing the magazine clippings and swatches into some semblance of a pile.

I tried not to take up too much space if I could help it, seeing as the house was already small enough and there were five of us crammed in here. The twins and Benny had enough crap lying around; I didn't need to add to it. Especially since I was the one doing most of the cleaning.

With his eyes closed and his head tipped back, I wondered if Dad had fallen asleep sitting up. It wasn't uncommon for him to come home absolutely wiped after a long day and be dead on his feet.

"Just a normal day at the office," he grumbled, standing back up to remove his utility belt and unbutton his stiff khaki button-down.

Once he had extricated himself from the bulk of his uniform, he walked over to the fridge, opened the door, and peered inside for something to eat.

"There are leftover enchiladas in the microwave for you."

I could see the tension in his posture relax as he closed the fridge door and walked over to where the microwave sat above the stove. He opened the door, took the aluminum foil off the dish, and started the timer to heat everything up.

Walking back over to the table, he stood behind my chair, leaning down and placing a soft kiss on the top of my head.

"What would I do without you, mija?" he asked softly, placing a gentle hand on my shoulder.

"Well, your uniforms wouldn't be clean, you'd probably eat takeout every night, and I'm sure the kids would have to walk or find their own ride to practice." I chuckled, but as I looked over at him to where he'd retreated to in front of the kitchen sink, I saw the tension he had just released a second before come back, tightening his shoulders toward his ears.

"Sorry, I was trying to make a joke, but it clearly didn't come out as I'd intended." Mentally sticking my foot in my mouth, I hoped I hadn't offended him.

I hadn't meant anything by what I'd said; I didn't mind helping out where I could. I lived there rent-free for goodness' sake; the least I could do was the laundry, cooking, and making sure the kids got to where they needed to be.

"It's fine, mija. I've just had a long day, and it hit me how much you do around here to help."

"I don't mind helping, Dad. It's the least I can do for you letting me live here rent-free."

"No. The least I can do as your *father* is allow you a safe place to stay that doesn't put you into unnecessary debt." He growled, clearly frustrated with the situation.

"Dad, it's fine. I don't mi—"

"It's *not* fine!" he yelled, slamming his hands down on the sink, causing me to flinch slightly at his outburst. "It's not fine." This time the sentiment was quieter, almost a whisper, but I heard it loud and clear.

"What happened at work, Dad?" I asked softly, knowing that something had clearly rattled him.

He tried his hardest to leave work at work when there was

a tough case, but he was only human, and sometimes things followed him home that were hard to shake.

"We ran a call today that made me seriously evaluate how much I rely on you to do the things a parent should be doing."

The microwave beeped, signaling his food was heated, so he grabbed the plate, bringing it back to the table. He sat down across from me but didn't touch his food.

"You know the trailer park right outside of town? The one I've always told you is best to stay away from?"

I nodded, afraid that if I spoke, he'd shut down, and I wanted him to feel comfortable talking about the things that stressed him out.

If I'd learned anything from Wade, it's that bottling everything up and shouldering all the guilt and blame for things beyond your control doesn't make them go away. It just piles them up until you're buried and can't find your way out.

"We got a call this evening that there was a domestic dispute in that area. When we responded, we found both parents high off their asses and the thirteen-year-old son caring for the one-month-old baby. The kid is just a baby himself, and he's having to shoulder the burden of parenthood because his parents can't put their wants aside for the sake of their own kids."

I could tell that the call had shaken him, but comparing that situation to what happened in our home was asinine. Nothing about what my father had done to keep our household afloat was selfish. He had run himself ragged trying to keep food on the table, a roof over our heads, and the lights on for the last fifteen years.

"Dad, I hope you don't think for a single second that there's any comparison between what you saw on that call today and what happened here after Mom died."

"But isn't there?" I could hear the pain flowing from his words as he pushed the full plate of food away, his appetite clearly gone.

Reaching across the table, I grabbed one of his hands and held it in mine. When our gazes met, I saw the shell of a broken man sitting across from me, similar to the one I'd just recently watched drive away toward healing.

"Papí." I squeezed his hand softly, holding back the tears that threatened to fall.

I'd done enough crying for the men in my life who couldn't stop being everything for everyone to take a second and take care of themselves.

"You are the strongest, most resilient, and wonderful father that *all* of us could ask for. Our family went through one of the most challenging tragedies a family can go through, and somehow, we all made it. Have I had to step up and, at times, act as a parental figure to the younger kids? Yes. Do I sometimes wish that things could be different? Also, yes. But the fact of the matter is that they aren't different. We've made do with what we have. And Dad, what we have is an abundance of *love*.

Each and every one of us has had to make sacrifices because of our circumstances. But you lost the love of your life. You made one of the biggest sacrifices a parent can make by setting aside your grief to make sure our family didn't fall apart. None of us can fault you for doing what needed to be done."

He sighed, squeezing my hand back gently and brushing away the tears that threatened to track down his cheeks.

"When did you get so wise?" he asked with a sad chuckle.

I laughed back, swiping at my own tears. "I don't know,

but lately I feel like I've been doing a lot of crying, and I'd like for that to stop."

"Mija, I'm so proud of you. I hope you know that."

"I know, Dad."

I stood from the table, walked over, and placed a soft kiss on his cheek before heading toward the stairs. I was emotionally wrung out after the week I'd had, and my bed was calling my name. After all, each day I laid my head down and closed my eyes, I was one day closer to Wade coming home.

Pausing at the foot of the stairs, I turned with my hand on the banister.

"Hey, Dad?"

"¿Qué, mija?"

"I think Izzy needs to hear that you're proud of her, too."

He nodded softly, pulling the plate back in front of him and picking at the leftovers. I could see the wheels turning in his head, digesting my words, but that wasn't my battle to fight.

I'd opened the conversation, and that would have to do for now. The ball was in their court, and I hoped their relationship wasn't too far broken to be mended.

WADE

I HAD COME to the conclusion that therapy was the universe's way of taking everything that was weighing you down, amplifying it by a hundred, and shoving it back down your throat for you to choke on.

I'd spent the last two weeks talking about my feelings more often than I had in my entire life.

At the end of each day, I crawled into bed, closed my eyes, and crashed. There were no nightmares, no thoughts of the past, just a void of darkness and an overwhelming sense of calm.

The first couple of days after arriving at the treatment center were rough. Settling into a new environment had exacerbated my nightmares, often leaving me gasping for air as I fought for each ragged inhale of breath.

Thankfully, the in-house psychiatrist had offered relief in the form of some sleeping pills to get me through the worst of it.

I fought tooth and nail against taking any sort of meds, but after talking with the therapist in individual sessions, she encouraged me to use them as a stepping stone, not a crutch, to which I'd reluctantly agreed.

After the first night of getting a full ten hours of sleep, I decided to only use them temporarily. As my therapist would say, "We're here to create good habits and coping mechanisms, not to create bad habits as a way of brushing off the things we need to deal with."

Each day at the center, we alternated between group and individual therapy in the morning, and a therapy-based extracurricular in the afternoons.

We weren't bound to a schedule, but for the duration of our stay, it was highly encouraged for us to focus on the suggestions of our therapy team and the assets provided. Keeping a strict schedule was something I was intimately familiar with, so I had no reservations about working within those constraints.

I was signed up for individual therapy and dreading every single moment as the clock ticked by. My therapist, Dr. Langford, was a kind woman—but her idea of healing involved what I could only constitute as psychological torture.

Locking the door to my room behind me, I walked down the long corridor to the wing where the offices were. I passed by other residents' rooms; people were milling about, chatting in between therapy sessions.

The interior of the center reminded me of its own little town. Each resident had their own apartment of sorts, and there were common areas for food, entertainment, and socializing.

Therapists' offices and conference rooms were kept sequestered to one wing of the center, maintaining the appearance of a nonclinical atmosphere.

I had learned that each therapist focused on only three

clients at a time to ensure everyone was given ample attention to their individual needs. Not only did they work in small numbers, but each therapist was also specifically chosen for each resident based on their expertise and background.

Dr. Langford, who insisted during each and every session that I call her Winnie, had grown up in the area and was highly familiar with the small-town lifestyle.

She had shared with me during our first session that she actually had been born and raised on a small ranch much like ours. We bonded over our love of horses and riding. It made confiding in her easier, knowing that she was able to correlate some of the daily stressors with experience.

She pushed me to join the equine therapy extracurricular as a way to push past mental barriers I'd put up around riding. Even though I couldn't ride, it was comforting to be around a ranch-like atmosphere.

Each day, I went out and mucked stalls, tacked up horses for riders, and washed them down when they came back in.

It was nice to feel needed and have something to keep my hands from sitting idle, but I struggled to see how it correlated to my healing. It often felt like a slap in the face to be so close but unable to ride.

I rapped on Dr. Langford's door, and a soft "come in" echoed from behind the wood. I turned the knob and removed my hat, setting it upside down on the table beside the entrance.

"Mornin', ma'am." Some habits were hard to break, and this was one I would take to my grave. Calling a woman ma'am, even if they weren't much your senior, was a sign of respect, and I wasn't going to give it up, no matter how formal it sounded.

"Good morning, Wade," she said with a smile.

Dr. Langford was a middle-aged woman with a warm personality and a gentle, motherly soul. Her wardrobe consisted of items that reminded me of the seventies. All long, layered pieces that swished when she walked, and rings on each finger. Her long blonde hair, graying at the temples, was always in a braid, draped over one shoulder. She was eclectic, but never off-putting.

As I walked into the room and took a seat across from her on the worn leather couch, she lowered her reading glasses that hung around her neck on a beaded string.

I noticed the soft laugh lines that webbed beside her eyes, crinkling with each soft smile. They reminded me of Pops and the way he'd earned every single one with a hard-fought smile and a welcome laugh.

"How are you feeling today?" she asked, her signature notebook seated in her lap. The small leather-bound book was where she kept all the important information on each of her clients.

From what some of the other residents had mentioned, it seemed like she was the only one who still hand-wrote her notes. Most of the other therapists had moved over to recording sessions and transcribing them after the fact.

I liked the fact that she was a little old-school, as I wasn't huge on technology myself.

"Better than yesterday," I sighed.

Each day that we had individual sessions, she asked me to focus on one thing that was better between sessions. So far, they had been minor, like not forgetting to get dessert at the cafeteria or making the acquaintance of another resident.

I hadn't felt much of a breakthrough toward healing, but I knew that the process wasn't simple or linear. I just needed to be patient and trust in myself and my therapists to help me get back to a place where I could see the light again.

"That's great. You had your appointment with the doctor yesterday, correct?"

"Yes, ma'am."

The previous day, I'd been able to miss out on my therapy sessions as I spent the day at Grady Memorial Hospital in Atlanta. I'd been poked, prodded, imaged, stretched, bent, and studied all day.

Coming back to the treatment center had been a relief after all the testing I had endured, and I'd flopped down in my bed, dead on my feet.

When I'd first arrived, and the intake coordinator noted that I never received a second opinion on my injury, the focus became making sure the doctors hadn't been wrong in keeping me from riding.

It had taken almost two weeks to get an appointment with each of the specialists, and the center gave me a day pass to be able to attend all of my appointments.

On a general basis, once you checked in at ERRC, you didn't get to leave until the end of your allotted thirty days.

I'd been accompanied by the intake coordinator, Lydia, whom I'd met on my first day, to each of my appointments. I didn't feel like a prisoner, but the reminder of having a babysitter kept things more clinical.

Throughout the day, I met with a neurosurgeon, a musculoskeletal specialist, an orthopedic surgeon, and a physical therapist.

Each one had run different versions of the same tests, and they would sit down and discuss their findings as a panel once the results were in. I was on pins and needles waiting for answers, but I hadn't allowed myself the opportunity to hope for a different outcome than the one I'd already been given.

Hope was too dangerous a feeling to allow myself the luxury of entertaining.

"How are you feeling about all of that?" the therapist asked, uncapping her pen and opening her notebook to a blank page.

"Nervous," I stated simply; no use in beating around the bush. I learned very early on that the sooner I cut to the chase in individual therapy, the sooner I was able to get out to the stables where I truly wanted to be.

"What has you nervous?" she asked gently, probing me for more information.

"What if they say I still can't ride?"

"What will that change about the way things are right now?"

I thought about that for a moment. Realistically, it wouldn't change the way things were currently; she was right. Things could only get better or stay the same.

There was a high probability that they would tell me what I already knew—that I wouldn't be able to ride again. But the tiny spark of hope that bloomed inside of me, no matter how hard I'd fought it, at the prospect of the original diagnosis being wrong was a hard thing to ignore.

"I guess it doesn't really change the way things are right now, but I don't want to get my hopes up to have them crushed again."

"I can see how that would be devastating, especially since a lot of your sense of self is wrapped up in the notion that riding is your one true love."

I nodded and relaxed, leaning back on the sofa and

crossing my arms. Talking about my inability to ride was still a sore subject, and thinking about it always made me tense.

"Let's change gears a bit. I wanna talk about Ray." She shifted, flipping back through her notebook to a previous session's notes.

My heart started pounding at the mere mention of her name. This had been one of the longest stints I'd gone without being able to talk to her, and both my body and mind were remembering how much I needed her in my life.

"What about her?"

"It seems like she's someone extremely important in your life. We asked at the beginning of your therapy to write down each person in your life waiting for the healthy version of you to come home. Besides your immediate family, she was at the top of your list. We haven't really had a chance to talk about her, and I'm curious to know more."

"What do you want to know?" I did my best to hide the defensive tone of my voice, but Dr. Langford was perceptive and caught on to the tightness in my posture and edge to my words.

"What do you want to share?" she asked, crossing her legs at the ankles and sitting back in her seat, mirroring my defensive posture.

"She's my best friend."

"I see." She hummed noncommittally, seeing through my bullshit with ease.

An exasperated sigh puffed past my lips. I knew that if I didn't give her a little more than just "she's my best friend," she would sit here and wait until I gave something up. It was better to get it out of the way and open up.

"Ray and I have been best friends since we were kids. She was the only girl I met who didn't look at me like I had something they wanted. It wasn't a secret that my brother and I were hot commodities with the girls in school. Even though she was younger than me, Ray didn't act like it. She is wise beyond her years and one of the best people I know."

The therapist nodded, urging me to continue.

What did I want to share about Ray?

I'm sure she didn't want to hear about how responsive she was to my touch, how her body reacted like it was made specifically for me. She probably didn't want to know about how sinking inside her for the first time had left me raw and emotional at how good it had felt, and how right. So, I settled on a version of all of the above.

"Rayna Cortez is the sun that shines, even on my darkest days. She is my anchor in the storm, keeping me from drifting. She's it for me, and she's the love of my life."

"It sounds like she's a very special woman. It takes a strong partner to stand beside you, encouraging you to be the best version of yourself. Can you tell me about the moment you realized that you loved her?"

I thought back, trying to remember the singular moment I knew that my feelings for her had veered from friendly to romantic.

There had been so many moments over the years that I'd seen her in a light that was more than just friends, but only one stood out that encompassed everything for me.

WADE - 27 YEARS OLD

THE COOL WATER rushed around my fingers as I trailed them through the creek's inky depths. The ripples waved around the traces of my touch, receding into nothingness as they edged outward.

Everything hurt.

I had come to the one place we shared since I was a little boy. Ma always brought Max and me to the cove when we needed a quiet place to chat, think, or just exist. It had become *our* place. It was the last place on earth where I felt as if I could still *feel* her.

I had discarded my suit jacket beside me as soon as I sat down on the riverbank, yet I could still hear my cell phone buzzing in one of the pockets. I couldn't bring myself to answer whoever was relentlessly calling. I needed to be alone for a while.

Everyone always expected me to be the happy twin. The one they could count on to lift their spirits when times got tough. Max was the storm cloud, and I was the sunlight.

But right now, I couldn't be that happy-go-lucky guy.

There wasn't a single ounce of happiness flowing through my veins that I could spare for anyone else. I was completely drained and exhausted.

The crunch of leaves and snapping of twigs behind me signaled her approach, but I didn't need to hear her to know who it was. I had an uncanny ability to sense Ray long before seeing her.

I'm sure the fact that we had been best friends for fifteen years had something to do with it. Or, it could have been the uncomfortable fluttering in my stomach that had started recently, heightening my senses to her presence.

"Want some company?" she questioned, plopping down beside me on the bank of the small creek that flowed through the cove.

Here's the thing about Ray: she rarely gave you a choice. Even if she posed something as a question, she really wasn't asking. She was inadvertently telling you what she was going to do. Hence, she was sitting beside me when I couldn't be bothered to be any sort of pleasant company.

We sat in silence for what felt like hours, but likely only minutes, before someone spoke. Neither Ray nor I was any good at expressing our emotions. We both repressed things until we exploded, often causing volatile blowups at each other that resulted in us tiptoeing around one another for a couple of days, before the person in the wrong apologized.

"The service was beautiful," she whispered, breaking the quiet serenity.

I grumbled in response, not bothering to speak. I didn't trust myself enough not to lash out after the emotional roller-coaster I'd been riding over the last week.

"I'm sure she would have loved it. All those people

coming to see her? She was always one for a little bit of theatrics."

I didn't bother responding as I stared off into the trees surrounding us. I knew Ray meant well. When the situation was reversed, I had done the same thing, sitting beside her, cracking jokes and hoping to make her smile—even if just for a second during one of the hardest moments of her life.

Giving it one last valiant effort, Ray stood from her spot beside me, cleared her throat, and in a booming, announcer-like voice, exclaimed, "Welcome to the dead moms club!" She waggled her fingers dramatically at her sides.

That was enough to get a small tilt of my lip and a breathy chuckle. I scrubbed my hand down my face and rested it on my bent knee.

"Fuck, Ray. That's not funny," I huffed, doing my best to hide the sound of the secondary chuckle that threatened to crawl its way up my throat.

There was nothing, and I mean *nothing,* funny about losing my mother. Ma had been the glue holding our family together for so long, and the mere thought of returning to normal life without her had my heart beating wildly in my chest.

We weren't even given a chance to say goodbye. She was here one minute and gone the next. She didn't even see it coming.

A fucking brain aneurysm.

Life could be so goddamn cruel when it wanted to be. Our vibrant, beautiful, and full-of-wisdom mother had been taken from us without warning. She had lived a good, healthy, and happy life—only to be robbed of the rest by a medical anomaly.

"Got you to smile, though," she said triumphantly as she sat back down beside me.

Her mood switched back to somber as she rested a hand gently on my knee. I ignored the tingle of desire that always niggled at the back of my mind when Ray's hands were on me.

"But really, Wade, I'm sorry." She sighed as she looked out into the water. The heaviness in the air was oppressive as the weight of the day settled around us.

The crickets and rustling of fall leaves became the soundtrack of our grief, dulling the ache ever so softly with each minute we listened to their quiet song. We fell back into a comfortable silence, neither of us feeling the need to fill the void with empty platitudes, comfortable to sit together in our grief.

Surprisingly, I was the first to break. After being friends with Ray for so many years, I knew what I wanted to say would be met with receptive ears instead of the judgmental looks I would receive from my family.

"I'm just so… angry," I said, plucking a blade of grass from the dirt beside me. "I don't want to be. But I'm fucking livid."

I could feel the festering rage burning inside of me, the lick of the flames flickering up my throat as I did my best to stanch their ascent. As the week had gone on, it had become more and more difficult to suppress the desire to destroy everything around me.

"Wade… It's okay to be—"

"It's not fucking going to be okay, Ray." Using her name, not the nickname I had been calling her for years, was a true testament to how far into my grief I had retreated.

I felt my resolve slipping as I stood, pacing the edge of the bank, hoping to quell the anger radiating off my body in vibrating waves. Undeterred, Ray sat steadfast on the edge of the water, giving me the space I needed to sort through my swirling emotions.

If anyone could understand my pain and anguish, Ray could. She had lost her own mother when we were teens. I could never fathom the hardship and emotional strain she had gone through until now.

"I know this isn't what you want to hear right now," she started.

With a mirthless chuckle, I cut my eyes to hers, imploring her not to continue that sentiment. But Ray knew me better than anyone, and she would never back down from my wrath. I could throw everything in the book at this girl, and she would stand, unshakable, beside me.

"I'm not going to sit here and bullshit you, Wade. Losing your mom fucking sucks. Don't I fucking know it." She let out a breathy, humorless chuckle.

"What I *am* going to tell you is that she wouldn't want you to be angry. You know that just as well as I do. Penelope Daniels may not have had enough time on this earth, but she treated me as the daughter she never had. I knew that woman longer than I had the pleasure of knowing my *own* mother."

She stood and walked over to where I was pacing. I kept my eyes averted from hers, not wanting to give in to the emotion threatening to spill over. I knew the second my eyes met hers, I'd break, and the dam holding back my tears would crumble.

Knowing I was listening, even if I wasn't looking at her, Ray took one of my hands.

"You boys were that woman's entire world. She thought

you and Max hung the moon and the stars. She was so proud of the man you have become."

I felt the softness of her touch as she used the pad of her thumb to wipe away the tear I hadn't realized was trailing down my cheek. I raised my eyes to meet the watery hazel gaze that would be my undoing.

"Grief is the price we pay for love, and love is always worth it," she whispered as she pulled me close, wrapping her small arms around my waist and laying her cheek on my chest.

I let the tears that had been threatening to spill over my bottom lashes fall. I knew that in this moment, I could break because Ray would be there to catch all my shattered pieces to put me back together.

WADE

SURPRISINGLY, my therapy session with Dr. Langford hadn't been too bad. Talking about Ray came naturally. She'd been in my life for so long that she had secured a permanent place there, regardless of our currently unresolved relationship status.

Our session had concluded with a series of breathing exercises to help regulate my emotions, should I feel that overwhelming pressure of an anxiety attack brewing. I hadn't had to use the techniques outside of practice yet, but I knew that being in the treatment facility was a controlled environment, and the true test would be when I went back to real life, and my triggers.

After grabbing a quick lunch in the large cafeteria, which surprisingly had delicious food, I made my way back to my room to change into some work clothes. I didn't need to be sullying my good jeans while mucking out stalls after group therapy.

I changed into one of my more worn pairs of Wranglers and a basic black T-shirt before throwing on my boots and grabbing my Stetson off the small desk in the corner of the room.

I took a second to marvel at how quickly I'd folded myself into a routine in the two short weeks I'd been there. The easy cadence of getting up, attending therapy, grabbing food, and going to work had kept my thoughts from drifting into uncomfortable territory.

Breathing came easier, the nightmares didn't wake me from a dead sleep, and for once, I felt like the weight of life wasn't holding me down.

Following the same routine as that morning, I locked up my room and made my way down the long corridor to the large meeting space reserved for group therapy.

Just like in the movies, everyone sat around in a folding chair circle, sharing the shit that haunts them. There were about ten people already seated, waiting for the session to begin.

Around the room, every face told a story. We had veterans, assault survivors, first responders, and then there was me—the lowly cowboy who'd been shot in a freak accident.

Most days, I struggled with feeling like I wasn't truly damaged enough to be here. That was a harrowing thought in itself. How did you judge someone else's pain and say yours doesn't match up?

I took one of the empty seats, leaning back in the folding chair and crossing my legs at the ankles in front of me.

The group therapist, Leslie, took a seat directly opposite the circle from where I was sitting and smiled at each and every one of us individually.

Even though we were here as individuals, there was a strong focus on camaraderie and finding common threads among our traumas. It had been preached to us that creating a support system was key to managing expectations for continued healing back in the real world.

Each group session rotated weeks and times, so you got to meet and hear from residents of varying walks of life. The group was never the same, but the emotional damage each of us carried with us was always a common thread.

"Hey, y'all!" Leslie remarked cheerfully. She was a petite, late-thirties, soccer-mom-vibe type of woman who, in my opinion, talked way too animatedly for a group therapist focusing on trauma and PTSD.

A mumbled greeting came from around the circle as each of us readied ourselves for the onslaught of sharing we were about to do.

Leslie didn't bother recording our group sessions. This wasn't something that was going to be analyzed by our individual therapists later.

Group therapy was solely focused on sharing your heaviness with those around you who may or may not have similar stories, but who had been through similar emotions.

"Would anyone like to start us off today?" she asked, looking from one person to the next, willing someone to speak up. No one seemed to take the bait, and the echo of silence in the room was deafening.

Who really wanted to be the first person to trauma dump all over their peers in group therapy? *Not me.*

"Wade!"

Fuck.

I looked up from beneath the brim of my hat, not having bothered to take it off. I had honestly hoped that I would get away from sharing unscathed and catch a quick power nap during the session.

Leslie looked back at me with a huge smile, pleading with her eyes for me to share something with the group.

"Um, hi, I'm Wade, and I'm emotionally damaged?"

A chuckle echoed through the room as all the residents loosened up a bit.

Leslie laughed loudly, shaking her head as if I were the most hilarious person she'd met. Something about her zest for life and her relentless happiness helped me relax a bit.

"Funny! You're funny, Wade," she chuckled. "If you don't mind, we'd love to hear a little bit about why you're here with us at ERRC."

This was the part I hated. I hated the constant need to relive the incident over and over again.

Dr. Langford had drilled into me since my first session that repressing the trauma surrounding the shooting and acting like it never happened didn't make it go away.

I needed to face the fact that it happened; it changed my life, and I was going to grow and move forward from it.

Clearing my throat and sitting up straighter in my seat, I leaned forward, resting my elbows on my knees.

"My name's Wade. I'm here at ERRC because I was shot in the back after helping rescue my now sister-in-law from drug dealers who were threatening to kill her daughter. I struggle with PTSD because of the incident and the subsequent loss of my ability to ride horses. I am a retired rodeo cowboy, so that pill was hard to swallow."

The room was silent as everyone nodded their heads and listened with rapt attention as if my story was the most riveting part of their week.

"I decided that I needed to make an effort to deal with what happened to me so I can move forward with my life. I've got a girl back home who has seen all the good and broken parts of me, yet somehow still loves me. She deserves to get the best version of me.”

“And?” Leslie prodded. I knew what she was hinting at, and I hated saying it. It sounded selfish, but I knew it was a pivotal part of my healing journey.

“And, I want to be the best version of myself because *I* deserve it.”

“Very good, Wade,” the therapist commended. “One last thing before we move on, I want you to take a second and reflect on your trauma. Can you tell me one *good* thing to come out of it?”

My eyes shot up to hers, and I swear I saw a hint of a smile playing on her lips. A subtle challenge.

Something good to come out of getting shot in the back? What the fuck good could have come out of that?

This wasn’t something I’d had to share before in group therapy, so I didn’t have a canned response at the ready like every question before.

I took a minute to think, picking at the skin around my thumbs as I batted around ideas in my head. Finding something good that came out of trauma seemed like an oxymoron.

As I sat surrounded by peers who’d gone through similar or more excruciating traumatic events, the only face I saw was Ray’s.

She was the best thing that had come out of all of this. The ache of unspoken love had lingered for what felt like forever. The reason for finally surrendering to it could always be traced back to the sharp, sudden sting of that gunshot.

If I hadn’t been shot, I would still be able to ride. I wouldn’t have turned into the grumpy asshole who snapped at anyone with a pulse. I would have continued using humor to hide the gnawing feeling of regret each time I neglected the swirl of emotions that surged when Ray was near.

If I hadn't been shot, I wouldn't have pushed her against that brick wall outside of Jack's and tasted her perfect lips, heard her needy moans, or felt how responsive she was to my touch.

Just thinking about her made me smile, and I looked up at Leslie, her smile now wide. I could see the lightbulb turn on in her head as she and I both realized the small breakthrough I was having.

At the end of the day, if I hadn't been shot, I wouldn't have Ray the way I'd been dreaming about for years.

Before I could answer her, one of the meeting room doors opened up and Dr. Langford came in, striding over to stand behind Leslie, whispering something in her ear. Both of their eyes flicked to me, and I felt my heart begin to race.

What had I done?

Was I in some sort of trouble?

"Wade, do you mind coming with me?" Dr. Langford asked, extending her arm toward the meeting room door. I could sense everyone's curiosity as to what was going on, but none of them dared speak.

I nodded silently, standing and following my therapist into the hall. She stopped right outside the door as it clicked shut behind us, putting her hand gently on my forearm.

"You're not in trouble," she said, and I felt my anxiety relax marginally.

Memories of being called to the principal's office briefly floated through my mind, and hearing that I wasn't in trouble quelled a bit of the terrible scenarios I'd been conjuring.

"Is everyone at home okay?" I asked breathlessly, my

body doing its best to catch up with my mind as my panic receded.

Had something happened to Pops?

Were Stella and the baby okay?

I closed my eyes, leaning into the box breathing that Dr. Langford had taught me in one of our first sessions.

Breathe in for four seconds.

Hold for four seconds.

Release for four seconds.

Hold for four seconds.

With each repeat of the breathing exercise, I willed my heart to beat regularly, slowing its rapid pace. Dr. Langford stood silently, letting me regulate my emotions. The knowledge that she was beside me was comforting as my heartbeat slowed.

"Yes, everyone's fine. I'm sorry to have scared you. We got the results of your diagnostics, and the panel wanted to meet with you to discuss them. The only time that worked for everyone was right now, hence my pulling you out of an important therapy session."

The results were in?

Fuck, I had just done my testing and scans yesterday. How had they gotten the results and come up with a diagnosis so fast? Surely that meant that the original doctor's suggestion stood, and they had been right in keeping me from riding.

Coming out of the swirling haze of thoughts clouding my mind, I noticed Dr. Langford was walking down the hallway toward one of the small conference rooms.

She must have instructed me to follow, but my brain was slow on the uptake, swirling with thoughts and emotions. I took a deep breath, steeling my resolve, and walked behind her to my inevitable execution.

WADE

YOU CAN RIDE AGAIN.

The words swirled around my mind in a constant loop, taunting me with the hope I'd spent the last two weeks keeping at bay. Had I heard the doctors right? I could ride again.

"Wade." Dr. Langford's gentle voice pulled me out of the haze of jumbled thoughts. "Did you hear the doctors?"

She moved her chair to sit closer, somehow using her psychologist's sixth sense to know that I was likely spiraling.

"Wade. I need you to breathe for me," she whispered, placing her index and middle fingers over the pulse point on my wrist.

I had no clue how long I'd been sitting here, zoned out, but my lungs felt like they were on fire, and I realized I'd been holding my breath.

Gasping, I pulled in a deep lungful of stagnant conference room air and focused on my breathing exercises again. I hated feeling like I was spiraling out of control with no brakes, and

somehow, evening out my breathing into four-second incre-
ments calmed me enough to focus on my surroundings.

Dr. Langford kept her fingers on my pulse as I worked to
slow my heart rate and calm my breathing, monitoring my
ability to self-regulate.

Breathe in for four seconds.

Hold for four seconds.

Out for four seconds.

Hold for four seconds.

I repeated the motions until I could feel the tension that
had wound itself through my muscles relax, and the sweat that
had broken out across my skin had dried.

"Good. You're doing fantastic, Wade," she praised,
removing her fingers from my wrist, clearly satisfied with the
slowing of my heart rate to a more acceptable rhythm.

It was then that I noticed that the doctors were no longer
on the large projector screen across the room. We had called
them in virtually to read off the findings of all the tests and
scans from the day prior.

Watching a team of world-renowned doctors and surgeons
pore over my chart had left me feeling severely undeserving.

My brain kept screaming that I wasn't worthy of all the
attention I was getting and that I should just suck it up and
accept that I wasn't meant to ride anymore. I couldn't ratio-
nalize why these important medical figureheads were so
invested in *me*.

I hadn't understood 90 percent of the medical jargon they
read off the chart in front of them. I didn't know the meaning
of all the results of the scans. But what I did understand were
the four words I'd been craving so desperately to hear since
the night of the incident.

You can ride again.

"Do you feel calm enough to talk through things a little bit?" Dr. Langford asked, pulling out one of her notebooks and spreading it open on the conference table in front of us. She uncapped a pen and wrote the date at the top. I guess we were having an impromptu therapy session.

I didn't trust myself to speak, so I nodded and pulled off my Stetson, setting it upside down on the table in front of me. I ran my fingers through my hair, realizing how long it had gotten. As soon as I got out of here, I was going to need a trim.

"So, while I am a healthcare professional, I am not a medical doctor. I don't understand all the terminology that the team was using, but I did understand quite a bit. Were you able to understand the majority of what they discussed?"

"I can ride again," I whispered, leaning forward so my elbows rested on my knees as I held my head in my hands, the weight of those words sinking in.

"Yes, Wade. You will be able to ride again. Not right away, but you will be able to get on a horse. How are you feeling about that?"

How was I feeling? I *should* feel on top of the fucking world.

When the doctor in Firefly Cove told me I couldn't ride, it ripped everything I had known and worked for my entire life out from under me.

Knowing I could get back out there, even if it took a lifetime, should have filled me with so much happiness I could burst.

But truthfully, I was terrified. What if I got back on a horse and the doctors were wrong? What type of life would I live if I ended up as a paraplegic? How could Ray ever love me if I needed to be pushed around in a wheelchair for the rest of my life and my fucking dick didn't work?

"Terrified," I choked out, the word catching in my throat as I fought for each labored breath. I focused on my box breathing again, feeling yet another panic attack rising to the surface. I hated feeling like everything I'd built by coming here was slowly crumbling around me.

Dr. Langford and I had recently discussed the possibility of setbacks in my therapy. Healing from trauma was not linear.

The key to successful healing wasn't curing the bad days so that they never showed up. It was about focusing on the good days when they came and taking the bad days one minute at a time.

Healing meant creating an environment where there were more good days than bad. The bad days would come, but knowing how to fight through them was the key.

"Feeling worried and scared about this is completely normal. What are you most scared of?" she prodded.

I hung my head as I whispered, "What happens if I get back on a horse and fuck my back up worse, ending up in a wheelchair for the rest of my life?"

"That is certainly a terrifying possibility. But how would you feel if you got back on a horse and nothing like that ever happened?"

I turned her challenge over in my mind. I could almost feel the wind whipping around me as I envisioned myself riding through the ranch, letting Joker take me out to the farthest parts of the property. I could feel the strong muscles of his haunches extending and contracting as he pushed himself to his limits, running wild and free through the fields.

A sense of calm washed over me at the prospect of being

able to feel the freedom I so desperately craved every time I was on the back of a horse.

"Free. I would feel free."

Her tight-lipped smile was hard to miss as she jotted a couple of things down in her notebook. She wasn't giving much away, trying to keep a professional demeanor, but I could tell she was proud, and that filled me with an effervescent sense of joy.

"Now, let's talk about what is going to have to happen to make sure you can get back on a horse."

I nodded, wishing I had something of my own to take notes on. I wanted to do this right so that the possibility of anything going wrong was minimal.

"The neurosurgeon and orthopedic specialist agreed that your lower spine and the surrounding muscles are going to need strengthening. They suggested some intense physical therapy over the next two weeks you're with us, and additional sessions once you're back home. They brought up your past rodeo injury where you twisted wrong getting out of the saddle, is that right?"

That had been the moment I knew it was time for me to retire from the rodeo. I had spent the majority of my adult life focusing on rodeo events. I wasn't crazy enough to put myself on the back of a bucking horse or a pissed-off bull, but I knew rodeo was my calling.

Sterling's dad had taught me how to rope, and I was damn good at it. I'd used my skills time and time again to help wrangle cattle on their family ranch when they needed to move herds from one pasture to the next. When his dad's small-time sponsors caught wind of my ability to rope well, they funded my first big event.

One event turned into two, two turned into qualifying,

qualifying turned into championships, and it all culminated with the NFR in Las Vegas when I was twenty-five. I had poured myself into training, telling myself I was going to bring home the championship buckle and winnings for the ranch.

That morning, something had felt off, but I ignored it, pushing back the thoughts and focusing on getting in my head for what I needed to do. For some reason, though, I couldn't shake the gut feeling that something wasn't right.

When Joker and I lined up in the chute on the timed end of the arena, waiting for the gate to open and the calf to cross over the scoreline, breaking the barrier rope to signal our predetermined go time, there was a weird tension in both of our movements.

We normally worked in tandem, feeding off each other's energy. We had been training together for my entire career, so I knew something was off the moment we lined up and readied ourselves.

When the chute opened, our sights homed in on that calf, waiting for it to cross the barrier rope. Once it did, we shot out like a light, and I swung my lasso over the calf's neck with ease.

Everything seemed to be lining up for a perfect score until I stepped out of the saddle and onto the ground to tie the calf down.

I twisted awkwardly when my boot got stuck in a rogue strap on Joker's haunch, and I lunged forward, the speed and momentum of my movement twisting my lower back at an odd angle.

The doctors told me that, with consistent chiropractic care and a long stint of physical therapy, I could go back to riding professionally, but I knew in my heart that I was done.

"Yeah, that's right. It was my last professional ride."

She nodded again, writing something down in her notebook.

"They mentioned you were given the opportunity for scheduled chiropractic care and physical therapy that would have let you continue riding professionally. What made you decide to stop?"

"My family needed me. Pops and Max were working their asses off to keep things running around the ranch, trying to make ends meet. I knew it was my time to pull my weight instead of chasing buckles."

"And so, you opened a training center on the ranch for up-and-coming rodeo stars."

I nodded. Opening a training facility had been the best of both worlds. I got to continue doing what I loved—shaping the next generation of rodeo cowboys and cowgirls. I got to be around my family and still bring in a consistent income to the ranch.

"That's absolutely something to be proud of. Taking the hand you were dealt, filled with adversity, and turning it into something beautiful to help not only yourself and your family, but the community you poured most of your adult life into."

I narrowed my eyes at her, and she chuckled. I knew what she was doing. She somehow turned everything into a learning moment, and it hadn't taken me long to catch on.

"I can see you get where I'm heading with this," she said with a smile. She placed her pen down on top of her notebook and folded her hands in her lap.

"Life isn't always going to be kind, but what you do with the hand you're dealt is key to continued happiness. You've been dealt blow after blow over the last couple of years. Between your mom dying, losing your rodeo identity, and getting shot, you've lost sight of everything good that surrounds you. You've forgotten who you are at your *core*. Now that you've gotten the go-ahead to get back to riding, it's almost as if you're being reborn. So, Wade Daniels, with this new lease on life, what are you going to do with it? What type of man do you want to be when you leave here in two weeks?"

Her words floated around me, swirling like a tempest of emotion as I grasped for a response. What type of man *did* I want to be when I left here? But deep down, I knew. I knew the type of man I was and the type of man I wanted to be.

"I want to be the type of man who looks the devil in the eyes when he's standing across a field and laughs because I've seen hell, I've walked through it, and I won't let myself go there again."

RAY

THREE WEEKS HAD CRAWLED by since Wade left for Ember Ridge. No matter what I did to pass the time, my mind always wandered back to him—wondering what he was up to, how his therapy was going, and if he missed me.

I wasn't generally one for self-doubt, but since our situation was so new when he left, I wondered what things would be like when he got back. Would he still want to be together, or would he want to go back to being just friends? Could we realistically go back to being just friends?

After knowing what it felt like to be wrapped in his arms, have his lips on mine, and feel the connection of our bodies when we fell into bed, I doubted we could go back to the way things were before he left.

Have faith. He's going to come back the same man, just a little less grumpy.

I repeated the same mantra anytime those self-deprecating thoughts started creeping in, threatening to take hold and cast a consistent shadow of doubt over everything. This was the longest we had ever gone without talking, and like an addict, I was itching to hear the sound of his voice.

Keeping myself busy had been key, and this day was no different. It was the twins' and Charlie's birthday. It was also the first anniversary of Charlie's kidnapping and, subsequently, the anniversary of Wade getting shot.

A large part of me wondered if he was celebrating or if he was spending the day hunkered down, thinking of all the things he had lost. Selfishly, I wanted him with us, celebrating another year around the sun, especially since this was the big 3-0 for him and Max.

Stella insisted on keeping things low-key this year, since Wade wasn't there to celebrate. We were just having a small dinner with the family at the big house.

Charlie was still too young to comprehend the concept of a large birthday party, so we just got her a cupcake and planned to sing *Happy Birthday* and open gifts.

As I stood on the porch of the big house, the ranch felt quiet. It was as if the land knew there was a piece missing, and it was biding its time like the rest of us until that last puzzle piece was back in place. There was no breeze, no snickering of horses, no buzz of insects. It was just silent. Every facet of the ranch and its inhabitants felt the weight of Wade's missing presence.

Securing Charlie's present under my arm, I knocked, pushing open the large front door into the foyer. The silence even stretched through the house, shrouding everything in an uncomfortable haze of grief.

Brushing off the prickling sensation of unease, I made my way into the large family room, looking for where everyone was gathered, hoping that seeing Charlie enjoy her birthday would help with the melancholy feeling blanketing the day.

Stella and Max were cuddled together on the sofa, staring at the baby monitor where I assumed Charlie slept. I couldn't imagine the restlessness they were feeling, knowing that this time last year, their world was upended and their lives forever changed.

Although it ended in happiness for them, the ever-present trauma would shroud this day like a low-hanging cloud, reminding them how everything could have ended so differently; for some, it did.

"Hey, guys," I whispered, setting the gift down on the fireplace hearth where the rest were stacked.

"Hey," Stella whispered back, angling her eyes toward me in greeting but not taking them off the monitor for longer than a second.

"How long has she been asleep?" I asked, sitting on the floor at their feet, laying my head gently on Stella's thigh. She reached her hand down, and I met her grasp, entwining our fingers in a gesture of solidarity. I could feel the slight tremor in her hand as I lightly squeezed three times.

"About an hour and a half. We wanted to sit in the room with her, but our therapist suggested sitting in a neutral space with the monitor instead."

Max and Stella went through intense therapy after Charlie's kidnapping. They still attended sessions once a week, even a year after the incident, and I was so proud of them for sticking with it.

It made me think about where Wade would be a year from now. Would he still attend therapy, or would he think he'd been cured and move on? Hopefully, that was a discussion he'd have with his therapist, and he wouldn't be too stubborn to take their advice.

I sensed Stella's body relax as Charlie stirred on the monitor. I could hear her babbling to herself, singing something that sounded like a gibberish version of *Jingle Bells*.

No matter what, that child always brought a smile to my face and joy to my heart. She was unfiltered positivity wrapped up in a tiny body.

I scooted out of Stella's way so she could stand. She moved around me, giving Max a quick kiss before padding down the hallway to retrieve the birthday girl. I gave Max's knee a soft squeeze, and he smiled gently down at me.

I never would have imagined the broody cowboy would find the love of his life, settle down, and become a dad all in one year.

He was so jaded after his ex-fiancée screwed him over that I was a little concerned he would end up a perpetual bachelor. Stella and Charlie were so good for him, and they had instantly meshed with our little misfit family.

Tiny feet thundered down the hallway as Charlie rushed into the living room, a huge smile on her face. Last year, she had insisted on a fairy birthday; this year, she wanted to be a cowgirl.

She was decked out from head to toe in Western wear, from her tiny Ariat boots, Wranglers, a pink button-down with pearl snaps and matching pink fringe vest, all the way to the child-sized Stetson that sat atop her head. Her wild curls were sticking up in every direction, clearly mussed from a good afternoon nap, beneath the brim of her hat.

"Happy Birthday, little one," Max cooed, opening his arms for her to climb into his lap. She bypassed everyone else, heading directly for her dad, climbing up and settling on his thighs with a contented sigh.

"Happy Birfday Mass Da!" she yelled, causing Max to wince in discomfort as she screeched. She was pure happiness, but I'm sure we could all do without the high-pitched, excited squealing.

Clearly having just clocked the number of gifts sitting on the fireplace mantel, most wrapped in pink paper, she scrambled out of her dad's lap and ran directly toward her presents.

"Mama, I open?" she asked, her little feet unable to stay still as she vibrated with excitement. I chuckled lightly, wishing I could bottle even just an ounce of her excitement to keep in my pocket for a rainy day.

"Yes, baby, you can open them," Stella said, sitting down and tucking herself into Max's side.

We all watched as Charlie tore into every gift with reckless abandon, flinging scraps of wrapping paper across the living room.

We'd worry about the mess later; for now, we were just enjoying watching her eyes light up with excitement as she opened each package.

After unwrapping a new baby doll, a miniature lasso set—complete with a steer's head to rope, a pretend camera, and a bunch of clothes—she sat down in the middle of the chaos and just smiled, taking everything in.

Unsurprisingly, she reached for the lasso set first, bringing it to Max to take out of the packaging.

"There's one more gift," Pops said gruffly, pushing out of his armchair with a grunt and holding out his hand for Charlie to follow him.

She placed her tiny palm in his as he steered her out the front door. At the top of the porch steps, he stopped and picked her up, carrying her toward the barn.

Max and Stella watched in utter confusion as we all followed behind the pair, everyone curious as to what sort of gift needed to be kept in the barn.

Pops set Charlie down outside the large wooden doors. "Wait right here," he instructed, sliding open the door and re-shutting it behind him.

All of us waited with bated breath, excited to see what this gift could be. Charlie stood stock still, dutifully following Pops' orders.

As the clomping of hooves echoed through the surrounding air, Max's head tilted back toward the sky, and a groan of frustration crested his lips.

"For fuck's sake," he grumbled.

"Mass Da, bad wo—PONY!" Charlie's scream of excitement could have been heard at least two counties over as she jumped up and down with giddy excitement.

Pops brought the small, speckled foal over, its legs barely stable, and stopped it right in front of our group. He motioned for Charlie to approach, and she did so slowly, walking on soft feet like she'd been taught to do when around new animals.

She was a natural with horses; I had seen it with my own two eyes. She walked closer to the foal, holding out her tiny hand to allow it to sniff her. The horse let out an excited whinny, and Charlie giggled in response.

Horses are very particular when it comes to their people. They can be exceptionally temperamental. The fact that an unbroken foal, with zero formal training, was letting Charlie get this close to it without so much as blinking an eye had all of us staring in wondrous amazement.

This was her heart horse—we all could feel it.

"Every cowgirl needs a horse," Pops explained, running his large, weathered hand down the horse's scrawny neck. "You're not quite old enough to be able to take care of it, so

I'll help you out with that, but this baby here will be *your* responsibility."

Charlie stared back at him unblinking as she nodded, listening with rapt attention to his instructions.

"Now, little one. What are you going to name him?"

We all waited anxiously as she tapped her finger to her lips in contemplation. Asking a two-year-old to name something often went over like a fart in church. After a couple of seconds of contemplation, her eyes lit up with joy, and a wide smile spread across her face.

"Hims name is Bubbles Flower Pancake."

A loud groan floated across the group, and Pops chuckled loudly.

"Welcome to the family, Bubbles Flower Pancake."

WADE

BREATHE *in*

> *Breathe out.*
> *Breathe in.*
> *Breathe Out.*

Standing there, the smell of hay and damp air filling my senses, my heart shouldn't have been racing, but I wasn't coming to the stables for my daily hour of grunt work.

I was standing on the precipice of the possibility that everything I'd been told for the last year wasn't true. The whinnying of horses ready to be set out to pasture or tacked up for a ride used to be a soundtrack that calmed me.

Now, those same sounds filled me with an unrelenting pressure of dread.

There was nothing in this world I wanted more than to step my boot into the stirrup, mount this horse, and go for a ride. The problem wasn't that I physically couldn't do it; it was that my brain kept conjuring worst-case scenarios, threatening to send me into a panic attack.

"It's not a race. Take it one step at a time." Dr. Langford

spoke softly from outside the stable, her reminder allowing me to take a baby step forward and grab the reins that dangled limply from their attachment point on the bridle.

The leather felt cool in my hands as I let the strap trail through my fingers. The once familiar feeling, now stiff and strained, as my body fought the trauma response.

I took another step further, allowing my fingers to brush across the coarse hair along the horse's neck.

Using techniques the therapists and I had discussed, I focused on one sense at a time, running my fingers once again over the horse's hair, cataloging the feel of it against my rough calluses.

Feeling the anxiety that had been building inside of me retreating, I took a fortified step forward, placing my hand in front of the horse to allow it to smell me before rubbing its long snout and ears.

The horse leaned into my touch, reveling in the attention and scratches. It nudged my hand upward, and I chuckled lightly at its insistence for more petting.

A cowboy never enters the stables unprepared, and I reached into the pocket of my jeans, pulling out a peppermint I'd managed to swipe from the front desk. I held it out flat in my palm for the horse's whiskery lips to gobble up.

"Good girl," I whispered reverently as the horse once again nuzzled her long snout into my hand, pushing me where she wanted me to scratch.

"How do you feel?" Dr. Langford asked from her spot outside the stable door. She stood to the side, watching closely for any setbacks in my ability to self-regulate.

"I've been around these animals every day for the entirety of my life, Doc. I feel at home. Even if the thought of what could happen when I put my boots in those stirrups sends me into a spiral, I feel like I'm right where I'm supposed to be."

Her gentle smile and slight nod of approval had me beaming with pride. I sensed what she was about to say before she said it, and for once, my heart raced with an excited giddiness instead of overwhelming dread.

"How would you feel about going for a short ride?"

"Excuse my language, but fuck yes."

She chuckled loudly, which caused a laugh to bubble out from my chest. It felt good to feel happy again, even if I knew that it could be temporary. The idea that I still had the capacity to smile, laugh, and joke meant that I wasn't as lost as I'd previously assumed.

GETTING BACK in the saddle felt amazing. Nothing felt as natural as getting on the back of a horse, even if it wasn't for a long ride.

Dr. Langford had promised I could take a quick trot around the small dirt arena they used for equine therapy if I felt like I could handle it. Nothing was holding me back, and I knew in my heart that I needed this ride.

I appreciated the fact that she let me make the choices and didn't handle me with kid gloves. She trusted me enough to know when something was going to be too much, and I was thankful we had been paired together on this journey.

Truthfully, I was going to miss her the following week when our sessions ended. She was such an important part of my healing journey, and I would forever be thankful for all of her expertise, even if it was painful getting to this point.

As I rounded the horse in a circle, relishing the warmth of the fading summer sunlight on my skin, I reflected on how far I'd come in just three short weeks at Ember Ridge.

I was nowhere close to healed, as there is no true threshold of complete healing when it comes to trauma, but I knew where my limits were and how to handle situations that pushed me beyond my comfort zone.

Instead of feeling completely paralyzed by guilt and anxiety, I felt strong and capable in my ability to battle through the tough moments. My journey with PTSD would be one that I'd take for a lifetime, and I would have setbacks along the way, but I was confident in myself to know they wouldn't end me.

I couldn't wait to share this new, emotionally mature, capable version of myself with my family—and most importantly, with my girl. If she was still my girl after waiting around for four weeks while I got my shit together.

There were still a couple of hurdles I needed to jump to be cleared for release, but I could taste the sweet freedom on the horizon.

AFTER MY RIDE, I walked the horse back to the stables, hosed her down, and turned her out to pasture for the night. The ranch hands would take care of all the grunt work in the morning.

I watched for a minute as the mare trotted around the grass, reveling in the fading sunlight and cooler air. She loped over to the other horses, nuzzling up beside their pack and grazing.

Making my way slowly back to the treatment center, I took in the setting sun as it fell behind the ridge. The beauty of the sunset stopped me in my tracks as I leaned against the wooden side of the stables.

I watched as the sky turned from brilliant blue to different shades of red, orange, pink, and even a hint of purple, streaks of color creating a watercolor image of serenity.

I'd never taken the time to truly experience the sunset, as most of the time, once I'd come in from working, it had either already set or I was dead tired and went straight to bed.

Now, sunrises? I'd seen my fair share of those over the years. I always marveled at how they crested across the flat plains of the ranch, promising beauty in the new day.

Standing there, marveling at the swatches of colors as they streaked across the sky, I realized there wasn't just something special about the sun rising, promising a new day. There was beauty in the sun setting, reminding us that endings can be beautiful, too.

As my time at Ember Ridge came to a close, I stood there, watching the sunset, and reveling in the beauty that this place has created for my new beginning. The sun might be setting on my time in treatment, but the sun was rising on my future, painting it in the warm promise of what was to come.

THE NEXT WEEK seemingly flew by, and my excitement ramped up with each passing day. I couldn't believe that I'd spent four weeks at a treatment center talking about my feelings.

Realistically, it was the first time in my adult life I'd been directly asked about how I felt.

This last week, we primarily focused on reintegration. Therapy consisted of talking about the things we were excited and nervous about as we headed back to our real lives, putting names to the important triggers we'd addressed.

Each one of us was armed to the teeth with tactics to deal with triggers in our everyday lives and resources should we need additional assistance. I had met with Dr. Langford about setting up a therapy appointment in Firefly Cove.

Unfortunately, the resources I needed weren't readily accessible locally, so we settled on once-a-month, in-person visits at her office at the center and virtual visits three times a week for the time being.

After my brief time back in the saddle, I met with the orthopedic doctor once again for final imaging. The team of specialists wanted to make sure I hadn't exacerbated any issues with my spine after getting back in the saddle.

After getting the all clear, he'd set me up with a physical therapist that I would see twice a week for a couple of months and then taper down as time went on.

Although it felt like I was going to be meeting with a specialist once a day for the remainder of my life, I knew it was temporary. After all, I didn't want to undo all the hard work I'd pushed through at ERRC, especially with all the painful reliving I'd been asked to do.

If I could go the rest of my life without talking about my feelings, I would love nothing more, but I knew it was an important part of letting the people around me in to assist in my recovery.

"Well, it's almost time to walk out of here," Dr. Langford said from the chair across from me. It was my final therapy session, and I'd have been lying if I said I wasn't nervous.

"Yep," I said softly, popping the "p" exaggeratedly.

"What are you going to do when you get out of here?" she prodded.

"I've got a couple of errands to run on my way home, but I think I'm most excited to get back to my family. I miss them, and I hope they're happy with all the work I've put in toward healing."

"Are *you* happy with all the work you've put in and where you're at mentally?"

I took a moment to ponder her question. I wouldn't say *happy* was the term I would use. I wished more than anything that I hadn't been in this position to begin with, but I was *proud* of the strength I'd shown in getting the help I so desperately needed.

"Truthfully, yes. I'm happy with where I am mentally and what I've done to get to this point. Most importantly, though, I'm proud. It might sound conceited to say that about myself, but I've done the damn thing, and I'm walking out of here a stronger man."

The therapist nodded with a wide smile. "I hope you know that *I* am proud of you, and I'm sure your family is as well. It's been a pleasure getting to know you in every form, Wade Daniels."

"That sounds like you're not going to see me again, Doc."

She laughed. "Sorry, but you're going to be seeing a lot of me in the near future."

"Looking forward to it."

RAY

THE DAY HAD FINALLY ARRIVED. I'd spent four weeks counting down the days, minutes, hours, and seconds, all culminating in Wade coming home. My body vibrated with giddy excitement, and I found it exceptionally hard to sit still.

None of us knew exactly when he would be back from the treatment facility, but we knew he had checked out that morning and would hopefully be on his way home soon.

It was already noon, and I was checking my phone for any signs of communication from him, only slightly disappointed every time my notifications came up empty.

I had crafted my entire day around spending every waking moment with Wade, but seeing as I had zero knowledge of when he'd actually be coming home, I was currently sitting on the living room sofa doom scrolling social media.

A text notification popped up, and my heart rate spiked as I scrambled to unlock my phone. Deflating when I realized it wasn't him, I sank back into the cushions of the couch.

Would he, though?

I'd been so positive when he'd left that we could go the distance with whatever we were calling the shift in our relationship, but it was so new that tiny speckles of doubt started to creep into my thoughts.

Would this new, healed version of Wade still want me?

I brushed off my asshole inner voice that threatened to derail all the happiness today brought as I walked back to my room to get ready.

What does someone wear when they're welcoming home their not-so-boyfriend-maybe-boyfriend after he spent four weeks working on his mental health in a treatment facility?

Settling on a pair of skinny jeans and a white fitted tank top, I snagged my cowboy boots from where I'd haphazardly thrown them in the closet. I tied a flannel shirt around my waist and sat down on the edge of the bed to tug on my boots.

I walked over to the floor-length mirror, inspecting my choice of attire. I brushed my thick hair back into a high ponytail, pulling out a couple of tendrils to frame my face. Content with what I'd chosen, I heaved a sigh, willing my mind and body into a forced sense of calm.

It was now or never, I guess.

I opted to walk over to D&D Ranch, hoping that a quiet walk through the woods would help ease some of the nervous energy that had built up while I waited for Wade to get home.

As I walked the worn path between our houses, I let the sound of the dense forest wash over me. The quiet chirping of birds and rustling of leaves helped my mind relax, and I could feel some of the tension easing from my muscles.

Maybe I could take Sunset out for a ride before Wade got home to keep the calm vibes going. After all, it could be late into the evening before he made it back from Ember Ridge, and I didn't want to look desperate, even if I was.

Cresting through the trees, the ranch was alive with activity as day-to-day duties continued as if nothing was amiss. Wade and Pops had created a well-oiled machine, and even though one of the pivotal parts was missing, they seemed to have made up the deficit just fine.

Nearing the barn, I could hear shouting from the training ring on the other side. Peeking around the corner, I spotted my sister sitting on top of Oakley, a deep scowl etched between her brows, and her arms flailing wildly as she berated the cowboy sitting on the top metal fencing rung.

Sterling's arms were crossed defiantly as she yelled. I couldn't make out exactly what they were arguing about, but it was clear they weren't each other's biggest fans. I could feel the tension in the air, and I chose to ignore it, walking back into the barn to tack up Sunset for a ride.

I didn't need to get in the middle of whatever fight was happening over there. My sister was a big girl, and if anyone could hold her own with a bronc rider, it was Izzy.

Sunset greeted me at the door to her stall with an excited whinny and enthusiastic head nod. I chuckled lightly, running my hand over her forehead and ears, brushing her forelock aside, and scratching the white blaze along her face, her favorite spot to be rubbed. She leaned into my touch, and I gave her one final scratch before heading to the tack room and grabbing everything I needed.

Normally, if Wade or Pops knew I would be coming by to ride, they'd have Sunset tacked up for me, but I had made sure to learn in case I wanted an impromptu ride. I grabbed the saddle pad, a saddle, and a bridle from the tack room, hefting everything over to her stall.

Thankfully, Sunset was a very easygoing girl, and I made quick work of getting everything in place. I double- and triple-checked that everything was secure without being too tight and then led her out of the barn to the mounting block.

Pops had built the wooden step-on area when the boys were young, giving them an area to safely mount their horses until they were tall enough to reach the stirrups without it.

Seeing as I was fully grown and couldn't reach the stirrups without help, I generally used the mounting block or, in a pinch, Wade's knee as a jumping off point; unless I was trying to show off, in which case, I often paid for it with screaming muscles for the following week.

I hitched Sunset to the wooden post in front of the block before stepping up the weathered steps, throwing my leg over the saddle, and settling myself on her back.

Sunset stood regally, waiting for instruction, a picture of the perfect beginner horse. I was thankful she allowed me to ride her each time I came to the ranch, and I made sure to bring along treats as a reward.

Clicking my tongue, I grabbed the reins loosely in my hand and urged her forward. She trotted past where Izzy and Sterling were still entangled in their heated debate. I made out "stupid fucker" and "stubborn cowgirl" before I was out of earshot.

Passing the hustle and bustle of the ranch, I made my way over to the trails, urging Sunset into a slow trot across the rocky terrain. She traipsed through the woods with ease, stepping over fallen branches and large rocks without a second glance.

I let the steady rhythm of her gait lull me into a serene calm, leaning into the movement and sound of her gentle clomps across the damp earth. Everything felt sticky and humid, but I let the warmth cast over my body, easing the tension of excitement coursing through my muscles.

Taking a trail ride was *my* form of therapy. I didn't need to sit in an office and pour out my emotions; I was very self-aware of the things that made me tick. But sitting atop Sunset, walking slowly through the quiet serenity that the lush forest provided, everything felt right.

The trails snaked through the vast acreage surrounding the ranch, and I took my time, enjoying the easy cadence as we worked our way back toward the stables. Sunset needed no guidance; she knew the way around these trails with her eyes closed, and I trusted her implicitly to make sure I got back unscathed.

As we left the coverage that the treelined trails provided, harsh sunlight blinded me, forcing me to pull down the brim of my hat to shield my eyes.

I kept my head down as we made our way back to the main barn, but just as we rounded the corner heading for the mounting block, a familiar voice called out—stopping my heart in its steady beat.

"You ridin' without me, Sunshine?"

I would have known the voice anywhere, and the sound of

it had tears welling in my eyes as I urged Sunset faster to the mounting block.

Finally lifting my eyes, my breath caught in my throat as I took in the sight of Wade and Joker waiting for me. A wide grin was plastered on his face as he gingerly shifted his weight to one side and used the saddle horn to dismount his horse. Joker whinnied in excitement, happy to have his rider back.

Before Sunset even had a chance to come to a complete stop at the mounting block, I was throwing myself off her back and wrapping the reins around the hitching post.

Willing my body to move faster, I used every ounce of pent-up joy to propel myself forward, eager to see my man.

Striding up to meet him, toe-to-toe, I looked my fill. He was still the tall, muscular, ruggedly handsome cowboy I'd fallen in love with—but different.

Instead of the hollow shell of a man who'd left this ranch in search of healing standing before me, I saw a strong and sure-of-himself vision in fitted Wranglers.

He had cropped his hair shorter on the sides, leaving the top long enough for it to be effortlessly sexy. I met his eyes, and seeing the light back in them nearly had me sobbing. He was back in more ways than one.

"Well, Sunshine. You gonna stand there looking at me like you wanna kiss me, or you wanna bring those pretty lips a little closer so I can fulfill the fantasies that kept me sane while I was gone?"

"You can ride," I stuttered, my brain not having quite caught up to the reality of the situation. "What...how... when?"

He took a step closer, caressing my cheek, wiping away the tears that had spilled over. "Yeah, baby. I can ride. I'll explain everything later, but right now I really need to kiss my girl."

Nearly throwing myself at him, I wrapped my arms around his neck, pressing my lips firmly to his. He wrapped his arms around my waist, tugging me tightly to him as he met my passion with the same fervent desire.

Our tongues tangled in a soft caress as our hands roamed, reminding ourselves that this was real, and we were together.

A throat clearing from beside us broke our heated embrace, and I could feel Wade's groan on my neck as he dipped his head to rest between my shoulder and chin.

"So, that's a new development," Max said, standing dumbfounded at the corner of the barn.

I chuckled lightly, pushing Wade off my neck and turning toward Max, reaching down to take my cowboy's hand. I squeezed three times and watched as a slow smile crept up at the corners of his mouth.

Damn, it felt good to see him smile.

"Not really; we've been in love with each other for years. Y'all are just slow to catch on," I teased.

Max's mouth opened and closed like a fish as Wade let out a hearty chuckle.

"We? Us? What the fuck is happening?" Max asked, looking between the two of us.

"I'm kidding, Max. Yes, it's new. Neither of us wanted to say anything because, truly, we didn't know where things stood when Wade left for treatment."

I looked over at Wade, whose smile couldn't have been scrubbed off his face if he tried.

"I knew, I was just waiting for everyone else to catch up," a voice crooned as Stella sidled up beside her husband, wrapping her arm around his waist. Over the last week, she'd definitely started to show. The little swell of her baby bump was evident beneath her top.

I didn't miss the subtle nod of acknowledgment and gentle smile Wade gave her, almost as if silently apologizing for all the pain he'd caused with his misplaced blame. Stella nodded back softly in response, not needing an overdone apology to forgive and forget.

"Yeah, cool, so can we save the family reunion for later? I really want to take my girl home and fu—" I slapped a hand over his mouth and felt the graze of his teeth against my palm. I laughed as he tightened his arms around my waist, pulling me against his growing erection.

"Yeah, we'll see you at dinner. The house is empty for another couple of hours," Stella said with an exaggerated wink.

Before I could insist on spending time with the family, Wade tossed me over his shoulder, placed a heavy smack to my ass, and started running toward the house, the sound of my laughter echoing across the ranch. The free and uninhibited way he laughed right alongside me had my heart swelling with love and pride.

WADE

FUCK, it felt good to be back.

Just breathing in the air of the ranch seemed to release any tension I had been holding since the moment I left Ember Ridge. Walking back into the "real world" felt foreign after being isolated for an entire month. I felt like I had to learn how to be a human being all over again, which, in a sense, was good.

I felt like I was getting a fresh lease on life as I drove away from the treatment center and toward my home.

Stopping at a barbershop on the way had been a spontaneous decision. I knew I needed a haircut because instead of a man bun, I was rocking a George Washington-esque ponytail, but the decision to cut it all off was spur-of-the-moment.

Something about watching each tendril of the hair I'd grown over the years fall to the ground felt freeing. It felt like I'd not only cut off a physical weight, but I'd released an emotional weight, as well.

The feeling of running my fingers along the buzzed sides

and mussing up the top had my cheeks pulling back into a wide grin. I felt lighter than I had in a long time.

As I walked through the large front door of the big house, calmness washed over my body, covering me in a warmth reminiscent of a phantom hug. It felt right to be there, in that home, with the love of my life's hand entwined with mine, and on the precipice of our forever.

"You okay?" Ray asked softly, a nervous lilt to her voice.

I turned, focusing all my attention on her down-turned hazel eyes. I used my index finger to lift her chin as I watched her lower lashes fill with tears.

"Baby, what's wrong?" I asked, cupping her cheek with my palm. She smiled softly back at me, and I felt my heart clench in my chest. This woman was so beautiful, so strong, and all mine. But I couldn't handle seeing her cry.

"I'm just so happy. I've missed you so much. There were so many times I looked for you or reached for my phone to send you a text, just to remember that I couldn't. I'm so fucking *proud* of you." She cupped both of my cheeks between her palms and brought my face down to hers in an unhurried kiss.

Pulling back, she rested her forehead on mine and closed her eyes. Relishing the feeling of us finally being together, I closed my eyes as I breathed her in. Her citrus and floral scent flooded my senses as we stood there, just feeling the comfort of each other's presence.

"I love you, Wade Daniels," she whispered, leaning back to look me in the eyes.

"I love you too, Sunshine."

"So… do you wan—" Her squeal of laughter as I once again hauled her over my shoulder and walked toward my room had a wide grin stretching across my face. There was nothing that made me happier than knowing I was the one making her happy.

"I can walk, Waddle!" she screeched. I smacked my palm hard on her ass as she let out a yelp and a whisper of a moan.

Well, okay, then. My girl liked it a little rough.

"What have I told you about that fucking nickname?" I growled, kicking the door shut behind me and flipping the lock.

I set her down in front of the closed door and backed her up against the wooden barrier. I could see her pulse fluttering in her neck, and I leaned forward, running my nose along the spot where it thudded rapidly.

"I asked you a question, Rayna," I growled, skimming my teeth along her throat. Her breathing intensified as her eyelids fluttered closed and her mouth dropped open in a soft exhale.

It had been too long since I'd felt the softness of her skin and tasted the sweetness of her lips. I was rock hard behind the denim of my jeans, ready to burst from just a couple of kisses.

"I don't remember what the question was," she mocked playfully, her hands flat against the door as if she was afraid to touch me, knowing how easily combustible the tension between us was. We were playing a game of tug-of-war where we were evenly matched, each of us giving and taking in tandem.

"What have I told you about that fucking nickname?" I reminded her gruffly, running my palm up between her breasts and resting my grip on her throat. I used my thumb and index finger to apply minimal pressure, causing a low moan to escape from her mouth.

"What nickname, Waddle?" she challenged with a grin.

A low groan rolled through my throat as I pulled her to me

by her neck, smashing my lips against hers. She met me stroke for stroke as our bodies collided, and she ground her core against my thick erection. There was nothing gentle as we let our bodies take over.

I took a step back, tugging my T-shirt over my head in a one-handed motion, slowly stalking back toward her. She stood, wide-eyed and panting, as I stepped in front of her, lowering my lips to hover over the shell of her ear.

"Lose the fucking clothes, Sunshine," I growled.

With unhurried ease, she pulled her top over her head, her heavy breasts swathed in white lace, a stark contrast to her caramel skin. As she reached to unbutton her jeans, I stopped her hand, slowly sinking down to kneel at her feet.

I placed open-mouthed kisses along the expanse of her stomach, my fingers deftly unbuttoning her jeans and slowly lowering the zipper. Her fingers tangled in the now-shorter strands of my hair, and I could feel her long nails scratching at my scalp.

My eyes involuntarily closed as she gently caressed me, and I torturously lowered her pants, tapping one foot and then the next for her to step out.

Looking up at the goddess before me, I took in the sight of her ragged breaths, her nipples peaked in pleasure, straining behind the lacy cups of her bra, begging to be lavished by my tongue.

Her trim waist and flared hips led down to matching white lace panties as I leaned forward, pressing my nose to her center and inhaling.

Fuck, how I'd missed this woman. How had I gone an entire lifetime without touching, tasting, and fucking her? She was perfection.

Standing at my full height, I reached behind her and

flicked the clasp on her bra, letting the lace cups fall to the floor. Her dusky nipples were stiff with desire, and I leaned down, blowing cool air on them.

She moaned, tipping her head back against the door, angling her body upward into mine, begging for my mouth to suck one of those pretty buds between my lips.

An idea sparked in my head, and I took a step back, pressing a finger to Ray's plush mouth. "Wait here."

She groaned, keeping her head back against the door as if waiting one more second would be her ultimate demise.

I rooted around in my closet, finally finding what I was looking for buried under forgotten rodeo buckles and a couple of pairs of jeans.

Stepping out of the door, I ran the braided nylon rope between my fingers. Ray's mouth dropped open in clear excitement as she watched me stalk slowly toward her, the piggin string flowing through my hand.

Standing in front of her, I trailed the string across her breasts and down one arm. Grabbing hold of her wrist and catching her gaze, I said, "Do you trust me?"

"With my life," she whispered reverently, no hesitation in her words.

I looped the string around one wrist, then grabbed the other and tied them together, tugging the ties into a quick knot. I slid the rope around, making sure it wasn't too tight.

Coincidentally, there was a hook on the back of my door, and content with her restraints, I tugged her hands up and secured the knot on the hook.

"You good?" I asked softly, making sure the string wasn't cutting into her wrists as she was stretched out before me.

"Never better," she crooned.

"If anything starts to hurt, tingle, or feel numb, let me

know immediately. All you have to do is say 'stop,' and I'll untie you," I commanded.

Consent and boundaries were exceptionally important if we were going to be exploring things like rope play in our sex life.

She nodded, tugging gently at the bindings on her wrists, testing her limits.

Having her spread out before me, unable to touch back, had my cock throbbing behind my zipper. Her arms strained against the restraints, and she had to stand on her tiptoes to reach the ground. The tightness it drew on her body had her breasts pushed forward, and I could see each deep inhale of air into her lungs.

"So pretty, bound up against my door, ready to take my cock," I said as I eased the zipper of my jeans down, shoving both my pants and boxer briefs to the floor.

Kicking them off my ankles, I stroked my cock languidly, using the drops of pre-cum that beaded on the tip as lube.

"Have you been waiting for this, Sunshine?"

Her tongue darted out and licked her plump bottom lip as she nodded. Leaning forward, I took that same bottom lip between my teeth, tugging gently before placing a soft kiss to her mouth to dull the sting.

"Yes," she whispered as I trailed kisses down her neck and across her chest. I hovered over one of her peaked nipples, using the tip of my tongue to flick the stiff bud. "Yes, Wade. Please," she begged, pulling at the ties, eager to put her hands on me.

"So responsive." I marveled at the way goosebumps erupted along her skin as I once again sank to my knees before her.

"Question for you, Sunshine."

"Yes, anything. Whatever it is, just put your fucking mouth on me."

Chuckling, I pulled her panties to the side, teasing my middle finger through the wetness that was pooled between her thighs. Her hips bucked as I swirled over her clit with gentle pressure. She moaned, pushing her hips forward, begging for more of my touch.

"So eager."

"You said... you had... a question," she panted as I stroked slowly through her wetness, paying special attention to the bundle of nerves at her core.

"Oh, yes. Did you know that Rayna roughly translates to queen in Spanish?"

She looked down, confused, as if she didn't speak the language fluently. I saw the arch of her eyebrow as she tried to discern where I was going with my train of thought.

I pressed a soft kiss to her inner thigh, my voice a raw whisper. "Good. Because you are my sanctuary, *mi reina*. You held me in your heart while I was fighting to come back, and now that I'm here... I'm going to worship every inch of the woman who brings me to my knees."

RAY

HOLY FUCKING SHIT.

Wade's words of reverence had me tugging at the cord around my wrists, begging to take him into my arms and show him just how much *he* deserved to be worshipped.

I did the bare minimum someone in love should do by waiting for him to heal himself and come home to me. He did the hard work of fighting the demons that plagued his thoughts, awake and asleep.

"Now, Sunshine. Your loyal subject would love nothing more than to taste the sweetness he's waited four long weeks to savor."

With a sharp tug, he ripped the side of my lace panties, tossing them across the room. Using the door as leverage, he lifted my legs over his shoulders and licked a long line up my core, stopping to suck gently on my clit.

I bucked against my restraints, a loud moan crawling up my throat as I pushed myself further into his long strokes with his flattened tongue and sharp flicks at the sensitive spot at my core.

Snaking one hand around my thigh, he used the pad of his thumb to massage my clit as his tongue darted relentlessly in and out of my entrance.

Loud moans continued to flow from my lips as I fought for purchase, but I was at his mercy. Losing the ability to touch had heightened my senses, and I was aching for release as he brought me to the brink of orgasm over and over again, but never let me fall over that ledge.

The familiar tingle crept down my spine, settling deep in my core as I thrashed against him, every sense in overdrive. With one final wrap of his lips around my clit, my body bowed, my head tipped back in ecstasy as my release flooded between us.

Lowering my legs, one at a time, Wade stood. He used his index and middle fingers to drag through the slickness between my thighs, bringing it to my lips.

I opened my mouth, wrapping my lips around the digits and sucking greedily, licking off the remnants of my release. As soon as his fingers left my mouth, his lips were on mine, the taste of my release swirling between us. I moaned into his kiss as my body arched into him, primed and ready for more.

"As much as I want to keep you tied up, I really want your fucking hands on me," Wade growled against my lips, reaching up to take my wrists off the hook and quickly unfastening the tie. He rubbed the red marks along my wrists and pressed gentle kisses to each one.

"You okay?" he asked. I could sense the hesitation in his voice. Had it been a lot to be tied up and unable to use my sense of touch? Yes. But was it the hottest moment of my entire adult life? Also, yes.

Wrapping my arms around his neck, I leaned forward, coasting my lips across his in a gentle caress. "Never better.

Now, are you gonna continue to talk or are you going to fuck me like you promised?"

He chuckled, picking me up with ease as he walked us over to the bed, setting me down on the edge. Standing between my knees, looking down at my flushed cheeks and wild hair, he caressed my jaw with a reverent gentleness.

"I love you so much," he whispered, leaning down and pressing a soft kiss to my lips.

I would never get tired of hearing those words from his mouth. Our lips were unhurried as we mapped each other's taste and feel after so much time apart.

Wade climbed to the middle of the bed, sitting with his back against the headboard. He crooked his finger, beckoning me, and with a wicked smile, I crawled slowly across the covers to settle before him.

I pressed a kiss to his lips, trailing down across his strong jaw, his taught stomach, and settling with my lips wrapped around his cock.

He hissed in pleasure as I swirled my tongue around the head, paying close attention to the way he tensed and gripped my thick tresses in his fist with each hollow of my cheeks. I took my time teasing him, bringing him closer and closer to the edge as he had so happily done to me.

Threading his fingers through the hair at the nape of my neck, he pulled me off him with an exaggerated pop. His thumb pulled down my bottom lip, and I took his thick finger into my mouth, sucking and licking the pad.

"Fuck, Sunshine. I need you."

I crawled over his legs, positioning him at my entrance, the thickness of his rock-hard erection between my thighs. Leaning forward, I pressed a gentle kiss directly over his heart as his strong hands gripped my hips.

"You have me, Wade. Always and forever."

Hovering over his length, I slowly sank down, allowing him to enter me inch by glorious inch. Once he was fully seated inside me, I leaned forward as our lips met.

There was nothing hurried about the way we came together. We used our bodies to express all the love and passion we had built through a lifetime of friendship.

I arched my back as he thrust into me deeply, pushing my chest forward. He took advantage of the opportunity and wrapped his lips around my nipple, sucking and flicking with his tongue. Moving over to the other nipple, he repeated the motions, giving each one ample attention.

As our thrusts grew sloppy and our moans louder, I could feel the impending tingle of release building in my spine as Wade reached between where our bodies were connected and applied pressure to my clit.

"That's it, baby. You were made for me. Soak my fucking cock, beautiful." As he guided my movements with one hand and stroked my core with the other, I felt my body tense as I fell over the edge into another blissful orgasm.

Wade thrusted a couple more times and then grunted loudly as his release spilled into me, flooding where our bodies were connected.

Realization hit both of us as we recognized that, in the heat of the moment, we hadn't thought to grab a condom.

"Fuck, Sunshine. I'm sorry. I wasn't thinking."

I put a hand on his chest and smiled as he sat up straighter, wrapping his arms around my waist, still inside of me.

"It's okay. After that first time, I went and had an IUD put in. We're good."

His sigh of relief as he rested his head on my collarbone had me laughing lightly. In mock exasperation, I brought my hand to my chest with a gasp. "What, you don't want me barefoot and pregnant in your kitchen?"

He cut his eyes up at me as he growled, flipping us so I was beneath him. Neither of us was worried about the mess we were making as his release dripped between my thighs.

He trailed feather-light kisses along my chest, grazing my sensitive nipples with his teeth as he looked up from between my breasts to where I lay before him.

"There is nothing I would love more after a long day of working out on the ranch than seeing you barefoot and pregnant in my kitchen. But this isn't 1950, and you aren't a housewife. When and if you want to have babies, I'll pump you so full of my cum you'll be leaking for weeks. Until then, I'm happy just to practice. After all, I *should* probably court you and ask your father for your hand in marriage."

I giggled, swatting at his chest as he laughed heartily.

"Wade Daniels, are you saying that you're currently sullying my virtue by deflowering me?" I asked with an exaggerated gasp.

He groaned, rolling over and lying beside me, propping himself up on an elbow as he brushed a stray tendril of hair from my face. The way he looked at me, so full of wonder and love, and knowing that the same sentiment was reflected in my gaze, had my heart content that things were going to be okay.

"All I'm saying, Rayna Cortez, is that you're it for me. Always have been and always will be."

"Right back at ya, Waddle," I joked, and with a growl, he rolled on top of me, pinning me down as he placed open-mouthed kisses along my neck.

Even knowing we only had the empty house for another

hour or so, neither of us wanted to leave that bed, content with making up for all the time lost to circumstances within *and* beyond our control.

WADE

"THIS IS FUCKING WEIRD," Max grumbled from across the room as I sat on the sofa with Ray perched on my lap.

We had spent the last hour lost in each other as we mapped every inch of one another's skin with our lips and reverent touches. It was surreal to finally have Ray in all the ways I'd only dreamed about for the last fifteen years.

Now that we'd had a taste of each other, we were disgustingly insatiable.

Everyone insisted on a quiet night at the big house for my homecoming. Stella made a lasagna that rivaled Ma's, and she had picked up a small cake to celebrate Max's, Charlie's, and my birthdays, since I hadn't been there for the first celebration.

Charlie was more than happy to indulge in more cake; after all, what two-year-old wouldn't be?

Surrounded by my family, I couldn't have been more at peace.

With my girl in my lap, my brother and his wife happily married and expecting a second baby, my niece playing with toy horses on the floor, and Pops content to watch all the chaos erupt around him, nothing felt more right.

I knew I still had a long way to go, and lots of groveling for the way I'd treated my family, but I'd take things one day at a time.

"Mass Da! Bad word," Charlie scolded as Max dug in the back of his jeans for his wallet, grabbing one of the bills from a thick stack between the leather. I cocked an eyebrow in his direction in silent question.

"I started keeping a stack of ones in my wallet because I can't seem to break the habit." He chuckled as Charlie grabbed the dollar from between his outstretched fingers and put it in the tiny pocket of her little Wranglers. That girl was going places.

I shook my head with a gentle laugh as she went back to playing with her toys, unfazed at how easily she'd swindled a dollar from my brother.

I took note of the number of things the little girl had spread around the living room. Building blocks were haphazardly stacked along the fireplace mantel, tiny shoes were thrown in the foyer as if taking the time to put them right side up was too much work, and a pile of tiny laundry sat on one end of the sofa.

What should have made me feel like an outsider in my own home instead gave me the confidence to broach a long overdue conversation. I cleared my throat, garnering the attention of everyone in the room.

Ray looked down at me and cocked her own eyebrow in question. I winked back at her, and she smiled, trusting me implicitly with whatever scheme I had up my sleeve.

"I wanna talk with y'all about something real quick," I started, making sure everyone was paying attention. Every set of eyes in the room was trained on me, and I breathed slowly, fighting the gnawing anxiety that started to build, realizing I was the center of everyone's attention.

Ray's hand found mine, and she squeezed gently three times, effectively slowing my heart rate.

"I know we really haven't had a chance to talk about it much, but I wanted to run something by you two," I said, my eyes darting to Max and Stella. Max nodded softly, and Stella's head tilted in a questioning gaze.

"I think it's time I moved out."

"What?" Max asked as if it was the most absurd suggestion in the world. The two of us had only ever had each other growing up, often sharing a room not out of necessity, but desire.

We were thick as thieves, and even though the thought of living apart filled me with a little trepidation, it was time that he and Stella had a space to build their own family.

"You're having another baby, and I think it's time I stood on my own two feet." Ray squeezed my hand in silent solidarity as a proud smile pulled at the corners of her mouth.

"But where will you go?" he asked, and I sensed a small amount of anxiety building in his voice.

"I own the back ten acres of the ranch, just as you own the other ten. I always figured when the time was right that we'd build houses side by side and raise our families together. But there's no need for you to uproot the home you've built here with your wife and daughter."

I could see Pops nodding from the armchair in the corner of the room in silent solidarity. I had talked with him before I left for the treatment center about the possibility of building on that land, and he'd been overwhelmingly supportive.

I knew it was the right time.

Max and Stella deserved to have a space that was wholly theirs, where they could raise their kids without their Uncle Wade and his girlfriend hanging around.

"So, you're going to build on the back half of the ranch?" Max asked, putting the pieces together. Stella's hand found his just as Ray's had found mine in support.

Both of us were lucky to have found the best women. Each of them complemented us in ways that we could only dream of.

"That's the plan. I've got some savings built up from rodeo events, even after footing the bill for the treatment facility. I haven't used any of it over the last couple of years, as the money from training sessions was plenty to keep things running around here. I haven't had a chance to reach out to builders about costs and timeline, but I'm sure we can find something that works around our schedules."

Max's hand softly went to the tiny swell of Stella's belly where she was growing their child. The love that passed between them was hard to miss as my brother looked at his woman as if she hung the moon and the stars. I knew that look because I imagined it was the same unfiltered bliss that passed across my face when I looked at Ray.

"We can be flexible. Even if it means things will be tight around here for a little bit until construction on your place is finished." His smile was tight-lipped, and I could tell that this was going to be tough for both of us, but we'd only be a stone's throw or ATV ride away from each other. "I'm proud of you, brother."

Tears welled up on my lower eyelashes, and I blinked rapidly to keep them from falling. Crying about my trauma in the confines of a therapist's office was one thing. Sitting in front of my entire family and the girl I loved while I became a blubbering mess was another.

"Fuck, brother," I choked out as the words caught in my throat through the emotions I was desperately trying to keep at bay.

"Unca Wade, bad word," Charlie scolded from her spot on the floor, her tiny finger waggling in my direction. Everyone chuckled, breaking the tension.

"Give the girl two fucking dollars, Max," I said through a laugh. "Unca Wade doesn't have any dollar bills, and you've got enough to fund the rent at a stri—"

Ray's hand slapped across my mouth as her eyes widened, threatening me silently if I continued that sentence. I licked her palm, and she squealed, pulling her hand back and wiping it on her shorts.

"Gross!" she exclaimed, laughing as she feigned disgust.

"Oh, don't act like you don't like it when my tongue—"

"And on that note! It's time for cake," she said quickly, standing from my lap and scooting over to sit on the floor and pull Charlie into her arms, effectively shutting me up.

Stella retreated to the kitchen, grabbing the small grocery store cake she had haphazardly put three candles in. It wasn't lost on me that this was the first birthday we had truly been able to experience together, and the weight that the day we all shared would stick around as time went on.

"I've got a suggestion," I said out of the blue. Every pair of eyes was trained on me as Stella stood poised over the candles, a long lighter in her hand. "How about we celebrate the three of us on this day, every year? There's so much negativity around our actual birthday; how about we create a new holiday? One that's filled with family and happiness."

"WadCharMass!" Charlie screeched, squishing all of our

names together like a Frankenstein version of Christmas. "Our day. Three a-mee-goo-s." She said the last word slowly, enunciating each syllable as if she were piecing it together in her mind.

Ray beamed with pride behind her as she butchered her way through the Spanish.

"Amigos, pequeño," Ray corrected. I watched as Charlie tried to emulate the way Ray pronounced the word with practiced ease, and her brow scrunched in frustration.

"Don't worry, little one. You'll get it," Max encouraged from his spot on the couch. Charlie rolled the word around on her tongue, trying to say it right. She was determined, and that little furrow between her brow was the spitting image of Stella when she was frustrated.

Charlie stood from Ray's lap, having given up on the mental Spanish lesson, and walked over to where I was sitting. She climbed up onto my lap, settling herself facing me on one of my legs as she looked me directly in the eye, a serious expression marring her features.

"Unca Wade," she said as if she were about to give me the fiercest lecture I'd ever heard.

"Yes, little one?" I prompted.

"You train horseys, right?"

"Yes…" I said hesitantly, confused as to where her line of questioning was coming from. She placed both of her tiny hands on my cheeks, pulling my attention directly to her.

"I need you train Bubbles Flower Pancake."

"Um…Okay. What is a Bubbles Flower Pancake?" I asked, confused as I looked around the room. Pops sat in his armchair, chuckling while Max threw himself back on the sofa in exasperation. Stella and Ray both hid their laughter behind their hands.

"Pops got me horsey!" she screeched, and my eyes widened as I looked over to my dad, who just shrugged his shoulders as if he hadn't just spent a giant hunk of change on a horse for a two-year-old.

"Welcome to the shitshow," Max groaned from across the room.

"MASS DA. BAD WORD," Charlie screeched. She held out her hand for another dollar, clearly frustrated at his lack of effort to quell his potty mouth.

There wasn't any place I'd rather be, shitshow or not. This was my family, my life, and my future all sitting here in this living room, and I couldn't have been happier.

WADE

THE AWKWARD MOMENT when you're sitting across the dining room table from the town sheriff, a man you admire greatly, the man who also saved your life, insinuating you've been fucking his daughter, was a situation I would have greatly loved to have avoided.

I had been home for almost two weeks, and acclimating back to everyday living had been a challenge.

Most of my trainees had been fine with Sterling taking over their sessions, but for some reason, Izzy had thrown the world's biggest hissy fit. Even Ray had mentioned how out of character it was for Izzy to be so defiant, especially when it came to her rodeo prep.

She was slated to race in the NFR in Vegas in a little over a month, so every moment was pivotal in her training.

Two weeks of playing catch-up while battling the stresses of ranch life made things beyond exhausting. I'd fallen into bed each night, wrapped in Ray's embrace as I drifted off into a nightmare-free slumber.

Neither of us wanted to be apart for long, so she'd all but

officially moved into the big house with me until construction on our place was finished.

Things were a little tight, but we made it work. After all, it was only temporary. After telling Max my plans to move onto the back ten acres of the property, I reached out to a local builder, someone we'd been friends with in high school, and inquired about getting plans drawn up.

Ray and I had pored over floor plans, design features, architectural styles, and so much more over the last week that my head was still spinning and my eyes were struggling to uncross. But watching my girl in her element had always been one of my favorite pastimes.

Truthfully, she could have said she wanted to live in a cardboard box on the side of the road, and I would have found the sturdiest one and staked it down wherever she'd asked.

Things had fallen into an easy rhythm as Ray and I adjusted to being a couple, rather than just friends. But the best part of our relationship was just that: being friends first gave us a solid foundation to build from.

Neither of us was without our faults, but it was easier for us to move past a disagreement since we knew each other backward and forward. She was my right-hand man, my better half, and the woman who could bring me to my knees with just a look.

That same look is how I ended up sitting across from her dad, awkwardly talking about my intentions with his daughter.

Emmanuel Cortez wasn't an inherently scary man. He was tall and thin with a thick head of dark hair and the same caramel skin as his daughter.

Yet, as he sat across the table from me, I felt like a

chihuahua trembling under his gaze. Neither of us had spoken yet as Ray finished prepping dinner.

She had somehow talked everyone in their household into a Friday night family dinner. Although over half of their family didn't live at home anymore and weren't able to come for a simple meal, she'd made sure that the twins, Benny, and her father made themselves available.

I'm sure this was her twisted way of indoctrinating me into their unit, but I couldn't deny I was a little terrified of the man seated in front of me.

"So, Wade." Emmanuel spoke slowly, drawing out each word as he crossed his arms across his chest and leaned back in his kitchen chair. I couldn't tell if he was playing good cop, bad cop, or if he was silently judging me across the weathered wood table.

"Yes, sir," I replied, sitting up straighter and fighting the urge to fiddle with the silverware lined up in front of me.

"You and my daughter?" His question was simple, but the answer was not. I wanted to express in great detail how much Ray meant to me, how much I cherished and loved her unconditionally, how often I had already thought about my ring on her finger, and her carrying my last name.

Instead, I settled for cordial, not looking to overwhelm the man since this was his oldest, his baby girl, the first one to be in a serious relationship—well, one we actually saw making it long term.

Izzy could insist six ways to Sunday that she and Tanner were headed to the altar, but they'd been engaged just under a year, and nothing about the two of them together made a lick of sense.

"Yes, sir," I nodded, taking a sip of the water in front of

me. Emmanuel casually reached for his beer, taking a sip without breaking eye contact.

I could tell why he was such a revered part of the law enforcement community; the man could make even the toughest of criminals break with his set jaw and unrelenting stare.

"I'm not going to lie and say I'm not worried, but I also can't say I didn't see this coming," he said, setting his beer back down with a definitive thump. Finally breaking eye contact, I took a deep inhale, thankful for the absence of his weighted gaze.

I'd never met the parents of a girl I'd been dating before, but I'd also never been seriously involved with anyone.

Even though I'd known Emmanuel for the majority of my life, he was no longer looking at me like his daughter's best friend. He was scrutinizing me as the man who would be responsible for her well-being for the remainder of her life.

I could only imagine the emotional toll this was taking on him, relinquishing his baby girl to the hands of another man.

"Sir, I want you to know that I love your daughter." I cleared my throat, sitting up straighter in my seat. "Ray has been my best friend for most of my life. She's been there for me in some of the happiest and, subsequently, the hardest moments I've ever lived through. She is the strongest, most loyal, and beautiful woman I have ever had the pleasure of being around. I can't promise you I won't fuck up. I'm human. What I can promise you is that for the rest of my life, it would be my honor to spend each day reminding her of her worth, cheering her on in all of her dreams and goals, and standing behind her every step of the way.

Your daughter is the reason I am half the man I am today. She has taught me to love without reservation, find the beauty in each day, chase after the things that are most important, and what it's like to be worthy of being loved."

I watched as he took in my words, his eyes downcast toward his lap, where he turned the gold band of his wedding ring around his finger.

In all the time since Ray's mom had died, he still kept his ring on. I hadn't really grasped the idea of a love that left you missing half of your heart until I stopped fighting what I felt for Ray.

"I'd like to ask for your blessing, sir. I wholeheartedly plan to marry your daughter. Not now, maybe not even a year from now, but as soon as *she* is ready, I'd like to spend the rest of forever with her."

He silently nodded, and I didn't miss the single tear that tracked down his cheek, even if he did his best to hide his emotions and wipe it away.

"You have it," he said softly, lifting his gaze back to mine. Swirling through his eyes, I saw hints of pride, pain, and happiness. "I'll have you know—that square fucker, Tanner, didn't have the balls to come and ask to marry my Isabella. So, thank you. Thank you for being a respectable young man that I'd be proud to have as part of our family… officially. After all, your ass has been hanging around this house for the better part of seventeen years. You're tough to get rid of, Wade Daniels."

Both of us chuckled as I stood, walking around the table and extending my hand out to him. He stood, gripping my hand in a firm handshake before pulling me into a tight hug.

"Welcome to the family, son. But if you hurt my daughter, I know the best places in and around town to hide a body and how to get away with it," he said, pulling back and looking me dead in the eyes.

A nervous chuckle crawled up my throat but died when I noticed the seriousness behind his gaze.

"Yes, sir." I nodded just as Ray breezed in from the kitchen, a pan of enchiladas in her hands.

"Dinner's ready!" she called out to the house as she set the dinner in the center of the table. Looking between her father and me, her brow furrowed in confusion, and she asked, "Why does it look like someone died in here?"

I let out another nervous chuckle as I placed a gentle kiss on her cheek, heading back to my spot at the table. Thundering footsteps echoed through the halls as Sofie, Lucy, and Benny made their way to the dining room.

Ray served everyone with pride, having orchestrated this whole ordeal. She filled each of the kids' plates, even though they were completely capable of doing so themselves.

She placed a plate in front of her father, leaned down to kiss him on the cheek, and then did the same thing to me before grabbing her own dinner and sitting beside me.

If there was one trait I loved most about Rayna Cortez, it was her ability to love and care for those around her unconditionally. She'd been thrust into adulthood way before she should have been due to circumstances out of anyone's control, but instead of letting life get her down, she grabbed the bull by the horns and took it for a ride.

There was no other cowgirl I'd like to spend riding through the rodeo of life with than the woman seated across from me, smiling at all the love and life that surrounded us.

RAY

DECEMBER HAD ROLLED AROUND before we knew it, bringing with it quieter mornings around the ranch and cooler temperatures. It generally didn't get *cold* in Georgia until around the end of January, but the cooler temperatures meant that the workload around the ranch had slowed down, and I could spend more mornings relaxing instead of being awakened by heavy footfalls and horses' thundering hooves outside my window.

That morning, though, I should have already been up and dressed, bags packed in the truck, heading to the airport.

Instead, I was lazily woken up with my boyfriend's head between my thighs, bringing me to the brink of an orgasm before I even opened my eyes.

What a way to start the day.

"Babe, we've gotta get going," I panted through moans as the familiar pressure of release coursed down my spine. I tugged at Wade's hair, still shorter on the sides and longer on the top, urging him from between my thighs before we were late for the airport.

"Sunshine, I'm a man starved, and the only source of food around is this delicious pussy."

I chuckled, throwing an arm over my eyes as he relentlessly brought me nearer and nearer to the edge of an orgasm. I felt my core tightening as he focused his tongue on my clit, pushing his fingers inside of me and pressing on that sweet spot that he knew would have me careening over the edge.

My back arched off the mattress as my thighs tightened around Wade's head. He greedily lapped at my core, savoring each pulse and flutter of my pussy.

As the waves of my orgasm faded, he pressed a gentle kiss to my inner thigh, edging his way up the bed to lie beside me.

"Good morning, Sunshine," he whispered, placing a tender kiss to my lips, allowing me to taste the remnants of my release. I stretched and wrapped my arms around his neck as he snaked his around my naked waist.

"Morning," I responded, laying my head gently on his bicep. Clearly, neither of us was in a hurry to get moving, content to laze the day away tangled in each other's arms.

A heavy pounding slammed on the door, and Wade groaned, throwing his head back in frustration.

"Hey, lovebirds, up and at 'em. We've got a plane to catch," Max called through the door, relentlessly knocking so we couldn't ignore him.

"We're up!" Wade yelled at his brother, throwing off the covers as he rolled over and placed his feet on the hardwood floor. "Keep banging on that door, and you're gonna catch something, and it won't be a plane," he grumbled.

I chuckled, extricating myself from the plush warmth of the bed and stretching in all my naked glory, while Wade's eyes drank me in from the other side of the bed.

"Keep teasing me like that, Sunshine, and we won't make that fucking plane." He grumbled. I sauntered over to his side of the bed, placing both palms on his muscled chest and standing on my tiptoes to whisper in his ear.

"Be a good boy, and I might help you join the Mile High Club later." A low feral growl left his throat as he darted out his arms, attempting to grab me around the waist. I giggled as I twirled away from him, heading for the en suite bathroom to get ready.

"You've got thirty minutes!" Max called grumpily from the other side of the door, one last tap of his knuckles for good measure.

"I only need ten!" Wade called back, chasing after me. He barely closed the door before setting me on the vanity and sinking inside of me.

FORTY-FIVE MINUTES and two orgasms later, we arrived at the airport and made our way through security. An hour or so after that, we were boarding the commercial flight headed for Las Vegas. We were all heading to the National Finals Rodeo, where Izzy would be competing in the barrel racing finals.

She left earlier that week, having to drive cross-country, pulling a trailer with Oakley behind her. Dad nearly lost his mind when she insisted she go alone instead of having someone ride along with her.

She said she needed the time to get into the competition

headspace, and the quiet would do her some good. He hadn't been able to take time off to come watch her, but we promised to take lots of pictures and videos.

We were a little confused as to why her fiancé, Tanner, wasn't making the effort to go with her, but no one dared question it.

Wade made mention of how important it was for a rider to stick to a routine and ritual before a competition. Apparently, they were a devoutly superstitious bunch, and deviating from a routine could throw off their entire ride.

The four-hour plane ride was uneventful, much to my dismay.

Apparently, it was Stella's first time on a flight, and morning sickness was kicking her ass, so I had ended up holding her hair back as she made good use of the included sick bags.

I shot Wade an apologetic look over the top of Stella's head as I rubbed gentle circles on her back, which he grumpily accepted. I'd make it up to him later.

After we checked into the hotel, Max and Stella retreated to their room, wanting to call Charlie and Stella's mom, who she'd recently reconnected with, who had stayed behind in Firefly Cove.

Wade and I quickly changed out of our airplane clothes and made our way out to the strip to find something to eat.

Although both of us were exhausted, and the time change would kick our asses in the morning, we walked hand in hand down the busy sidewalk, taking in the sights. We had been to Vegas previously; I'd come out when Wade competed in his second-to-last NFR at twenty-five.

"What cha' thinkin' about?" I asked, noticing the Cheshire grin that had spread across his face.

"Do you remember the last time we came to Vegas?"

"How could I forget, hubby?" I chuckled as I tucked myself into his side.

WADE - 25 YEARS OLD

WINNING a buckle at the NFR in Las Vegas was a cowboy's equivalent of earning a Super Bowl ring. There was no greater accomplishment than being named one of the best in the nation.

With the win came perks: a huge gold buckle you could wear with pride, sponsorship and brand deal opportunities, a huge winnings check, and buckle bunnies galore.

What was better than any other event I'd competed in before? I won the fucking buckle, and the girl I couldn't stop thinking about was there to see it.

No matter that she wasn't my girlfriend, I wouldn't be taking her home at the end of the night, and she'd forever friend-zoned me. She was there, cheering me on in lieu of my family, who hadn't been able to make it, and that's all that mattered.

We were both currently drunk off our asses at some night-club on the strip, and Ray was dancing to obnoxiously loud techno music like we weren't from the middle of nowhere, Georgia.

We definitely weren't in our element—me in my cowboy hat, starched Wranglers, pearl snap button-down, and boots, and her in a frilly sundress, her hair in a high ponytail, and white rhinestone boots of her own.

The majority of women here were dressed in skimpy, form-fitting dresses that left nothing to the imagination; then there was Ray, shining bright in the middle of the packed dance floor like the shiny beacon of sunlight she was.

She danced with reckless abandon, moving her hips in a circle to the beat. She was mesmerizing to watch, but I averted my eyes because I wasn't supposed to be staring at my best friend like she was the most beautiful girl in the place, even if she was.

Catching her attention, I waved her over from where I stood on the edge of the dance floor. The bass thumped as she made her way to me, every man's eyes watching the subtle sashay of her hips and heart-shaped ass.

I cut my eyes in their direction in warning, but this wasn't Jack's back at home, and I wasn't a threat to them.

"Why don't we find something a little more our speed?" I shouted over the raging music, hiking my thumb over my shoulder toward the exit. She leaned in closer to hear what I was saying, but I could barely hear myself think, much less have a conversation.

Grabbing her hand, I pulled her off the dance floor to the edge of the bar, where it was marginally quieter. I signaled the bartender for two glasses of water, and he filled two small plastic cups with the soda gun before shoving them in our direction.

Clearly, their priority was to keep people drunk, not hydrated.

I leaned forward, my lips nearly pressed to the shell of

Ray's ear as I repeated the question. "Why don't we find something a little more our speed?"

She nodded gently, taking my hand and pulling me toward the exit. Once we were outside, the air flooded our lungs with much-needed coolness. We both relished the breath of fresh air as we got our bearings back from the sensory overload we left behind.

"Wow, that place was insane!" Ray shouted, not having quite regained her hearing yet. I chuckled, taking her hand and walking away from the club and down the strip.

I'd seen a honky-tonk bar down that way earlier, and I thought we'd enjoy that more than the earthquake-inducing bass we'd just endured.

Both of us walked in companionable silence, letting our ears readjust to normal levels of hearing. As we stumbled down the sidewalk, both of us drunk enough to be feeling good, but neither drunk enough to make shitty decisions, we came to the heavy wooden doors of the cowboy bar.

The place was packed with cowboys and cowgirls, everyone wearing some form of hat and boots. It was definitely more our speed.

The bouncer at the door checked our IDs, scrutinizing Ray's a little longer than mine as if she were freshly twenty-one. After verifying we were of age, he ushered us inside.

The bar couldn't have been more stereotypical country, with its steer skulls, cowhide pool tables, lasso-wrapped bar stools, and Hank Williams on the old-school jukebox in the back corner. We made our way through the crowd, heading toward the bar to snag drinks.

I signaled the bartender, ordering both of us a whiskey shot and a beer. After all, whiskey before beer, you're in the clear. The volume was less oppressive as we each grabbed our shot glasses, ready to cheers.

"Cheers to the heat! Not the kind that brings down shacks and shanties, but to the kind that brings down panties," I yelled, earning a chorus of cheers and clinking glasses as all those within earshot toasted along with us.

I tapped my small shot glass to Ray's as she laughed loudly. I smiled at the warmth that bloomed in my chest at the sound.

Fuck, I needed to get laid.

THE SUNLIGHT WAS relentless as it blasted through the curtains I'd apparently forgotten to close the night before. Rolling over with a groan, my hand met the warm softness of another body, and I froze.

I'd had my share of one-night stands over the years. I'd taken many buckle bunnies back to my hotel rooms.

Never in my entire life had I let one sleep over. That crossed a line into something more than just sex, and it was a hard line in the sand for me.

Refusing to open my eyes, I lay perfectly still, hoping I was imagining the feeling of a woman's body next to mine. I hoped and prayed I hadn't made a huge mistake, and that it was Ray sleeping next to me.

That would have been a bigger can of worms to open that I didn't feel like dealing with, especially with how shitty I felt due to the obnoxious amount of whiskey I drank.

"Good morning, stud," the woman purred, rolling over

and scratching her long nails along my chest. She nuzzled up close to me, and I could smell the sickly-sweet scent of too much perfume mixed with an insane amount of hairspray.

"Uh, mornin'," I mumbled back.

"What a wild night. You're quite the stallion," she teased as she ran one of her long nails over my nipple, causing a pained hiss to escape my lips.

"Yeah, wild night, um, excuse me, I've gotta take a piss." I fumbled out of the bed, snagging my phone from where I'd thrown it haphazardly on the nightstand, sending up a silent prayer that there was enough charge to send out an SOS text.

Slamming the door to the bathroom behind me, I unlocked my phone and pulled up the contact for the one person I could trust to get me out of a shitty situation, no questions asked.

The dial tone rang once, twice. "Fuck, Wade. How much did we drink last night? I feel like I got hit by a truck. Izzy didn't even make it back to the room. She sent me a text letting me know she'd met someone at the rodeo and would meet up with us later before the events."

A sigh of relief flowed past my lips at hearing Ray's voice on the other end of the line. "Sunshine, I need your help."

"Are you okay?" I could hear the frantic edge to her voice and the rustling of sheets on the other end.

I willed my mind to avoid conjuring images of Ray, half naked in her bed, hair mussed and hungover. Unfortunately, Las Vegas luck clearly wasn't on my side because my dick was rock hard beneath my briefs.

"Yeah, I'm fine," I said quickly. "I fucked up."

"Wade, you're scaring me," she said softly.

"Apparently, I took a girl home last night. I normally don't let women stay the night, but I must have been seriously fucked up. I don't remember much after dancing at the cowboy bar on the strip and then walking you back to your room. I must have gone back out and ended up bringing someone back with me." I groaned as the fluorescent lights of the bathroom assaulted my senses when I flicked the switch to get a look at myself.

There were claw marks down my chest and back, clearly from the woman's talons that she called nails. I had a giant purple hickey on the right side of my neck, and lipstick smeared all over my face. I looked like a rodeo clown who had gotten in a fight with a bobcat.

"And how do you want me to help?" she asked pointedly, clearly irritated at my lack of responsibility.

"I don't know! Come up with something! Please," I begged.

Her sigh of frustration was followed by the clanging of a belt buckle as I assumed she was putting her clothes on. I willed my dick to stand down as she rustled around on the other end of the line.

"Give me five minutes, and somehow slide one of the room keys under the door."

AFTER A HUNDRED EXTRICATIONS of Daisy June's, as I'd learned her name was, hand from my dick and five excruciating minutes, the electronic lock on the door whirred and unlatched with a click.

I watched the woman's eyebrows furrow in confusion as she tried to put the pieces together of who might be entering my room, especially someone who so clearly had a key.

"Babe, I know I'm not supposed to see you the day before the wedding, but—What the FUCK!"

Ray's screech as she entered the room had Daisy June scrambling off the bed, grabbing for any item of clothing she could find scattered across the floor. She was thankfully in her underwear and a T-shirt of mine that barely covered her tits and ass as she gathered her belongings.

"You shitbag!" she screamed at me, tossing one of the pillows that had fallen off the bed in my direction. "You're married?!"

"Technically engaged?" I asked, looking in Ray's direction for confirmation. She gave me a sly nod as she struggled to hold in her laughter, watching the woman fumble around on the floor.

"Fuck you!" Daisy June added and turned toward Ray in womanly solidarity. "Good luck, honey. He wasn't that great of a fuck anyway," she spat as she stormed from the room, slamming the door behind her.

As soon as the door shut, both of us burst into hysterical laughter. I groaned, gripping my head and falling back on the pillows as the throbbing pain bloomed behind my eyes.

Ray walked over and flopped herself down on the bed beside me, a similar wince escaping her lips from the pounding in her own skull.

"So, what time's the wedding?" I joked, only to be met with the plush thud of a pillow as it whacked me directly in the face.

WADE

MY PULSE THUNDERED with excitement as I entered the Thomas and Mack Center for the start of the ten-day-long rodeo event. The smell of the pungent, wet dirt of the arena wafted through the air like a familiar perfume.

I stopped right outside the grandstands, closing my eyes and relishing the feeling of being back here after such a long hiatus. It was like being greeted by an old friend.

There were days I missed the rodeo: the adrenaline coursing through your system as you wait for your time to shine, the camaraderie, the thrill of a new buckle added to your stash, the drinking, smoking, and fucking.

It was an aphrodisiac. But that life was behind me, and I wouldn't change things if I could. I was happy sitting beside the love of my life, watching one of my riders compete in the biggest event of their career and possibly their life.

Ray's warm hand landed on my forearm, and I opened my eyes with an easy smile.

"You okay?" she asked softly, a concerned look brushing across her features. I took her hand gently in mine and squeezed three times as I pulled her toward me and pressed a tender kiss to her forehead.

"Yeah, Sunshine. Never better." I breathed against her skin.

My phone buzzed in my pocket with a text, and I pulled it out, thumbing it open to read the message.

Sterling: BR up 1. IC riding 3.

I laughed at his inability to type out a full sentence, but I knew exactly what he was trying to say.

"Barrel racers are up first. Izzy's riding third," I relayed to Ray as we scoured the crowd for the rest of our crew. Max and Stella had wandered off to check out some of the food vendors before the event started.

Ray's arms wrapped around my waist as she settled herself into my embrace. I could feel the nervous energy radiating from her. It was one thing to experience the rodeo as a best friend. It was another thing to have a family member competing.

Even though barrel racing was generally safe compared to some of the other rodeo events, riders and their horses were still pushed to their limits as they raced for the best time.

Anything could go wrong at any minute, and I just hoped that at the end of the day, Izzy and Oakley had trained enough to score decently and come home unscathed.

"You nervous?" I asked, running my hands up and down Ray's back.

"Yeah," she whispered. "I just worry. That's my baby sister out there, and as much as I trust Oakley, I can't help this gut feeling that something's off."

She shook her head as if she were being ridiculous, and I

gripped her chin between my thumb and index finger, holding her attention.

"Do you want me to go down and check on her? I will if it will make you feel better," I offered, genuinely concerned about anxiety radiating off her.

"No, I'm sure she's fine. Sterling would have said something if she seemed off, right?"

"I'd hope so, but I'm not sure how close he's willing to get to that spitfire right before an event, Sunshine. She's pretty scary on a daily basis. Add in the stress and anxiety before the biggest rodeo of her career? I'd stay clear out of her way."

Ray chuckled, standing on her tiptoes to press a gentle kiss to my lips. I snaked one arm around her waist, pulling her flush to my body, and deepened the kiss just a fraction.

Before things got too hot and heavy, I pulled back, placing another tender kiss to her plush lips. I could have spent the rest of my life with my lips on hers, but we had a rodeo to watch and a cowgirl to cheer on.

Spotting Max and Stella behind Ray, I spun her around and tapped her on the ass to head toward the stands. She turned her head over her shoulder and flashed me a wicked grin that screamed of all the dirty things we planned to do later.

I subtly adjusted myself in my jeans and groaned as she walked toward my brother and his wife, her Wranglers molding to her curves and thighs like they were specially made for her.

We all climbed the grandstand stairs and found our seats. The view from up there was magnificent. The arena floor was freshly raked, dirt spiraling around in even swirls. The barrels had been placed in their appropriate spots, each one labeled with the name of the business that sponsored it.

The crowd grew louder with excited chatter as the announcer instructed everyone to take their seats.

Ray's hand found mine from her spot beside me. Her ability to read my emotions without my having to say a word was astounding.

We were anxious for different reasons, and we leaned on each other in silent support as riders and their horses took their places in order of turn.

Even from up high, I spotted Izzy immediately. She and Oakley were third in line, just as Sterling said. She sat stoically, zeroed in on her pre-race ritual, visualizing the cloverleaf pattern she and Oakley would run.

After the national anthem was played and everyone returned to their seats, the first racer shot out of the gate. A dappled mare with a short, stocky rider rounded each barrel, kicking up dirt behind them. They managed to time out at fifteen seconds, which wasn't anything to write home about.

Back at the ranch's makeshift arena, Izzy was consistently running high thirteens, on a slow day, a low fourteen. She was hoping for at least a high thirteen to place among the top three, carrying her through to the two other rounds.

She would race a total of three times that week, and the average of the three scores would determine who would take home the national championship.

The second rider narrowly missed one of the barrels, knocking it over with the edge of their stirrup. That would incur them a five-second penalty, which was a death sentence in a high-stakes event like this one.

Izzy was up next, and I watched closely as she entered the

alley where she and Oakley would gain their momentum ahead of their turns.

Something was off. Oakley looked uncomfortable as she danced back and forth on her feet. Izzy ran her hand down her neck, trying to calm her, but Oakley wasn't having it.

Thankfully, their time didn't start until they crossed the start line, and Izzy was able to get Oakley zeroed in on her task. They shot out of the gate, and the clock started ticking. The crowd cheered as Izzy and Oakley took to their cloverleaf.

They rounded the first barrel with ease, Izzy's body fluid as she used her heels to kick Oakley's midsection, encouraging her to run faster. As they rounded the second barrel, Oakley's gait faltered, and Izzy didn't have time to adjust for the shift as she slid to the side, falling out of the saddle and hitting the ground with a thud.

The arena went silent as we all watched with bated breath, waiting for Izzy to get up.

One second.

Two seconds.

She still didn't stand. Ray gripped my shirt as she clung to me desperately, watching her little sister lie lifeless in the dirt. I met my brother's eyes and gave him a subtle nod as I transferred Ray to his arms and raced down the stairs toward the arena.

"Stay with Max. I've got her," I yelled behind me.

I could hear Ray's wails as she fought against my brother's grip, thrashing her body in an attempt to follow me.

The truth was, though, if Izzy didn't get up, I didn't want that to be the last vision Ray saw of her sister.

I knew she would be furious, but I'd rather that than the

mental image of her sister's dead body being played on repeat in her mind every single time she closed her eyes.

RAY

I WAS REALLY tired of everything going right in our lives, and then finding myself sitting beside one of my family members in a hospital.

Thankfully, Izzy hadn't been seriously hurt. She'd been knocked unconscious when she fell off Oakley and was sporting a nasty concussion, but it hadn't stopped her from asking every five minutes when she could leave.

"For the millionth time, Isabella Cortez, you are *not* going home until the doctor releases you, and he has made it exceptionally clear that you're going to be here for at least a full night to monitor your concussion symptoms," I scolded, standing beside her bed and tucking the blankets and sheets back around her body from where she'd thrown them off, insisting that she was checking herself out against medical advice.

"I'm fine, I need to go check on Oakley," she grumbled, pushing herself to a seated position with a sharp hiss as pain radiated through her head. I gently pushed her back against the raised bed and shot her a look that said, "I'm not fucking around."

Her sigh of frustration was loud enough to be heard from the hallway as Wade came back into the room carrying two cups of coffee, chuckling at her dramatics.

I had been furious at him for leaving me in the stands back at the arena to go check on Izzy, but after he'd had a chance to get her situated and we'd started following the ambulance in an Uber, he'd explained why he'd done it.

Although I was still frustrated at him for trying to shield me from the truth—I was a big girl, after all—but I couldn't be mad at him for having my best interests at heart.

He knew better than anyone how sideways rodeo events could go, and he was trying to do me a favor by keeping me from seeing something that may or may not have haunted me for the rest of my life.

At the end of the day, I loved him for doing what he could to care for my sister and protect me at the same time.

"As your trainer, I'll have to agree with your sister on this one. You've got a nasty concussion, Izzy, and they can turn from bad to worse quickly. It's better for you to stay here and be monitored overnight. I had Sterling head down to the stables and check on Oakley. She's spooked, but physically fine. I've already got a farrier lined up to come check out her shoes in the morning, and the vet is heading over there tonight to run a few tests. We've got her."

My sister's shoulders slumped in defeat as she'd been properly chastised. She'd been fighting with us for the last five hours to let her check out and go back to the arena. I feared, though, that if we let that happen, she'd demand a re-ride and do serious damage to herself or her horse.

She was reckless when it came to winning, and the NFR

had taken so much to prepare for, that not placing was a hard pill for her to swallow.

A knock sounded on the door to her room as it slowly eased open. Slightly shocked, I watched as Tanner let himself in, coming to Izzy's bedside and taking her hand.

"Babe, I'm so sorry I'm just getting here. Finding a flight last minute was insane, not to mention obnoxiously expensive, but I'm here. How are you? Do the doctors think you'll make a full recovery?"

Wade and I looked at one another, rolling our eyes at his exaggeration of the severity of Izzy's condition. He was acting like she was dying, and it had taken everything in him to make it here before she croaked.

When we'd spoken to him on the phone earlier, we'd let him know what was happening and made sure to tell him that it wasn't necessary for him to fly all the way out there, and that we'd keep him updated.

"I'm fine, Tanner. I thought we told you that you didn't need to fly all the way out here."

The way her body recoiled at his touch had me on edge. Something about him had always given me the ick.

I didn't know if it was his straitlacedness, how he was overly doting, or something else, but he had always had an air about him that unsettled me.

"I couldn't let my fiancée wither away in a hospital bed without her man by her side."

I closed my eyes to keep from rolling them, but Wade's groan of annoyance was loud as it rumbled through the small room. I shot him a look to keep his thoughts to himself, and he stuck his tongue out at me.

So mature.

With his juvenile response, my eyes rolled on their own accord, no stopping them this time.

Tanner raised Izzy's hand to his lips, leaning down to kiss where her engagement ring should have been, but instead met with an empty ring finger on her left hand.

"Where's your ring?" he asked sharply.

She pulled her hand from his grasp, rubbing at where she generally wore the gaudy piece of jewelry.

It had shocked us all to see how large and obnoxious the ring Tanner had proposed with looked on Izzy's slim fingers. It was a huge three-carat solitaire diamond that was flanked by smaller diamonds on each side and a diamond-encrusted band. I'm sure the thing cost a fortune, but money couldn't always buy sense, and it was clear that he'd lost his mind the day he thought that was the type of ring my sister would have wanted.

"I don't wear it when I ride. That thing's a fucking hazard," she grumbled, pulling the covers up around her like a shield.

"Watch your language, Isabella," he scolded, as if he had any right to tell her how to speak.

She nodded demurely, and Wade and I looked at each other in confusion. I'd never seen my sister shrink under the gaze of anyone, much less a man, and seeing how defeated she looked after being scolded by her fiancé had my hackles rising.

"Knock, knock!" the nurse cheerfully called as she pushed her way into the room, grabbing a pair of gloves as she entered. "How are you feeling, sweetheart?" she asked.

"Like all of this is unnecessary, and I want to go home."

"I understand, sweetie. But I promise we will get you out of here as soon as we can."

The nurse took a set of vitals, listening to Izzy's breathing, pulse, and checking her reflexes. Everything seemed to check out as she stripped off the gloves and made notes on the chart at the end of her bed.

"While I'm in here, we were having a little bit of trouble billing your insurance." She looked down at the chart and flipped one of the papers over, looking for the information. "It looks like the billing department contacted the policy owner to sort a few things out, and we just need a signature or two to send it back over. It looks like your—"

I didn't miss the stiffness that fell over Izzy's demeanor and the wild look in her eyes. Something was off. She was old enough to be on her own insurance. I had assumed she'd been given insurance through one of her sponsors or that she had signed up for her own policy once she'd been removed from Dad's.

Another knock came from the door, interrupting the nurse, and we looked around, wondering who else could be showing up.

Pushing into the room, Sterling looked around from person to person, clearly uncomfortable. He was still dressed in his riding gear, obviously having left the arena and going directly to the hospital after checking on Oakley. His flannel shirt stretched across his broad chest, the sleeves rolled to just above his elbows, straining against his biceps and accenting the sleeves of tattoos that swirled around his forearms. He wore a leather vest littered with rodeo sponsorships and a black felt Stetson, which he respectfully removed.

"Ah, yes! Mr. Morgen, I was just telling your wife about the issue with the insurance."

You could have heard a toad fart with how quiet it got in the room.

Wife?

What the actual fuck was going on?

"Uh, hey… wifey," he choked out nervously.

Tanner looked from Izzy to Sterling, his face reddening with pent-up rage as he worked to figure out what in the world was going on. Welcome to the club, bud.

"Wife? You're married?" he screeched, throwing Izzy's hand back down in her lap. She clutched at her forehead, wincing with pain as he raged beside her.

"How about we all take a walk?" the nurse asked, giving Izzy the quiet she needed while recovering. "I'll show you where the cafeteria is," she said, guiding Tanner to the door.

I walked over to Izzy's bedside, leaning down to whisper in her ear, "We're gonna talk about this later." She nodded.

Wade and I walked out the door, leaving her and Sterling to work out whatever the hell had just happened back there.

"And I thought we were the only ones who got married in Vegas," Wade joked. I chuckled, nervous energy coming off me in waves as I looked back at the door, wondering if we should wait around.

"Sunshine, let's leave them to sort their shit out. Sterling's a good man, and Izzy is smart and strong enough to handle herself. I'm sure it's just a misunderstanding." He ran a gentle hand down the back of my head as he pulled me into a hug.

Yeah, I hoped it was all just a misunderstanding, because explaining to my father that my sister was married while engaged to another man wasn't going to go over well.

IZZY WAS RELEASED from the hospital that evening with strict doctor's orders to go home, rest, and stay off the back of her horse for a couple of days.

Wade and I hadn't stuck around for the conversation between her and Sterling, but whatever had transpired, he'd offered to drive her truck and Oakley back to the ranch so Izzy could fly home with us.

None of us was comfortable approaching the subject. Clearly, the two of them knew each other better than they had let on, especially since they were somehow married.

Tanner had stormed out of the hospital, not bothering to come back or offer to fly home with us. I could tell the exhaustion of the day's events and Tanner's fury were weighing on my sister.

"You okay?" I asked softly, the dashboard lights of Wade's truck illuminating just enough for me to make out her down-trodden features.

"Fine," she snapped, turning to look out the window, shutting me out. In the reflection of the glass, I saw the subtle swipe of her hands across her cheeks, brushing away tears as they fell.

I reached my hand over the seat, grabbing hold of hers, squeezing three times. She returned the gesture, never taking her eyes off the passing landscape around us.

"WHAT A FUCKING DAY," Wade groaned, throwing himself backward onto the plush mattress, not bothering to remove a stitch of clothing.

"You got that right," I replied, climbing into bed next to him, snuggling into his side, and resting my head on his bicep.

"You know what I'm most disappointed about?" he asked, a devious grin pulling at the corners of his mouth.

"What's that?"

"I didn't get to join the Mile High Club."

A loud laugh bubbled past my lips as I leaned over, crossing my arms across his wide chest, resting my chin atop my hands. I grabbed his hat off his head, plopping it down on top of mine.

"My poor cowboy," I crooned. "How about I give you eight seconds and see if you can hold on instead?"

He growled, rolling on top of me as he stared down into my eyes.

"I love you, mi reina," he whispered, never breaking eye contact.

"I love you too, Waddle."

EPILOGUE

RAY - 4 MONTHS LATER

"SUNSHINE, WE'VE GOTTA GET MOVING!" Wade shouted from the foyer as I tacked paint samples to the living room wall. Trying to find the perfect shade of green was proving harder than I'd expected it to be.

We had moved into our new house the week before and were putting the finishing touches on everything before moving all our belongings and furniture in.

We settled on a four-bedroom, craftsman-style house with a wide front porch, white siding, and black shutters. It was everything I'd ever dreamed the perfect home to be. Wade gave me free rein on decorating, and I was overwhelmed by all the possibilities and a blank slate.

"I'm coming!" I yelled back.

Wade stood in the foyer, typing furiously on his phone, as he waited for me to get ready. I took a second just to drink him in. My husband.

Neither of us had wanted to wait to get married; we had known for long enough that this was it for us. Wade proposed a month after the rodeo, surrounded by our family at a normal Sunday dinner.

We opted for a small ceremony out by the pond behind the big house, with just those important to us in attendance.

Construction of our forever home had taken precedence over a honeymoon, but neither of us was too upset with a quiet start to our future after the whirlwind of the last year and a half.

"Max just texted and said they're all settled in, and we can come whenever."

I could see the excitement on his face as he pocketed his phone and reached for the front door. Stella had given birth to their baby boy this morning, and we were all on pins and needles waiting for the green light to go and meet him.

They had opted to wait on finding out the gender until delivery, something I still, to this day, commend both of them for. I don't know that I would have been able to wait nine months to find out what I was having, but I had a while before I had to start thinking about that.

Wade and I had discussed when we wanted to start trying for kids. We both agreed that we wanted to be married for at least a year before we actively started trying.

We were focused on our budding careers, his training facility's success taking off heavily after the last NFR, and mine steadily growing as we branched out into a larger online presence.

Until then, we were both more than happy to spoil our niece and new nephew unconditionally and obnoxiously, until it was our time.

AS WE KNOCKED on the entrance of the hospital room, I could hear soft chatting from behind the heavy door. I smiled, taking Wade's hand in mine as we entered, balloons and a blue teddy bear in our grasp.

"Hi, Mama," I whispered to Stella, who sat holding a blanket-wrapped bundle in her arms.

She was glowing, exhausted, but glowing. You could feel the happiness radiating from her with the pride of welcoming her son into this world.

Max stood at the head of the bed, brushing Stella's hair back gently, looking down at the two of them with soft reverence. His eyes were red —he'd clearly been crying—and it warmed my heart to see their happily ever after coming true.

"Hi," Stella said back with a soft smile.

"Congratulations, brother," Wade said as he walked over to Max, tugging him into a tight hug.

"Thank you," he said, sniffing away the tears that welled in his eyes. "Stella was a fucking rockstar."

He leaned down and kissed the top of her head as she beamed back up at him.

"Can I hold him?" I asked. Stella nodded, and I walked over to the sink to wash my hands, making sure to scrub well. I took him gently from Stella's outstretched arms and peered down at his cherub face.

His long lashes brushed against chubby cheeks as he slept soundly, swaddled in my arms. A striped hat covered his head, and I pulled it back slightly to be met with a full head of dark brown hair. He was perfect, and although Max wasn't Charlie's biological father, the kids looked almost identical.

"So, we wanted to talk to you guys about something," Max said, clearing his throat and taking Stella's hand in his.

I walked over to the armchair in the corner of the room and sat down, tucking the tiny bundle into the crook of my arm. Wade washed his hands and came over beside me, running a gentle finger over the baby's brow as he stared down at him in wonder.

"Anything," I said softly, looking up at two of my best friends.

"We were wondering if you guys would do us the honor of being his godparents."

Tears welled in my eyes as I reached for Wade's hand. I looked down at the tiny boy in my arms, and there was no question that the answer was yes. I could hear Wade sniffling, holding back tears himself as we both marveled at the baby.

"We'd be honored," he said softly.

"Good, because it would have been really awkward to name a kid after a man who didn't want to be his godfather."

Both of our eyes shot up to where Max stood with a wide grin on his face.

"I want you to meet Holden Wade Daniels."

"We wanted him to have a name that represented strength, and there's no stronger person we know than you," Stella added.

I stood from the chair and pulled Wade to sit where I had been, placing the baby gently in his arms. He looked down at him, tears streaming unabashedly down his face.

I could see the pride and joy emanating from his gaze as he took in the moment. He looked to his brother and his wife, mouthing a silent "thank you" before training his gaze back on his new nephew.

"It's nice to meet you, Holden. I'm your Uncle Wade."

COMING SOON FROM FIREFLY COVE
FIREFLY SECRETS

GETTING my dick sucked enthusiastically by a bottle-blonde buckle bunny in my truck should have given me a much greater sense of excitement.

After all, I'd just secured my twentieth gold buckle, added another ten-thousand to my already padded bank account, and been riding the post-win high when she approached me outside the stables, using nothing more than her flirty smile to reel me in.

It had been so long since I'd let myself indulge in a mindless fling that I didn't think twice when she suggested we go back to my camper. We hadn't even made it out of the truck before she was unbuckling my belt and pulling out my dick.

Except, as I watched her manicured hand twist its way around my shaft where her plush lips couldn't reach, and the lewd sounds of her wet mouth echoed through the cab, all I could think about was how much I'd rather take matters into my own hands — literally and figuratively.

Leaning my head back against the headrest, I forced my mind to try to focus on the woman with my dick currently halfway down her throat. Instead, that fucking traitor decided it was the perfect time to remind me of the last time I'd been in a situation similar to this.

Long, dark hair wrapped around my fist as another woman —in another time—wrapped her lips around my tip, slowly sliding down inch by glorious inch until I could feel my crown hit the fleshy softness at the back of her throat. With a determined swallow, she edged further, taking my entire length like the champion she was.

As she reached between my legs, cupping my balls in her slender fingers and rolling them gently, I felt the build of my release at the base of my spine and it threatened to overtake me. Stars dotted my vision as everything tunneled in on the sensation of the brown haired vixen expertly stroking and sucking in perfect tandem.

"If you don't want me coming down your throat, you better slow down, cowgirl," I growled as the pressure became almost too much to bear.

Instead of backing down from the challenge, I felt her body tense beneath me, as my dirty words spurred her on. She hollowed her cheeks and took me deep as I spilled my warm release down her throat.

"Fuck... Iz..." I groaned.

The hand around my shaft faltered slightly but kept a steady rhythm as my hips bucked into the warm heat of her mouth.

After I was sufficiently spent, I kept my head leaned back against the headrest, allowing my body to come down from its post-release high. Tucking my dick back into my pants and buckling my belt, I gazed down at the sight before me. I was met with blue eyes instead of hazel, blonde hair instead of brown, and a scowl that would have had most men scrambling for any semblance of apology.

"Tara," the woman snipped. "My name is Tara."

"Sorry 'bout that, darlin'," I drawled with a timid smile, doing my best to lean into the southern drawl and gentlemanly persona that drew her in to begin with.

Resignation lined her face, and a nagging feeling of guilt washed over me. "It's okay. I know I'm not the first or the last woman you've been with or will be with," she sighed.

As if the universe was throwing me a bone, my phone rang from where I'd tossed it on the dash. I fumbled around to grab it and unlock it with a quick swipe of my thumb. My eyebrow cocked up on one side at the name flashing across the glaringly bright screen.

Wade Daniels.

Taking a quick peek at the time, I did the mental math to calculate the time difference from where I was in bum-fuck-egypt Arizona, to back home in Georgia.

While the sun had long since faded over the desert, it was just about quittin' time back on the ranches.

I looked over at... what was her name again? Tracy? *Fuck.*

I looked over at the girl sitting across the bench seat of my truck, typing away on her own phone, clearly done with me and the situation.

I had made things clear at the beginning of our time together that this would be a one time thing and that I wasn't looking for anything more than a quick fuck. She'd been more than eager to comply, clearly punctuated by the fact that we were still sitting in my truck instead of inside my camper in a bed.

"Uh... so, I've gotta take this call. I don't want to be an

asshole and—" I started, rubbing a hand nervously over the nape of my neck.

She didn't look taken aback in the slightest as she gathered her things and shot me a smile, her hand already primed on the door handle.

"It's all good, I hope whoever Iz is, she knows she's a lucky fucking woman to have you so wrapped up in her." The look of placation across her face was borderline patronizing.

I'm sure she'd been with her fair share of cowboys in her day that were hung up on other women. Generally speaking, buckle bunnies were one of two things—down to fuck or trying to tie you down. She seemed like the type to float on the wind, happy to live life to its fullest, never settling down.

A raw ache bloomed throughout my chest as I fought the memories of a woman with a similar take on life. Would there ever come a day that the image and thought of her wouldn't haunt my every waking moment? A part of me wanted to hold onto the ghost of her presence for as long as possible, but she'd made her decision and she'd moved on.

I watched as she slid into the driver's side of her small sedan, turning the engine over and pulling off with a small wave. Her taillights lit up the dark sky and I watched until they retreated to nothing but tiny red specks in the distance. I sent up a silent prayer that she found what she was looking for.

Glancing back down at my phone in my hand, I pulled up my recent call log and pressed redial on the missed call.

"Hey, man," Wade's voice cut through the speaker as I placed my phone on the dash and cut the engine.

"Hey, been awhile," I replied as I pushed open the heavy door of my truck and stepped down onto the running boards and onto the sandy ground. I walked the few remaining steps to the door of my camper that I traveled with to rodeo events.

After ten years on the circuit, you learn that there's no better preparation for getting on the back of a pissed off horse, than a good night's sleep. I had done my fair share of sleeping in my truck in the early days of my career, and I'd leave that up to the newbies.

"Yeah, sorry to bother you. I know you're out on the road right now, but I was checking the rodeo schedule and it looks like you might have a couple months off coming up."

I sat down on the small sofa right inside the door and pulled off my boots, setting them neatly off to the side.

"Uh, yeah. I've got a couple months off. I was going to R&R at the ranch before we head out to Vegas." I tried to keep the skepticism from bleeding through my voice, but it was weird that Wade was following my schedule close enough to know that I had time off. We were friends, sure, but we didn't often run in the same circles.

Wade had retired from competing a couple years prior and although we'd gotten close on the circuit, we didn't see much of each other outside of competing. Even if we only lived a couple of hours from each other.

He was busy running a training facility for up-and-coming rodeo stars back in Firefly Cove, a small town about two hours away from my hometown of Ember Ridge. I was busy chasing buckles and living out my glory days while my body still had the ability to attempt eight seconds on the back of a bucking bronco.

"I was wondering if I could call in a favor," he said softly. I didn't miss the hesitation that lined his words, and it had me perking up on instinct. Something didn't seem right.

"Sure, man. What do you need?" I responded without hesitation.

"I'm sure you're aware of what happened last year with my brother's fiance's kid and my incident." The venom dripped off his words as he spoke.

Even if our towns weren't connected by miles, we still shared a lot of the same circles, and I hadn't missed the news about Wade being shot. There had been talks that he wouldn't ever ride a horse again, and that thought gutted me to my core.

Taking a horse away from a cowboy was a fate almost worse than death. I couldn't even begin to imagine how I would feel if I weren't ever able to ride again.

"Yeah, I heard." I wasn't one for empty apologies, and that was something that Wade and I had always agreed on. There was no need to apologize for something beyond your control. I wasn't the one who'd shot him, so I wasn't going to say, "I'm sorry," as if it would make any lick of difference.

"Well, I've been going through a lot over the last year, and I've decided that I'm going to check myself into an inpatient facility that specializes in PTSD and panic disorders."

I didn't have the words to express my profound pride in my friend. I imagine that it wasn't a decision he came to lightly, and if there was some way I could help out, I sure as hell was going to do it.

"This doesn't have anything to do with the Cortez girl you were mauling behind Jack's a couple weeks ago, does it?" I asked, lightening the mood.

I could hear his grumbling and growling on the other side of the phone, and I let out a hearty chuckle.

"I'm just messing with you, man. I'm proud of you. Takes a strong-ass man to admit when he needs help, even if his woman pushes him in the right direction. What do you need me to do?"

I could hear papers rustling in the background, and I pressed the phone between my shoulder and my ear as I tugged my buckle open and slid my belt from its loops. I tossed it on the small dresser in the corner as I traded my jeans for some gym shorts and my button-down for a plain grey T-shirt.

"I've got a couple of trainees who have sessions scheduled through the next couple months. One of them is heading to Vegas in December. She doesn't need…"

His voice faded into the background as the reality of whom he was talking about flooded my veins.

Isabella Cortez.

"Sterling, you there?" I heard him call through the receiver as my mind rushed back to the situation at present.

"Yeah, sorry. I'm here." I responded, shaking my head and focusing on Wade.

"I'm sure everyone will be okay with having a substitute trainer for a while, but I'll have Pops reach out to each of the trainees and give them the option of continuing lessons or rescheduling them until I'm back."

"Okay. Just shoot me the dates so I can look at places to stay that offer long-term rentals." I added, putting a burrito I'd pulled from the freezer into the microwave to heat up.

"We've actually got an empty, furnished, bunkhouse on the property that you're welcome to use. That way you don't have to find somewhere to stay and commute every day."

"Works for me," I said, opening the microwave as the timer hit one second remaining, challenging myself to catch it before it beeped.

"I really appreciate it, man. I'll have Pops call in a day or so and give you the rundown on all the trainees and their schedules. We will have the bunkhouse ready for you by Thursday. Can you be here by the weekend?"

I quickly checked the calendar on my phone, doing the mental math on how far of a drive it would be and how long it would take me to do it.

"Yeah, no problem. You do what you need to do," I responded, already mentally calculating how I was going to deal with the fallout once Izzy found out I'd be training her instead of Wade.

"Thanks man. I owe you one."

I grunted a response as we hung up, my mind swirling with images of long brown hair, tender smiles, slender fingers, and the loud, boisterous laugh that had haunted my mind daily in the year since I'd last seen Isabella Cortez.

But I was a bareback bronc rider, and I'd learned at an early age how to get bucked off and get right back on. Maybe this was the universe's way of giving me a boost back into the saddle.

ACKNOWLEDGMENTS

Wow, a whole ass second book. I still can't believe I've written almost 150,000 words and published them out into the world.

I wouldn't have been able to do it without the unwavering support of my circle.

Thank you to my Alpha/Beta Readers: Cera, Mandi, Kelly, Emily, Laura, and Paige.

Without you guys breaking down each chapter, Firefly Embers wouldn't be what it is. I'm incredibly thankful for your support and advice. Especially when I come to you complaining and you hype me up without question.

Thank you to my husband who has seen first hand the amount of stress and work that goes into writing and publishing a book. You've made writing, editing, and publishing this easy as you've helped keep our household running.

Thank you to my parents for always supporting my dreams and sharing my successes. Just a reminder, skip over the spicy chapters.

Thank you to all the readers, the book shops, the book clubs, and social media communities who have supported Firefly Cove endlessly. I hope that I can continue to write things that bring you joy, even through the emotional damage.

Last but not least, Thank you Monster Energy - you've fueled lots of long nights. You da real MVP.

ALSO BY ASHLEY TEMPLIN

<u>Firefly Cove Series</u>

Firefly Wishes

Firefly Embers

Firefly Secrets - Coming Winter 2026

<u>Ember Ridge Series</u>

Wildflowers & Weeds

ABOUT THE AUTHOR

Ashley Templin was born and raised in Fredericksburg, Virginia where she spent the majority of her adult life. Upon marrying her high school sweetheart, Jacob, she relocated to wherever his Army career took them. They have lived in New York, Virginia, and Georgia as of current and can't wait to see where they will end up next. Together, they have a daughter named Mellie, four cats, and a basset hound named Toby. As an avid reader, she found herself constantly bombarded with characters wanting their stories written, hence the dream of being an author. She enjoys a romance novel that brings you to your knees with emotional storylines, spice, and characters that are relatable. In her spare time, she owns a handmade children's clothing boutique, plays Animal Crossing, and spends time finding ways to annoy her husband.

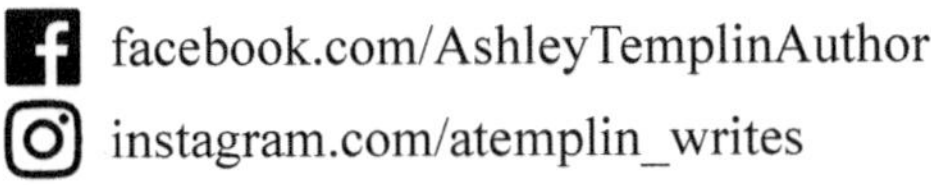

www.ingramcontent.com/pod-product-compliance
Lightning Source LLC
Chambersburg PA
CBHW071533110726
47908CB00007B/1865